SILENT COUNTRY

DAVID WOLF MYSTERY THRILLER
BOOK 18

JEFF CARSON

Cross Atlantic Publishing

ALSO BY JEFF CARSON

The David Wolf Series

Gut Decision (A David Wolf Short Story) – Sign up for the new release newsletter at http://www.jeffcarson.co/p/newsletter.html and receive a complimentary copy.

CHAPTER ONE

Tammy Granger's voice drawled out of the SUV's speakers. "We have a report of a stolen trailer at twenty-one County Road 30, a.k.a. Powerline Gulch Road. Nearby units, please check in."

Wolf sipped his coffee in the gas station parking lot and listened to the silence that followed while staring out the window toward the spot Tammy was speaking about. The road, a red slice in the green carpet of sage and juniper, led up and over a rise no more than a few miles away.

He picked up the radio. "Wolf here. I'm nearby. I'll check it out."

"Thank you."

"Who called it in?"

"Andy Tallbaum."

Tallbaum. The man grew up with Wolf down south in Rocky Points, both attending the same schools. But Tallbaum was two years younger and had run with a different type of crowd, so Wolf didn't know much about him, other than after his schooling, he used to frequent Beer Goggles Bar and Grill.

That was back when Wolf used to hang out there a lot himself. Jack had been just a kid. Now, a couple of decades later, Jack was a father to his own kid. And Wolf was a grandfather.

My God, time kept on flying.

The Toughbook computer mounted on Wolf's dash told him Tallbaum was convicted of DUI five years prior.

"Okay, I'm on it," he said and hung the radio on the hook.

He fired up his engine and headed north on Highway 734 to the next exit, which forked off the road a mile onward.

As he hung a left onto the dirt, he swerved around a deep puddle, a remnant of the showers they'd had over the last few afternoons. Over the first two weeks of June, the valley here and down south in town had exploded in green. Flowers dotted the landscape, sometimes quilting it in swaths of purple, blue, or yellow. He lowered the windows and enjoyed the scents of grass and sage flowing in.

The road rose and fell a couple of times over rolling hills. On the third rise, a glint of metal caught his eye down on the left at the bottom of a ravine that paralleled the road.

He climbed the next hill, bouncing through more potholes, and came to a stop. Leaving the engine running, he got out and stepped to the edge of the road, his work boots squishing into the soft shoulder.

Twin tire tracks led off the road, gouging the wet earth, matting the grass, and plowing through bushes, where it met the ravine. At the bottom, in a shallow trickle of water, sat a trailer. Its steel frame bent from the ride.

A box of asphalt roof shingles had fallen off halfway down, leaving a trail, along with a bonanza of pine wood of various cuts, loosely held together by bright orange tie-downs. A torn cardboard box bent on the breeze.

Like the sunflowers dotting the valley, he shut his eyes and pivoted toward the low-angled morning sun, raising his face to drink up the warmth. A refrigerator breeze hit his back.

The cerulean sky was devoid of clouds, save a strip of mist clinging to the river far to the south. The forecast was calling for sixties and sunny, and it looked like they had it right. Not bad for the middle of June.

He climbed back in and drove. A mile later, he pulled up to his destination, a single-wide trailer parked next to a partially framed house.

He parked next to a beat-up Chevy pickup. In the truck bed was a pile of wood strapped in using familiar bright orange tie-downs. The concrete foundation of the house had been poured, and framing was underway, albeit sparse for now. Surely, it was ready to rock and roll with the new shipment of wood.

Wolf shut off the engine and got out.

The trailer door opened, and Tallbaum appeared. Short and rail-thin, he wore Carhartt pants and a black Megadeth sweatshirt.

"Oh, hey, Wolf!" Tallbaum hopped down the two steps and met him with an outstretched hand. "What are you doing here? I figured they'd send some young grunt or something."

Wolf shook the offered hand, feeling heavy calluses and too much moisture for his liking.

"Tallbaum."

"They sending out the big guns to figure this out, eh?"

Tallbaum pulled out a box of Marlboro Reds and lit one.

"Where's your uniform?"

"I'm a detective. We don't need to wear them."

"Aha."

"Why don't you tell me why I'm here, Andy?"

Tallbaum exhaled, and the sour stench of a long night of drinking cut through the smoke. His eyes were bloodshot, and the right half of his beard was matted flat.

"Yeah." Tallbaum walked toward his truck. "So, I wake up this morning, ready to get a jump on my framing. And I see here that some dickhead stole my trailer!" He shouted the last words to the horizon as if the thief were perched behind a bush, having returned to his perfect crime to watch how it played out.

Wolf went to the back of Tallbaum's truck and eyed the trailer hitch. The mount was still inside the receiver. The ball was an over-worn globe. On both sides of the hitch, rusted chains dangled, broken away from the underside of the frame.

"When were you last driving?"

"I drove home last night after getting the lumber up in Brushing."

"And you stopped for a few drinks on the way home, did you?"

"Nope. I learned my lesson in that department, Sheriff. I drink here in my place now. It's so much better. Got me and the beautiful country to keep me company." He windmilled his arms, stumbling slightly.

Wolf nodded and pointed to the ground behind the trailer. "I don't see any extra tracks. Do you?"

Tallbaum walked over. The wind had deposited fine, orange dirt in the driveway. The vague outline of Tallbaum's truck tires as they came in were there, but no telltale signs of theft. Fresh footprints where Tallbaum had stood that morning, presumably cooking up his explanation for the prior night's events before calling the sheriff's department, were also visible.

Tallbaum squinted. "No."

"So, what do you think happened then?"

"What do you mean?"

"You think somebody was able to come in here and steal the trailer off your vehicle without leaving any tracks?"

Tallbaum smoked his cigarette.

"Hop in," Wolf said, walking to his truck.

"Hey, wait a minute. I'm not going to the station or anything."

"Why not? Your trailer's been stolen. You have to make a report."

"Don't you have a...I don't know, report here with you or something I can fill out?"

Wolf shook his head. "Just get in. I know exactly who stole your trailer. I'll take you. It's just over the hill there."

"Over the hill? You think Jake Jackson stole my trailer?"

Wolf ignored him and sat behind the wheel.

Firing up the engine, he turned down the radio and waited for Tallbaum to suck another drag, flick away the cigarette, and then climb into the passenger's seat. Backing out, Wolf rolled down the windows to counteract the stench and drove out the way he came in.

"I should have known that piece of crap would take my

stuff," Tallbaum said. "I've never liked him. Him and that wife of his are always giving me looks whenever I see them."

Wolf drove, ignoring the incessant talk as he went over the first hill.

"Hey, aren't you getting married soon?"

"Yeah."

Tallbaum snapped. "What's her name again?"

"Piper."

"Yeah, that's it." He whistled softly. "She's good-looking."

Wolf gave him a glare that told him to watch his next words. Tallbaum missed the warning.

"No, she's hot. That's what she is. Nice work, Wolf."

The dashboard screen changed, indicating a radio message coming in, and Tammy's voice came out of the speakers once again.

"Wolf, come in."

"Wolf here," he said. "I'm with Tallbaum now."

"You're with him now?"

"Yes."

"Oh..." she paused. "Okay, well...we have a Code Frank. South of the pass."

Code Frank meant a dead body, which sent a jolt of adrenaline through his system, but he kept his reaction nonchalant. "Okay, I'll get back to you ASAP." He turned down the radio dial, silencing the speakers.

Tallbaum was staring at him now. "Who's Frank?"

Wolf ignored him as he slowed at the top of the hill and shifted into park. "Here we are."

"Where? What's going on?"

Wolf pointed down the slope past Tallbaum.

Tallbaum looked, then leaned into the glass. "What the hell?" He opened the door and got out.

"Shut the door," Wolf said.

"Huh? Why?"

"That's your trailer, isn't it?"

"Yeah."

"Shut the door," Wolf said again, this time more forcefully.

Tallbaum closed the door.

Wolf let off the brake and drove.

"Hey! Wait! Where are you going?"

Wolf rolled up his window and called Tammy on his cell phone, ignoring a flailing Tallbaum in the rearview mirror.

"Wolf," she answered.

"What's going on?"

"Are you still with Tallbaum?"

"No."

"What happened with his trailer?"

"I found it. What's happening? Who died?"

"I don't know. Got a call from Ashland PD. Apparent bear attack. That's all I know. Patterson and Rachette are already on their way."

The information shocked his nerves a bit. In over two decades at the department, he had never been called to a bear attack. "Okay. I'm on my way."

He turned back onto the highway, this time headed south at speed, flashers blinking along the top of his windshield, and dialed Patterson.

CHAPTER TWO

"Okay, see you soon." Detective Heather Patterson hung up her cell and put it in her pocket.

Rachette looked over at her. "Was that Wolf?"

She nodded.

"What did he say?"

"He's on his way. He was up north. He's a few minutes behind us."

She bounced hard in her seat as Rachette hit another rock. He seemed to swerve into bumps rather than around them. "Easy! Watch where you're going."

"I'm doing the best I can!" Rachette said. "You want to drive?"

"Yeah. I do. I did. Remember?"

He scoffed. "If you were driving, we'd still be back on the pass. Just hang on."

Patterson's forearm and bicep were cramping from hanging on. She turned to her open window, sucking in a breath of the biting fresh air streaming in, and reminded herself things could have been much worse. She could have been sitting behind that sheriff's desk, delegating instead of being there herself.

"Pretty great, huh? Being in on the action instead of cooped up in that office?" Rachette said, clearly reading her thoughts. "Ass parked firmly in that leather chair, going over talking points you were going to cover in your lunch meeting with the county treasurer?"

She frowned, keeping her eyes out her window, but inwardly shocked at the accuracy of his ribbing. She had traded the sheriff's job for this moment at the cost of a lot of public scrutiny that bordered on humiliation. But at that moment, watching the trees, meadows, and shrubs skate by, the smell of pine and the cool air hitting her face, for the first time in a while, she knew for certain it was all worth it.

"How much longer?" Rachette asked.

She poked the GPS unit screen. "Less than a mile."

"I gotta take a piss so bad."

"Of course you do." Her nine-year-old son had a bigger bladder.

Rachette revved around the next turn, fishtailing the back end on the washboard dirt, and the view opened up as they exited a patch of forest and entered a wide meadow.

A group of vehicles were parked along the road ahead: Two Ashland Police Department vehicles, two county sheriff's department units, and a black Ford F150.

Sergeant Gantrell stood near the front APD vehicle. He turned and walked their way.

"Finally," Rachette said, skidding up behind the first vehicle. As they rocked to a stop, Rachette launched out of his seat and jogged to the back bumper.

She got out and shut the door, turning to the front and walking quickly, trying to ignore the noises coming from her partner. Behind her, he moaned to the sky while the sounds of a frantic stream hitting the road told her he was relieving himself. She would need to scrub yet another Rachette experience from her mind. They were stacking up. There wasn't enough time left in her life for the meditation necessary.

As she stepped away, nearing Gantrell, the sounds of nature took over. Rushing water echoed from somewhere in the dense woods to her left. Her gaze climbed above the officer's approaching form to the thirteen-thousand-foot peaks. They were still slathered in snow from the wet winter.

It had been a long time since she'd been in this part of the county, this far south of Rocky Points and out in the wilderness near Ashland.

"Sheriff," Gantrell said. His smile was forced, distracted.

She'd gotten to know Gantrell during her time in office and her regular visits down to the Ashland Police Department. He was a father of three girls and had a dry sense of humor that she hadn't detected until well into their first meeting, but ever since, she'd gotten to like the man.

"It's detective now," she said.

"Right." He shook her hand with a warm, soft grip. "How are you liking the demotion?"

"I'm on the job instead of at the desk." She shrugged as if the rest of the answer were self-evident.

"I'm not sure that desk would be too bad today." He shook his head.

Rachette came up with quick footsteps. "Sup Gantrell?" Rachette held his hand out to shake.

Patterson pulled on the sleeve of Rachette's jacket,

making them whiff the formality. "Were you not just relieving yourself with that hand?"

Rachette looked at his palm like it was a foreign object.

"There's hand sanitizer in the center console," she said.

Clearly annoyed, he went back to the SUV, then walked back, rubbing his hands together. She waited patiently, then asked, "So? What do we got?"

"Two bodies," Gantrell said.

"Two?" Rachette frowned. "They told us one."

"Yeah, well, we found another one."

"Both bear attack?" Patterson asked.

"I don't think so," Gantrell said.

"Then what are we looking at here?" Rachette folded his arms. "Where is everyone?"

Gantrell pointed to the trees on their right and the thin path leading into them. "They're down the trail." He rubbed a sleeve over his nose, his eyebrows pinching together. His skin was pale. "Let's get back in the vehicles. Follow me." He turned to leave.

"Wait a minute," Patterson said. "Where are we going?"

"Just another half mile or so up the road."

She gestured to the trail. "Isn't everyone down there?"

Gantrell let out an exhale, again wiping his face with his sleeve. Any harder, and he was going to draw blood.

"It's okay," she said. "Why don't you start from the beginning."

"Okay. A wildlife photographer, a guy named Pontowski or Polski, or something like that, he called in the DB. The first one. We met him here. That's his truck." He pointed to the Ford F150 without markings on it. "This guy apparently camped nearby, and this morning walked down that trail there to a meadow, where he saw and photographed a bear eating a...a corpse."

Rachette made a noise somewhere between a grunt and a heave.

"The guy ran back here and gave us a call. And here we are. The bear was gone when he led us out to the spot, but the body was still there. Mangled to all hell."

"Okay," Patterson said.

"From the body, you can see a cabin in the trees. We walked to it, you know, to see if everyone was okay. First thing I thought was maybe it had been somebody living there."

"And?" Patterson asked.

"We found the other body."

Patterson let out a sigh, nodding. "And this cabin's up the road."

"Yes."

"Got it."

Rumbling tires approached, pulling their gazes back the way they'd come in.

"Wolf," Rachette said.

The chief was rolling in at speed in his unmarked, black Interceptor. He slowed and pulled in behind Rachette's SUV.

"Okay," she said, turning back to Gantrell. "You lead the way."

Gantrell nodded, walking up the road to his vehicle, while Patterson and Rachette walked to Wolf.

"What's happening?" Wolf asked as he rolled down his window.

"We were just about to find out. Follow us."

CHAPTER THREE

Wolf followed the dust as the road curved in a long C. A group of uniformed men and women standing out in the meadow flitted in and out of view behind the trees. A blue tarp was stretched out on the ground near them, undoubtedly covering the body.

Brake lights bloomed through the dust ahead as Gantrell and Rachette's SUVs pulled over near a driveway that led to a red cabin. The cabin was small, one-storied, and squatting in a dense thicket of ponderosa pines that lined the meadow where the rest of the uniforms stood.

No other vehicles were present, but two APD officers milled about by an attached garage at the side of the cabin. Another uniform Wolf recognized as Deputy Nelson of the sheriff's department stood at the back of the place, looking down at a dark shape on the ground.

Wolf parked, shut off the engine, and got out.

Gantrell led them down the driveway. "Looks like two or three gunshot wounds. The bear didn't touch this body. But you can see the one in the meadow was here originally. At least, I think so. They're dressed the same. Bikers."

Wolf wanted clarification but could sense that Gantrell was unsettled. Walking a few yards further would tell him everything he needed to know, so he nodded and let the man talk.

They reached the two APD officers. They exchanged names and greetings and walked toward Nelson at the back of the cabin. He appeared mesmerized by the dead body.

"Nelson," Patterson said as she put on some nitrile gloves pulled from her pocket. "You okay?"

The multi-decade deputy of the Sluice-Byron County Sheriff's Department blinked as if coming out of a deep hypnosis and turned toward them. "Hey."

"Mind if we take a look?"

Wolf and Rachette followed Patterson as she walked past Nelson and knelt at the body.

"Damn," Rachette said.

Wolf knew what he meant. The body was twisted in a position that looked to defy the law of physics. The man was leaning against a tree, face-first, with his right shoulder pushing into the trunk of a towering ponderosa, his arms hung down, and his back was arched. Greasy black hair hung limp and past his shoulders, covering his face. His knees were locked, and his heavy motorcycle boots had skidded out behind him until they dug in enough to catch in the soil. He had been frozen in the act of falling.

The man wore a black leather vest that read *Sons of the Void* on the back. A patch involving a skull and fire was sewn in the middle. He wore jeans and a T-shirt underneath the vest, chains hanging from the pockets.

Wolf counted two holes in the leather, which was

streaked with dried blood. The dark liquid had flowed down the tree, over the ghostly white skin of his arm, and across his jeans before pooling in clumps on the dirt beneath him.

Wolf rounded the body to look at his face. The man had a beard almost as long as his hair. His eyes were open, the irises clouded. The mouth in a silent moan.

"James Whitcomb," Patterson said, looking inside the wallet she'd pulled from the back pocket. She fiddled with the attached chain and handed the wallet to Rachette.

"What's Lorber's ETA?" Wolf asked, referring to the county medical examiner and his team.

"He's on his way," Patterson said.

Wolf looked back at the two APD officers and Nelson. "Did any of you touch this man?"

"No, sir," one of them answered. The other two shook their heads.

"Good."

Patterson touched the other pockets of the man's jeans.

"Careful," Rachette said. "Looks like he's gonna fall any second."

"I'm being careful."

Wolf watched Patterson tug out a set of keys. Rachette stepped forward with a plastic evidence bag, and she dropped them inside with a thud.

Rachette looked, then handed the bag over to Wolf. One of the keys had a Harley-Davidson logo stamped into the head and was attached to a small metal keychain ornament, a grenade replica. He handed the bag back to Rachette.

Patterson lifted the shirt, exposing heavily tattooed skin on a hairy back with a sagging belly in front. "One gunshot wound to the back."

Wolf eyed the cabin, then Nelson. "Did you check inside?"

"I knocked," Nelson said. "Rang the doorbell, but nobody answered."

"We were just talking about going inside," one of the officers said.

"Your name?" Wolf asked.

"Redman, sir," he said.

Wolf looked at the other man.

"Barrington, sir."

Wolf nodded. "Could you two please take a look around and see if you can find the vehicle this guy came in on?"

They nodded and walked away, heading back down the driveway toward the road.

Wolf walked along the garage toward the cabin, passing a patch of weeds sprouting from the corner of the house and up to a front entrance crowded by overgrown aspen branches. The door was shut. Behind the aspen tree was a darkened window. The glass was covered in streaked dust like it had never been cleaned.

He pulled his gun, stepped up onto the small wooden porch, and pressed the glowing doorbell button with his knuckle, hearing the chime inside.

Like rushing water, the wind whipped through the aspen leaves, obscuring any sound that might have come out of the interior. Nobody answered.

"Got your six," Rachette said, stepping up behind him.

The brass of the knob was worn and cold, loose and unlocked. Wolf pushed, and the door opened, creaking on its hinges.

Raising his gun, he stepped inside onto a cracked linoleum floor. The place smelled of dust. He flipped the light switch on, illuminating a family room with an ancient green velvet couch. The carpet was red shag, and the walls were stacked logs with plaster-filled gaps. Dusty paintings of wildlife in mountain scenes hung on the walls.

"Sheriff's department! Anybody home?" No answer.

Wolf hung a right, heading into the living room toward a doorway that led into a dark space.

"I'll take this way," Rachette said, heading in the other direction.

The floor creaked under Wolf's feet. The place was sparsely furnished. The end tables flanking the couch were brand new, modern designs that failed to match the rest of the place. It looked like a rental, not lived in.

"Clear!" Rachette said.

Wolf rounded the corner and found himself facing Rachette inside a smallish kitchen.

"Check this out," Rachette said.

He pointed to a black duffle bag lying on a kitchen table. It was unzipped and open, with a butcher's knife next to it, along with a dismantled electrical device lying in pieces.

"What's going on here?" Rachette asked.

Wolf picked up a piece of plastic and turned it over. It was a rectangular housing roughly the size of a USB stick that had been cracked on one side like it was smashed open. A tiny green electrical board lay next to it; the board itself also cracked. Bits of solder, multicolored particles of plastic, and tiny wires dusted the table.

"GPS device," Wolf said. He pulled open the bag and looked inside, finding nothing.

"Looks like somebody didn't want to be tracked," Rachette said.

Wolf turned to a doorway behind them.

"There's a single bedroom back there," Rachette said. "Bed's been slept in. Piss in the toilet of the bathroom. Other than that, it looks uninhabited."

Wolf walked over to look for himself. "No luggage? No clothing?"

"Nope."

Holstering his gun, he went back to the kitchen, took out some gloves, put them on, and opened the refrigerator. It was empty. A trash can sat in the cabinet under the sink. He pulled it out and found a wadded-up bag of McDonald's inside. He unraveled it and found no receipt.

"Here's a key," Rachette said.

Gingerly, with gloved fingers, Wolf picked it up off the counter by the edges and walked to the front door. The key fit into the lock and twisted easily.

"So the key goes to the front door," Rachette said. "The place is all clean and vanilla. Like it's used for a rental. Maybe it's a rented place. Or, I guess it could be the owner."

Wolf pulled the key back out, went to the kitchen, and set it back down on the counter. He toured the bedroom, bathroom, and living room again, then went outside with Rachette.

Officer Barrington came from the direction of the vehicles, slightly out of breath. "We found two bikes. Harley-Davidson's. Stashed in the trees up the road a hundred yards or so."

"Plates?" Wolf asked.

"One of them was Wyoming, the other Colorado. Redman stayed up there while I came back to tell you. Deputy Nelson went ahead up the road to see if he could find anything else."

"Thank you," Wolf said.

Patterson was still over by the dead body. She stood up from studying the ground and walked over, taking off her gloves. "Three gunshot wounds total. One in the shoulder, one in the chest, last one in the back. Found some brass on the side of the house." She dangled a bag tinkling with casings inside. "Five shells total. Hornady 9mm. It looks like somebody else was shot here." She pointed to a dark spot on the ground, surrounded by a smattering of signs in the dirt.

"That's blood. And those are bear prints." She pointed at a large paw print in a soft patch of ground. "Clearly, our other victim was shot here and was dragged out there by the bear." A long scrape mark streaked over to the trees and disappeared into the long grass of the meadow, which began where the trees stopped—a few yards away.

Out in the clearing, another fifty yards, the group of law enforcement personnel already on the scene watched them with interest.

"Let's leave the motorcycles for now," Wolf said. "I think it's time we go see who the bear drug out of here."

Wolf led the way, following the signs the bear left without stepping on them. Fresher-looking blood smeared the grass, the stalks bent toward the tarp lying near the four uniforms.

"Still no word from Lorber?"

"I talked to him thirty minutes ago, and he said he was on his way," Patterson pulled out her phone, looked at the screen, and pointed it at the sky. "No reception."

Rachette walked next to them, looking ahead.

The air was still, and the scent of death suddenly saturated the air.

"So, how's living with Piper going?" Rachette asked.

Wolf looked at him, but the detective's eyes were locked on the tarp ahead. Tom Rachette had never liked the sight, smell, or scent of death and was trying to keep his mind off it.

"Nice," Rachette said. "She's what?"

"I didn't say anything."

"Oh."

Patterson stopped. "Look at this." She picked up a vest made of black leather, torn by raking claw marks. "Same vest as the other guy."

They walked.

A single boot poking out from the plastic sheet came into view. Buzzing flies grew louder, along with the smell of death and viscera.

Patterson wasted no time, stepping in front of them and folding back the plastic sheet, revealing the mangled corpse.

"Phew," she said.

Wolf seconded the sentiment but kept silent as he eyed the body. The clothing was torn to shreds, what was left of it. A black T-shirt was ripped open, revealing a chest torn by claws, the rib cage hinged apart by a breaking force, claw marks gouging the cartilage and bone. Organs were exposed, missing, or half-eaten.

The man's face was turned away from them on a neck wrenched around at an unnatural angle, and Wolf made no move to see better. He was a fellow biker and member of Sons of the Void. And now he was being digested by a bear. That's all he needed to know.

Wolf looked over at the uniforms. They were holding fast upwind, far from the sight below, making no move to join them.

"Shit," Rachette said, the word sounding more like a guttural spasm. "I'm out." He walked away.

Patterson stooped, scanning the body from a close distance. "I can't tell what killed him. I'm not seeing any gunshot wounds."

"I'm not sure it's possible," she said. She shook her head, then looked at Wolf. "You good?"

"Please."

She folded the tarp back over the body. They followed Rachette toward the group of men standing nearby—two more Ashland police officers, Deputy Vickers, and a man dressed in flannel and jeans, clearly the civilian that had called in the body.

Immediately, the smell dissipated on the opposing wind, and Wolf felt grateful for the scents of life filling his nose once again.

They did a round of introductions.

"This is Jeb Pontowski," Vickers said.

"Detective Wolf." Wolf shook the man's hand.

Pontowski was thin, dressed in flannel and Carhartt pants, a Patagonia baseball cap covering shoulder-length hair.

"You called this in," Wolf said.

"That's right."

"Do you mind telling us about it from the beginning?"

The man told his story; waking up before sunrise at a campsite down the road and coming out to this meadow to take some photographs.

"I heard the grunts from the bear," Pontowski said, his blue eyes wide, haunted. "I took a bunch of photos. It's pretty rare to see a bear, much less one scarfing down on a meal." He swallowed. "Then I saw the arm."

"The arm?" Patterson asked.

"I couldn't see what it was eating, you know, because of the long grass until it lifted one of the arms of the body. And that's when I freaked out."

Wolf nodded. "I'm sorry. That must have been tough to see."

Patterson approached the camera bag lying on the ground. "You have any of those photographs you could show us?" she asked.

"Yeah." Pontowski went to his bag, pulled out a large-bodied camera, and presented the LCD screen.

After a few button pushes, a picture came on the screen showing a bear with a human arm in its mouth.

"Here's what I was talking about."

"Mr. Pontowski," Patterson said. "We're going to have to confiscate this SD card."

"What? No way."

"I'm sorry, sir..."

Wolf and Rachette backed away, letting Patterson take the lead on dealing with the now angry photographer, and turned their attention toward the road. Two vans rumbled into view, pulling up to the driveway of the red cabin.

"Lorber," Rachette said.

Patterson came over to them. "Thanks for backing me up there, you two."

"Looks like you had it under control," Rachette said.

"We need to call animal control," Patterson said.

Wolf nodded, then shook his head with disdain. The bear that had taken advantage of this easy meal could have a newly acquired taste for human flesh, overriding its normal fear of the species. Protocol said the bear would need to be euthanized.

"Right," Rachette said. "I'll make the call."

"And we gotta check out those bikes," Wolf said.

"Yes, sir. Of course."

"And talk to any neighbors."

"Yes, sir."

––––––

Lorber and the CSI team took over, processing the cabin for forensic evidence and bagging the bodies.

The two motorcycles parked up the road in the trees were Harley-Davidson Wide Glides, beaten in and used as primary means of transportation like only a biker gang member could. The well-worn leather saddle bags contained tobacco products and ammunition for a .45 caliber handgun, which weren't found on scene.

A mile beyond the cabin were two houses, both of them vacant. A mile back toward Ashland, an elderly couple living on a ranch had not heard anything as far as distant gunshots but had seen and heard the two bikers drive by, exhaust pipes chuffing loudly three days prior.

Lorber and his tech evidence man confirmed the dismantled and destroyed device on the kitchen table was a GPS unit.

The lack of cell service was hindering their online search for an owner of the cabin.

"And that's where we're at," Wolf said.

Sheriff Waze stood next to Wolf at the end of the driveway, nodding. His mirrored sunglasses reflected the image of Patterson and Rachette as they helped load evidence into Lorber's van.

Standing downwind of the sheriff, Wolf could smell

mint gum and cologne. For the first two weeks in office, after taking over for Patterson, Waze had rolled into work with a visible and smellable hangover.

Wolf wasn't sure what Patterson had said, but it was something effective. She had gone in and shut the blinds. He'd heard the yelling. Wolf suspected it was something like: *I dropped out of this race to give the sheriff's job to a good man, and right now, you're not it. Sober up, or get out.* She had probably added a threat in there that she wasn't going to sit back and watch the people working inside that building that she cared about so much be taken under the wing of a checked-out drunk.

Whatever it was, it worked. And going on seven months now, the man seemed to be dead dry.

"Sons of the Void," Waze said. "What kind of history do we have with these guys?"

"None," Wolf said. "They're thick up north, near Walden. Wyoming, Montana, up in Idaho. But they've generally steered clear of here."

"Until now." Waze pulled out his phone, read something on the screen, and shook his head. "Damn it," he said under his breath. "Is it always like this when something happens?"

"What's that?" Wolf asked.

"The governor's up my ass on this."

"Sounds about right," Wolf said.

Waze jammed the phone back into his pocket, lips moving.

Wolf had spent a few years as sheriff himself and felt for the man. Initially wanting the role, Wolf had backed himself out of the position. Sliding back into detective had been like putting on an old, comfortable shirt. One that he was sure he would wear until the day he either retired or died. Hopefully, the former before the latter.

Lorber approached. "We're wrapping up here." The county ME pulled off his circular lensed glasses and wiped them on the tie-dyed shirt underneath his monkey suit.

"So, what does it look like?" Waze asked. "Did you get any prints inside the place?"

"The occupant feasted on fast food, which might help us with identification. We've pulled a bunch of partials, and it looks like we have three different sets."

"You said occupant, but there were three sets?"

"I'm saying there're three sets," Lorber said. "But it looks to me like there was one person there."

Wolf nodded. "I agree. The three sets could be the owner of the place, the occupant, and somebody else entirely unrelated."

"A cleaner or something," Lorber said. "Hell, none of the prints might be who you're looking for."

"Right, right." Waze waved a hand. "Time of death of these two outside?"

"I'd go with two days. Maybe three."

Rachette walked up.

"You spoke to the people down the road?" Waze asked.

"Yes, sir," Rachette said.

"They definitely think three days ago they saw the bikers?"

"The old guy said it was Saturday. The two males he described match those of our deceased: hairy bikers. He heard the bikes go by his house and looked out his window."

Waze scoffed. "And he didn't hear a bunch of gunfire after that and think something of it?"

"The guy wears hearing aids," Rachette said.

"But he heard the bikes."

Rachette shrugged.

Waze pulled out his phone, shaking his head as he read something on the screen. "Sounds like he needs his hearing aids adjusted."

Patterson walked up. "You guys are all loaded."

Lorber nodded. "Thank you."

One of the forensic vans fired up, turned around on the road, and drove away.

"So what are we thinking here?" Waze asked.

"Looks like whoever was here figured out he was being tracked when he smashed that GPS tracker," Rachette said.

Waze nodded. "And these two guys found him."

"But that guy got the jump on these two," Rachette said. "And shot them before he could be shot."

"Probably something to do with loud motorcycles," Waze said. "Kind of tough sneaking up on somebody when your Vance and Hines pipes give away your position."

"These guys had no weapons," Patterson said.

"But there's ammo in their saddle bags," Rachette said.

She shrugged.

Waze looked at his watch. "Alright, I'm heading back. Secure the scene, and we'll let APD keep an eye on it. I've already spoken to the chief about that. Keep us posted on your report," he said to Lorber.

"We'll get started on the autopsies this afternoon."

"Thank you." Waze walked away, mumbling to himself.

"I'll keep you posted, too." Lorber broke off, leaving Wolf with his two detectives.

"What's next?" Rachette asked.

Wolf eyed his watch, which read 3:25 p.m. They'd been

there for five and a half hours, and he was ready to get behind the wheel and then put his feet up on a couch somewhere. He stifled a yawn.

"You two head home," he said. "It's been a long day, and by the time we get back, it will have been even longer. Let's let Lorber do his thing. I'll do the database checks and then see you two tomorrow first thing."

"I'll check on the bike plates and the man with the wallet," Patterson said. "We'll be driving by your house on the way back. You may as well turn off and head home. Besides, you probably have a lot to do with Piper moving in and all that."

Wolf considered the offer.

"Seriously. It's no big deal," she said.

"Thanks. I guess I'll take you up on that."

"How's that going with Piper's move anyway? I haven't had a chance to ask," Patterson said.

"She's almost all in." Wolf smiled. "It's nice to have her there."

CHAPTER FOUR

To the north, over Williams Pass, the Chautauqua River flossed a deep ravine into the granite earth, sliding down in elevation into a valley widened by millennia of catastrophic erosion events, where the town of Rocky Points lay sparkling in the late-spring sun.

Before reaching town, Wolf hung a right and crossed over the river on a narrow two-lane bridge before heading back south along the Chautauqua on the opposite side of the highway.

A few miles up the dirt road, he slowed at a familiar clump of bushes that had grown so big over the last half-century they now blocked the view of the river below. He rounded the next corner and turned at a drive that led up a steep rise.

The ranch gate at the apex of the hill framed the thirteen-thousand-foot peaks, snow shining like glass in the late-day sun, and then his house that sat on the acres he had inherited years ago.

His father used to raise cattle on the wide-open field in

front of his house, but now it served as a yard, mowed every now and then with his old riding John Deere parked in the red-painted barn next to the house. The grass was getting long, and he would have to carve out some time to mow it that weekend. He enjoyed the chore and saw it as more of an artistic creation to lay down a pattern of stripes he would enjoy looking at for the next couple of weeks.

Piper's Toyota Highlander sat parked under the carport's roof, the hatch lifted, revealing a large cardboard box inside.

He parked and got out into the bright afternoon sun. The air was comfortable, though, cooled by a northerly breeze.

"Hi."

Wolf shielded his eyes and looked at Piper coming out of the kitchen entrance. She skipped down the stairs and walked to him.

They embraced and kissed.

"You're looking at the last box from my house," she said.

Wolf folded his arms, appraising the cube of cardboard. "Wow, you've been busy today."

"Yeah. Sorry about what it looks like inside."

He put his arm around her. "It'll take some time. I'm not worried about it."

She kissed him on the cheek. "How was today?"

They each took one side of the box and lifted. Wolf cringed as a bolt of electricity traveled up his right leg, ending in an explosion of pain in his lower back.

"Are you okay?" she asked.

The pain disappeared as quickly as it came, and he kept hold of his side of the box. "I'm fine."

"Your back?" she asked.

"It's acting up a little again."

"Probably from lifting those boxes. I told you to let the movers take care of it."

They went up the kitchen stairs and inside. As they lowered the box onto the floor, he kept his face neutral but felt another twinge. He pushed a fist into his back as he straightened, alleviating the tightness.

"You should sit down," she said, stepping behind him and rubbing his shoulders.

"I think it's too much of the sitting down that does it," he said. "Too much driving. And I'm behind my desk when I'm not doing that."

Her hands dug deep into his back muscles, and the tension melted away. "That's the stuff."

"So what's happening south of the pass?" she asked.

He told her about the day's events.

"Holy cow," she said. "I've never heard of biker gang violence down here. Up north, maybe. But here in the county?"

For the first time, Wolf noticed the kitchen. It had been transformed from a bland vision of Wolf's unartistic eye to a tasteful, color-bound space filled with light and warmth. She had hung two bright paintings, added vases with flowers, and neatly stacked a set of bowls on a normally blank shelf.

"Do you like it?" she asked, hopeful.

He smiled. He did like it. "I love it."

"Great. I have some ideas for the living room, too. Just... just tell me if I'm...you know, moving in too much."

He laughed. "Please. Move in thoroughly. We both know my blank white walls, accented by my maroon blanket hanging over the back of my Barcalounger, is, as they say, *in* right now. But I'm willing to compromise on style."

He turned to face her, relieving her of her masseuse duties. Piper stood with her hand on her hip, looking around at the boxes. Her hair was pulled back in a tight ponytail, her face tan. She wore yoga pants, a T-shirt, and sneakers, sweat glistening at her temples.

She looked up at him. "What?"

He smiled. "You look good."

She wiped her forehead self-consciously and then received Wolf as he embraced her.

After a long kiss, she stepped back. "It's really nice to be here."

"It's nice to have you here."

"Oh. Wait. I have something to show you." She reached over and picked up a bright turquoise folder from the couch. "Remember I was meeting with the events company today?"

"Yeah."

"Well, they've made some preliminary sketches of what the wedding will look like."

"Oh."

"Do you want to see?" She moved toward the front door.

He nodded, following her out.

"Okay, so they came out, and I know we had talked about putting the wedding tent here, in front of the house, and the reception tent out over there. But I got to talking to the woman, and we both thought it would be better to reverse the two tents."

Wolf nodded again, smiling at her enthusiasm.

"Because it's a better view for the ceremony there." She gestured. "You can see more of the valley."

"Okay."

"Here's what it would look like."

She opened the folder and pulled out a piece of glossy paper showing an artist's rendition of the space in front of them with the two tents overlaying the image. It was uncannily real-looking. Almost impossible to tell if it had been rendered by software or some sort of AI tool. That, and it was familiar.

More than that, it was as if one of Wolf's most terrible memories had been plucked from his brain and printed on glossy paper, even more detailed and specific than his own mind could recreate.

Unbidden, the memory of Lauren leaving in her car came to mind, her daughter Ella waving goodbye out the back. Wolf watching all of it through windows of tears.

"What do you think?" Piper asked, ripping him from his thoughts. "So, the wedding tent goes there, see? And the reception right here, in front of the house. It's also logistically better for the caterers, who will have easier access to the kitchen. They can—" She stopped talking, looking at him. "You don't like it."

"What?" He frowned, shaking his head. "No. It's great."

She went quiet, lowering the picture.

"No. Sorry, I was just thinking about the case for a second. I'm sorry." He shook his head. "I'm here now. It looks great. I love it." He moved behind her and wrapped his arms around her. "I think it's going to be great. Good job."

Why was he lying? There had never been a time in their relationship that he'd refrained from telling Piper something that bothered him. But he'd never really spoken about Lauren, at least, not ever conveying the depth of the hole he still had inside from her leaving him a few short years ago. About how he'd grown to love Ella as if she were his own daughter before she'd been ripped from his life. It had been too much to ever thoroughly process himself. He wasn't going to lay that on Piper.

Stop complaining. That had been the mantra repeated by his mother growing up anytime he was upset for any and all reasons. Fall on the ground and scrape your knee? *Stop complaining.* Your dog died? It happens. *Stop complaining.* Be grateful for having had a great pet at all.

Piper leaned into him, raising the photo again. "It makes everything more beautiful and easier."

"Yeah," Wolf said, his voice like raking sandpaper.

She turned around, studying his eyes. "You're sure nothing's bothering you?"

Clearing his throat, he shook his head. "None of this really matters," he said, plucking the papers from her hand. "Nothing's going to be as beautiful as you."

She rolled her eyes, rose up on her toes, and kissed him.

Their bodies latched together like two magnetized and perfectly fitted puzzle pieces. To him, their embraces always felt so familiar and yet so new every time.

"I'm tired," he said. "I think I'll go take a nap."

"Okay."

"Are you coming?"

She smiled. "Okay."

———

The next morning, Wolf woke at sunrise and headed out for work. The dew that had covered his windows when he left was mostly dry by the time he reached the southern end of town.

He stopped at the Dead Grounds Coffee Shop and bought a breakfast burrito, then made his way three blocks further north and parked behind the county building.

The air was cool, carrying the scents of pine and river water. After entering the warm interior of the building, he rode the elevator up to the third floor.

His office was cold and smelled of cleaning agents. He pulled open the blinds, letting in the visage of the ski resort and town. The ski lifts hung still, but the town bustled silently on the other side of the triple-paned glass.

Putting down his bag of food and coffee, he sat down at his desk, his backside fitting deep into the well-worn chair.

He pushed aside his computer mouse, waking the machine while he ate his breakfast burrito. One bite in, somebody knocked on his door, and Rachette poked his head inside.

"Morning."

"Morning." Wolf waved him in.

Rachette sat on one of the chairs. "Patty's on her way."

Patterson walked in, cradling a travel mug of coffee and carrying a stack of manila folders. She sat next to Rachette and slapped them on the desk.

"They got the bear," she said by way of greeting. "Shot and killed it yesterday evening."

"That sucks," Rachette said. "We shouldn't be leaving dead bodies lying around to tempt wildlife. Hey, did you see Thatcher's here with some guy?"

"Yeah, I did," Patterson said, a hint of bitterness in her

tone. "Waze and Thatcher are longtime buddies now, I guess."

Before the last election, the one she had ultimately dropped out of, Waze had the backing of Thatcher, the eccentric billionaire living twenty miles north of town.

"We've positively ID'd our two bodies." She opened the top folder and splayed two rap sheets with color photos attached to each. "The first here is our man found against the tree. James Whitcomb, a.k.a. Jack Whitcomb. And our bear snack was a man named Benny Cruz."

Wolf put a palm on the pages and twisted them, looking at the pictures. They both had mugshots attached, white males, heavily laden with facial hair. Benny Cruz smiled maniacally into the camera lens.

Patterson read aloud. "Aggravated assault, attempted murder, robbery, multiple traffic citations. Failure to appear in court. These guys have it all."

She set the sheet aside and picked up another.

"Last known address of Jack Whitcomb is Cheyenne, Wyoming. For Benny Cruz, it's Doyle, Colorado. The bike with Colorado plates is registered to a man named Donald Cruz, same last name as Benny here."

"What's that?" Waze's voice came from the doorway. He walked inside and sat on the couch, sipping coffee. The fabric of his crisp sheriff's uniform rustled as he lowered to the cushion. His hair was wet-looking, combed precisely, like a silver field of corn.

Patterson cleared her throat. "We were just talking about how we ID'd the two victims found at the cabin. One of them is James Whitcomb, a.k.a. Jack Whitcomb. The other is a man named Benny Cruz."

Waze crossed his legs, leaning back heavily. He checked his watch, then waved his hand. "And?"

"One of the motorcycles had Colorado plates registered in Doyle, Colorado, to a man named Donald Cruz, who I found out was Benny Cruz's brother. The other motorcycle was unregistered. Last known address of Donald Cruz—the owner of the motorcycle—is Doyle, Colorado."

"Doyle?" Waze asked. "Where's that?"

"North," Wolf said. "Near Craig. Almost to the Wyoming border."

"Never heard of it."

"Anything on those prints inside the cabin yet?" Wolf asked.

"No," Patterson said. "Haven't heard from Lorber yet."

"And the cabin itself?" Waze said. "Where's the owner?"

"I looked online and found the place for rent through a property management company," she said. "A place called High Lonesome Management. They have no record of anybody renting through their system. So we've put in calls with the owner himself."

"And?"

"His name is Jim Everson. Seventy-three years old. Lives down in Ashland. He's not gotten back to us yet."

Waze scooted forward on his seat. "Okay, well, I'm off to a meeting." He stood up, straightening his jacket as he looked down at them. "Also, Thatcher's not pleased."

Roland Thatcher and the case of his missing-in-action security manager, Xavier Jorel, from nine months prior still hung over Wolf. The presence of Jorel's brain matter and blood at the crime scene told of the man's fate, but they still had no body to show for it.

"We've followed every lead, and we'll continue to follow

every lead," Wolf said. "Short of using magic..." He splayed his hands.

Waze nodded, resigned. "I know. I know." He walked to the door but turned around before he opened it. "And speaking of Thatcher and that whole case...how's Detective Yates doing?"

The question sucked the air out of the room. Detective Jeremy Yates had been shot in the chest on duty by the same woman who had killed Jorel. After numerous surgeries and walking the edge of life and death, the wounds were closed, but he was still struggling psychologically.

Wolf was not as versed in the saga of the man's journey of healing as Rachette, but he'd heard Yates had begun a relationship with Gemma Thatcher, Thatcher's daughter. Then there came news that Yates had somehow sullied that relationship, hampering his progress in getting back on his feet.

Wolf had gone to visit Yates at home a few times over the last six months. The last time had been the most appalling, discovering how low Yates had dropped. Once a specimen of health, the detective had been overweight, pale, unkempt, and unwashed. His eyes had been dead like they were ready to shed from his skull. Wolf had tried a pep talk but he was unfit to undertake such a task and had called Dr. Hawkwood to help. Wolf had set up a meeting between the two, and Rachette had volunteered to follow up on that front, giving him a ride to and from the psychologist's office. But that had been weeks ago. With Piper moving in and the wedding coming up, Wolf had completely forgotten about it.

Waze looked at them in turn, ending on Rachette.

"He's doing better, sir," Rachette said.

Waze smiled. "That's not what I'm hearing."

"Well, he's getting there."

"I heard he didn't show up for his appointment with Hawkwood."

Rachette said nothing.

"Weren't you going to take him there? What happened?"

Again, Rachette remained silent.

"And he still hasn't come in to talk to me."

"Have you gone to talk to him?" Rachette asked.

"No. But I've called him. I've left multiple messages, and he's never once returned any of them."

"He was shot on duty, sir," Rachette said. "In the chest. Ambushed by some psycho bitch who would have killed me if it weren't for him. And I think we should cut him some slack while he heals."

"It's been three months since he's been physically cleared by the doctors to come back, not back on full duty, mind you, but he's been cleared. So, where is he? He hasn't set foot in this building. Again. No answer to me, his new boss who's reaching out." Waze shrugged theatrically. "I understand that he might be struggling mentally, but he has to show some initiative here."

Waze turned back to the door. "I'm all for cutting some slack for our deputies, especially somebody in his position. But the writing's on the wall here, and at some point, I'm going to have to move on. We're in a situation right now where we need our fourth detective." He twisted the handle and opened the door. "Keep me posted on everything. I've got to talk to the press, and I have meetings all morning." He left and shut the door behind him.

They sat gripped in silent guilt.

"I'll go talk to him today," Wolf said.

"No," Rachette said. "I'll talk to him."

"We can both go."

"That's okay. I'll go myself."

Wolf and Patterson exchanged a glance.

"You think that's a good idea?" she asked.

"Yeah, I do. Or else I wouldn't have said it. I was his partner. I was the one who spent every day, for hours on end, for years on end with him. So, I'll go."

"Okay. But—"

Rachette shot her a glare.

"Okay, yeah," she said. "That's probably best. If anybody can get through to him, it'll be his partner."

"Let's talk about something else," Rachette said. "Like it's amazing we haven't had a run-in with these bikers before."

Wolf picked up his coffee. "Let's get on the owner of the cabin."

"Yes, sir," Patterson said.

Wolf nodded. "And did you call the sheriff in Doyle?"

"I did. But I got a deputy named Larkin, who took a message. I haven't had a return call from them, either."

"I'll call them."

"Yes, sir."

Rachette's eyes were on the floor next to him.

Wolf knocked on the desk, bringing his gaze up. "And Yates."

Rachette nodded.

"We have to reach him."

"I know we do."

"Let's get to work."

CHAPTER FIVE

"Brandenburg," the voice came through Wolf's phone.

"Sheriff Brandenburg?"

"Yeah."

"Hello, this is Chief Detective David Wolf from the Sluice-Byron County Sheriff's Department up in Colorado. My detective, Heather Patterson, left you a message yesterday afternoon. I'm just doing a follow-up call here."

"Ah, yes. The dead bikers. What can I do for you on that front?"

Wolf relayed the full story of finding the dead bodies and the two motorcycles and how one of those dead men had a last known address in Doyle.

"Okay," Brandenburg said, his tone unreadable.

"Does any of this mean anything to you?"

"Yes." Brandenburg's voice sounded tired now. "In fact, it does."

Wolf stood up and looked down at the street below, waiting.

"We had a shootout up here involving Sons of the Void."

"Oh?"

"Yeah."

"When was this?"

"A few days ago." The phone rustled. "What day is it?"

"Wednesday," Wolf said, unsure if the man was being rhetorical but wanting him to keep talking.

"It happened Friday night. Actually, early Saturday morning, about three a.m. So, five nights ago, yeah. One of the victims was Donald Cruz."

Wolf sat back down. "Dead?"

"Yes. In fact, there were four deaths. Three more injured with gunshot wounds." Brandenburg chuckled mirthlessly. "I guess the action must have bled south to you guys."

"So we're looking at retaliation against whoever shot them up," Wolf said.

"Sounds that way to me."

"We found an empty bag," Wolf said. "A canvass duffle. And a GPS tracking unit that looks like it was pulled out of it and destroyed."

"There you go," Brandenburg said. "Must have tracked him down there with that."

"Him?"

"Or them."

"Four people killed and three others injured," Wolf said. "That's seven victims. That sounds like multiple perps. What happened exactly? A bar shootout? Or..."

"The shootings happened at their compound. So, we're not exactly sure what happened, except that we responded in the middle of the night when they called for medical help."

"So, it was at their compound. An inside altercation?" Wolf asked. "A disgruntled member?"

"We're still in the dark there."

"What are the bikers saying?"

"They're not. That's the problem."

Wolf put a foot up on his desk. "Any idea what would have been in the bag we found down here?"

"Money? Drugs? Guns?" Brandenburg chuckled again. "If I had three guesses, I'd guess in that order."

"Have you reached out to the FBI or ATF for support?"

"No, sir." The answer came immediately.

"I have a few contacts in the FBI," Wolf said. "They're good people. I could put in a call and see if they have anything new on their end."

"Could be a good idea," Brandenburg said. "But we certainly do not want to be inundated by suits, so I'd appreciate you keeping that in mind."

"Of course. It's your county. Your call."

Brandenburg said nothing.

"Well," Wolf said. "I'd appreciate you keeping us abreast of any changes in the situation. Any new information you come across, like who the hell might be down here killing people in our county."

"Will do," Brandenburg said. "And the same goes for you."

"Of course."

They said their goodbyes, and Wolf hung up.

He stared out the window for a few minutes, his thoughts turning to the next person he was going to dial. He could call Special Agent Kristen Luke or, more straight to the finish line of where he wanted to go, Special Agent Archie Hannigan, Luke's partner. A year ago, Hannigan had been in a relationship with a man who was undercover with a motorcycle gang. What had been the man's name? *Billy.* That had been it.

Wolf decided there would be no end of Luke's wrath if she caught wind that he went over her head, so he dialed her number.

"Hey," she said, answering after two rings.

"How are you?"

"I'm good."

"*Where* are you?" Wolf asked.

"Sunny Southern California, actually."

"Wow. Work or pleasure?"

"Work. Always work." A male's voice murmured beside her. "It's Wolf...Archie says hey."

"Actually, that's kind of why I was calling," Wolf said. He explained the situation.

"I'll give you over to him," she said, handing the phone to Hannigan.

Wolf and Special Agent Hannigan exchanged some pleasantries, and then Wolf repeated the situation, adding details about the gang's clubhouse in Doyle being shot up five nights prior.

"Wow," Hannigan said. "Yeah, that sounds like something Billy may know about. But I'm not seeing that asshole anymore, so I wouldn't know about what he knows."

Wolf sat back. "I see. Anyone else you know who would know?"

Hannigan remained silent for a beat, then huffed, "What do you want to know from him?"

"The violence is bleeding down into our county, and I'd like to know why. If something is going on I need to know about, I'd like to know before rather than after there's more violence."

"Yeah." Hannigan sighed, sounding like he was being berated by his mother to clean his room. "Okay, okay. I'll reach out to him and let you know what I hear. I can't guarantee anything useful from that asshole, or anything timely for that matter."

"I appreciate it."

"Yep. Here's Luke."

The phone rustled, and Luke came back on. "Is that all?"

"Yeah. I guess so."

"How's the wedding planning going?"

He lied without pause. "Good. We never did get an RSVP from you."

"I know."

The line static crackled in his ear.

"Look, I have to go," she said. "We're due into a meeting in a few minutes."

"Good talking to you."

"You, too."

The call ended, and Wolf set down the receiver.

I know. Her lack of explanation said volumes. Wolf just wasn't sure he knew what to read into them. Was she upset he was getting married? Whether or not she still harbored relic feelings for him from their attempt at a relationship a decade prior crossed his mind whenever he saw her. But, just like back then, they rarely ran across one another. They were on different career paths, traveling in wildly different directions, crossing every once in a while for brief moments.

Patterson poked her head inside, snapping him out of his daze. "Lorber's here. Sit room in five minutes."

CHAPTER SIX

The situation room was laid out like a college class auditorium, albeit a small one, with a semi-circular row of seats rising from a stage area. Dr. Lorber and his assistant, Daphne, were hunched over their laptops at the front of the room. The projector screen pulled down behind them, showing the title *Benjamin Cruz and Jack Whitcomb*, along with the day's date.

Wolf walked down the center aisle to the empty front row, passing District Attorney White, who was seated next to his two assistants. The DA was on his phone, lost in a conversation, but Wolf nodded to ADA Dan Warhola.

On the other side of the aisle, Waze typed a message to somebody on his phone. Next to him, Wilson also tapped his fingers on the screen of his cell, the undersheriff just as lost in technology as the rest of them.

When Wolf's phone vibrated insistently in his own pocket, as if he were missing a phone call, he ignored it out of principle. He settled into the chair next to Rachette and Patterson.

"All going well on Instagram?"

"Huh?" Rachette looked up from his own phone. "What? No. I'm looking at TJ's baseball schedule. He's playing Patty's kid's team for the league championship tomorrow night. You ready for that, Patty?"

Patterson raised a thumb.

"She's just disturbed at how bad TJ's team's gonna kick their ass."

"We'll see," Patterson said.

"Yeah. We will. I'm excited. The team has worked real hard this year. Improved a lot."

The screen at the front of the room changed from the placeholder text to a picture of the mangled dead body overhead.

Rachette turned to the front of the room as the murmur of conversation died down. Cell phones disappeared into pockets.

"Thanks for your attention," Lorber said, lazily clicking a laser pointer in his long-fingered hand. "This is Benny Cruz. Our bear attack victim. As you can see, the animal did some serious damage to the bone and tissue." He clicked through some photos. "The chest cavity was pried open to reveal the goods beneath. The arm was completely shredded and then ripped from its socket. Plenty of teeth marks everywhere."

A photo of the face came next. It was untouched, eyes closed like in a peaceful sleep.

"But all this definitely wasn't the cause of death. I found two gunshot wounds and retrieved two bullets. Both 9mm FMJs. Both shots to the chest lodged in his spinal column."

Lorber clicked through more photos showing different angles of the man and various body parts. There were tattoos on every square inch of skin except hands and face: skulls, fire, guns, demons.

"On to Jack Whitcomb."

The next body came on screen. This time, the face was frozen in the surprised expression of a D-list actor, both eyes open, one eyebrow raised. He lay straight now, no longer twisted as he had been against the tree.

"Three gunshot wounds. Chest, shoulder, and back. We found five corresponding casings at the rear corner of the cabin."

Lorber clicked the pointer, and pictures of the brass shells appeared. "No usable prints after firing. Not even a partial."

DA White raised his hand in the air, morning light glinting off the Rolex affixed to his wrist. "Time of death for these two?"

"I think Saturday fits." Lorber moved to the other side of the floor, crossing his arms, the laser pointer dangling from his spindly fingers.

"Any prints inside the house?" Patterson asked.

"We found some layered prints on the doorknobs, but they were too convoluted to yield any match. We found one soda can and a half-eaten bag of McDonalds. The soda can was covered in condensation at some point, which we know is bad for prints. The fries container, the burger wrappers, all of it was a smudged mess." Lorber shrugged his bony shoulders. "We tried. What can I say? If there's any usable prints in that place, we couldn't find them."

"Any receipts inside those fast-food bags?" Waze asked.

"No," Wolf said.

Waze's eyes slid to him. "Did you speak to the sheriff up in Doyle?"

"I did." Wolf relayed the substance of the conversation between him and the sheriff of Anniston County and the shootout they had at the biker gang compound near Doyle.

"Sons of the Void," Waze said. "They're some of the worst."

Pictures of the shattered and dismantled GPS unit came on screen, and Lorber continued talking. "This is a compact personal GPS tracking device from a company called Stonehouse Security. As you can see, it was disabled and destroyed in the process. No information is stored within, so there was none for us to find."

"Can you tell what was in the duffle bag?" Waze asked.

"We think money. We found numerous red and blue security fibers and traces of linen and cotton, like what is found in US paper currency."

"Ahh," Waze said, looking around. "So, somebody is shooting up the Sons of the Void and stealing their money. They come down south, then find the GPS tracker and smash it. But it's too late. They've been followed."

"But whoever was in that cabin was better than these two," Lorber said.

"It's one gun that shot and killed these two?" Waze asked.

Lorber nodded. "Correct."

"And what about the owner of the cabin?" Waze asked. "Have we gotten hold of him yet?"

"No, sir," Rachette said.

"What's his name?" Waze asked.

"Jim Everson," Rachette said. "Seventy-three years old. Lives down near Ashland."

"We don't think he's our man, do we?"

Undersheriff Wilson scoffed. "Not likely."

"We have his name, phone number, and address," Rachette said. "We'll go to him if need be."

"It need be," Waze said.

"Yes, sir."

"So, all we have are the names of the dead guys," White said.

All eyes landed on Wolf. He nodded.

"No witnesses. No weapons. No prints." The DA upturned his hands. After a theatrical pause, he stood up and left the room, his two assistants in tow.

When the doors clapped shut, Waze got up, descended the steps, and stood next to Lorber, crossing his arms as he faced the room. Wilson remained seated.

"Alright," Waze said. "So, we basically have nothing concrete."

"We'll talk to the cabin owner today, sir," Rachette said.

"You'd better. Because I'm not going on camera today, telling people to be on the lookout for stray biker gang members. We have to get on top of this. Or, at least, make it look like we are."

"We'll get on it," Wolf said.

Waze relaxed his position, unbuttoning his formal coat. "Just see what this guy says. I'm not expecting you guys to jump into a firefight between warring factions of psychos on motorcycles. I'm just..."

"You need something to tell the governor, who called you again this morning," Patterson said.

"That's right. How'd you know?" He feigned astonishment, wiped his forehead, and turned to leave. "Keep me posted."

Waze left up the stairs with the undersheriff in tow.

Wolf, Patterson, and Rachette followed into the squad room, gathering around Rachette's desk.

Next to them sat Yates's desk, vacant and clean.

Rachette slapped his pocket and pulled out his phone. He looked at the screen and answered. "Detective Rachette...yes I did...yes, Mr. Everson," he eyed them. "Thank you for calling me back."

Wolf and Patterson watched patiently while Rachette coaxed the man into coming into the station.

"Thank you, sir. We look forward to seeing you then." Rachette pocketed his phone. "He says he can be here by three o'clock this afternoon."

CHAPTER SEVEN

Wolf spent the rest of the morning and time after lunch at his desk catching up on a mound of paperwork and emails. When that was done, he took to staring at the wall and then fell asleep.

His cell phone buzzed on the desktop, jerking him awake. He picked it up. Piper.

"Hey," he answered.

"How's the case coming?"

He wiped the drool from his chin and stretched an arm overhead. "Good."

She chuckled. "Sounds like you were just sleeping."

"Only a little."

"Listen, not to wake you up too much here, but I just had an interesting conversation with your mother."

"Oh no. What now?"

"She seemed to think we should be inviting her cousin or someone to the wedding. I didn't recognize the name or how we knew or didn't know the person. I told her we'd talk about it and get back to her."

"Oh. Okay." He sighed, standing up and stretching an arm over his head. The muscles in his back felt like they were poked with a red-hot iron rod. "I'll deal with it."

"Thank you. I told her you'd call. I didn't know what to say...but we're pretty much tapped out on capacity as it is."

"I know. I'll talk to her."

"Thank you. So, are we good on what I showed you yesterday?" she asked. "I have to drop off a check by next week if that's how we want everything. I was thinking about dropping it by today when I come into town."

He stared at the wall, thinking of the plans again.

"David?"

"Yes."

"Yes, you're okay with everything? Yes, I should deliver the check today?"

He went to the window and looked outside.

"Or..." she said, "I could wait a few days. Like I said, we don't have to give them the check until next week. You definitely don't sound convinced. If it's not a hell yes, then it's a hell no."

"Okay, sure," he said. "Whatever you think."

She scoffed, then said nothing. He didn't blame her as he repeated what he just said in his mind. She obviously wanted to get this piece of planning out of her hair, and he was acting like an idiot. Still, this wasn't the time to open up about his troubled past.

Stop complaining.

"Listen," he said, narrowing his eyes with resolve. "I'm sorry. I'm just a bit busy. Go ahead and drop the check off. I'm good. Everything's good. Let's do it."

"You're sure?"

"Yeah."

"O-kay," she said slowly. "Well, have a good day. I'll see you later."

"Okay, bye."

He hung up, noting the pain from his back rapidly moving to his head. Rubbing his temple with his free hand, he dialed his mother and put the phone to his ear.

The phone rang eight times and went to a voice recording that told him her voicemail box was full.

He hung up, and a second later, the phone rang. It was his mother.

"Hi," he said.

"You called me?"

"Yes," he said. "I hear you called Piper. Something about inviting a guest to the wedding? Somebody that's not already on the list?"

"I did?"

He sagged back into his chair, closing his eyes. His mother's dementia was steadily growing worse, with more reminders every time he interacted with her. "She said you wanted to invite a cousin of yours."

"Shirley?" she asked.

"I don't know. Is that your cousin?"

"Yes. Did you invite her?"

"Mom. Is Derek over there?" Derek, the in-home nurse, visited her apartment five days a week.

"He just left."

Two knocks hit the door, and Patterson poked her head inside. "Hey—" she stopped talking and waited.

Wolf pulled the phone from his ear. "Yeah?"

"Cabin owner's here."

Wolf nodded. "Listen, Mom. I'll call you later, okay? I have to get back to work."

"Have a good day," she said and hung up.

He looked at the phone and sat it down.

"Everything okay?" Patterson asked.

"No."

"What happened?"

"Nothing. The cabin owner's here? Where?"

"Reception. You want us to bring him in here?"

"Yes, please."

"Be right back." She left.

Wolf stood up and stretched his arms overhead again, sucked in a deep breath, then blew out. Stress from the last few minutes left his body, but not all of it. Some still squat on his chest like a stone gargoyle.

He turned at the sound of the door opening. "This way, sir."

Patterson came in, followed by an elderly man dressed in a flannel shirt and jeans. A trucker hat with a picture of a jumping trout perched precariously on his head.

"This is Mr. Jim Everson," Patterson said. "Mr. Everson, this is Detective Wolf."

Everson nodded, eyes squinting in a distrustful glare.

Wolf shook his hand and gestured to one of the chairs in front of his desk.

Everson took off his hat, revealing a wispy combover, and sat down. Patterson sat next to him.

Rachette came in last and perched on the couch armrest.

"Thanks for coming in to speak with us today, sir," Wolf said.

"You're welcome."

"I take it you've heard what happened at your property."

"Yes." The man held his hat in both hands on his lap,

looking around at the stark walls of Wolf's office, landing his gaze on the CSU Rams clock. "I graduated from there myself."

Patterson cleared her throat. "Sir, we spoke to the property management company for your cabin to get your number, and they informed us they had no knowledge of anybody staying there. But we also found a key inside the property. No sign of forced entry."

Everson rarely blinked as he watched Patterson speak.

"Were you there in the last couple of days?" she asked.

"No."

"Okay. Does that mean you gave somebody access to the property without giving notice to your property managers?"

"I did."

"And who was that?"

A hint of anger narrowed Everson's eyes. "I don't have to explain myself to anyone. It's my property, and I can rent it out to anybody I want." Everson pointed at a wall with his hat. "This property management company's doing a terrible job. Dropping the ball all the time. Not cleaning the place right, and then I get the bad reviews online for it. One time, they didn't even hand over the key. Straight up had the tenant waiting at their office, which was closed for some godforsaken reason on a Tuesday afternoon! They stink."

Wolf put up a hand, nodding with sympathy. "Sir, I get it. These companies can be a pain. What we're trying to ascertain is who rented the place. That's all. You've heard about the two dead bodies. We believe the person who rented the cabin could be responsible."

"Yes. Of course. I heard." He looked down at his hands, nodding profusely. "I don't know exactly who he was. He called himself Adam."

"Adam?" Patterson wrote down the name in her notebook.

"But I don't think it was his name. He said, 'You can call me Adam.' Which I took to mean, don't ask me my name."

"Doesn't that raise any red flags for you when you're considering renting the cabin to somebody?"

Everson twisted the hat in his hands. "Normally. But when he pulled out a banded wad of ten thousand dollars in cash, I didn't really care what his name was. I asked him how many nights he wanted it."

Rachette whistled softly.

"And there was just one man?" Wolf asked.

"Yes, sir."

"Was he on a motorcycle?"

"No, sir. In a pickup truck."

Patterson and Rachette looked up from their notes.

"A truck?" Patterson asked.

"That's right. He said he wanted the place for a week and would decide if he needed it longer after that."

"And so he paid you, and then what?" Patterson asked. "You didn't ask any questions? Took no information from him? A license plate, a phone number?"

Everson shook his head.

"I'm confused," Rachette said. "How did this man get ahold of you if not through the property management company?"

"I have a friend down at the gas station that told me about him. This guy came in asking around for a place to stay, and my friend told him about me."

"What gas station is this?" Wolf asked.

"Prickly Pines Pumps on 734."

"That's the one just north of Ashland," Patterson said, writing furiously in her notes. "Right?"

"That's right," Everson said. "That's the one."

"Which day was this?" Patterson asked.

"Let's see." He looked at the ceiling. "Saturday."

"Time?"

"Just after lunch. I remember because my friend called me right as I was washing the dishes."

"So, noon?"

"I eat lunch at noon every day, on the dot. So must have been more like 12:30."

"What kind of vehicle was he driving?" Wolf asked.

"A Ford F-150. Kind of beat up. Had a big dent and scratch on one of the rear sides."

"Color?" Patterson asked.

"Dark blue."

"Did you take down a license plate number?" Rachette asked.

"No, sir. And I can't remember. I know it was Colorado plates. I do remember seeing that because I wondered. But that was when he was driving away. And my eyes aren't what they used to be."

"Tell us about the meeting," Wolf said. "How did it go down?"

"I got the call from my friend at the gas station. I went there and met him. We went outside to chat, and that's when he showed me...how he planned on paying me. After that," Everson shrugged, "I led him by vehicle out to my cabin. I gave him the key and left him be."

"This is all very helpful," Patterson said. "How about what he looked like?"

Everson shrugged. "White guy. Tall. Kind of overweight."

"Tattoos?" Rachette asked.

"No. No tattoos."

"Long hair? Short hair?"

"Short. Gray and black. Mostly gray."

"Age?" Wolf asked.

"Old guy. Older than you. But younger than me. He was probably in his sixties."

Wolf exchanged glances with his detectives. The description was anything but typical of a biker gang member or somebody who would go on a killing rampage.

"Clothing?" Patterson asked.

"Uh, let's see. I think he had a gray T-shirt with some kind of writing on it, something or other."

"Harley-Davidson motorcycles?" Rachette asked.

"No. More like...something with palm trees. Yeah. Some island. Something you get on a vacation, like that. And he had dark sweatpants on. I remember thinking somebody dressed like him and driving that beat-up piece of junk had no business having ten grand in cash."

"Didn't that set off any alarm bells for you?" Patterson asked.

"Maybe." Everson shrugged unapologetically. "Ten grand. The money did the talking."

"Did he have any luggage?" Wolf asked. "A duffle bag?"

"Nothing that I saw. I showed him how to get in, gave him my phone number in case he needed anything, and left him be."

Patterson wrote in her notes.

"I haven't done anything wrong," Everson said. "It was my place. I can do what I want with it."

The property managers would probably have something else to say, but Wolf didn't care how that turned out for the man. They'd gotten a lead.

"I'm going to get on the horn with Ashland PD," Rachette said, leaving the room.

Wolf nodded, standing up and holding out a hand. "Thank you, sir."

Everson grunted as he stood, offering a frail grip.

Wolf and Patterson walked him to the door.

"Sir, if you wouldn't mind filling out a form for me, I'd be very appreciative," Patterson said, leading him down the hall.

Wolf left the door open and sat back down, swiveling to look out the window. The sky was darkening in the west, threatening rain.

"Okay," Rachette said, marching in. "I called Ashland PD. They've got a unit on the way to the Prickly Pines Pumps. They'll check the surveillance and let us know."

CHAPTER EIGHT

An hour after Everson's visit, Wolf, Rachette, Waze, and Patterson congregated in the squad room around Patterson's desk, summoned by a group text message from Patterson to meet her there.

"What's up?" Waze asked.

She turned in her chair, shaking her head. Her hands splayed open. "They don't have any footage at the Prickly Pines gas station."

"What?" Waze asked. "That's impossible."

"Their system turned over yesterday and erased the footage from the previous week."

"And they don't have a backup or something?" Rachette asked.

"No," Patterson said. She raised a finger. "But I did talk to the gas station manager and the owner and confirmed that a man calling himself Adam did come in. According to the owner, he was driving a blue Ford F-150."

"Dent on the side?" Waze asked.

"He didn't know about that."

"Of course, he didn't."

"The owner said he engaged him in a conversation about the cabin for rent, and the owner handed over the number."

"What was the description of the man the manager and owner gave?" Wolf asked.

She turned around, picking up her notebook. "Not much different from Everson's, but...I'd say a bit more vague." She shook her head, tapping the page. "Gray hair. White male. Late fifties or early sixties. Wearing sunglasses and a baseball cap, so they had no idea about eye color. Height of five-eight to five-ten. No identifying tattoos or scars they could recall." She dropped the notebook.

"Damn it," Waze said.

"How about a receipt?" Wolf asked.

"None."

"He paid cash, of course," Waze said. "Have you called the men up in Doyle to ask about the Ford F-150? Maybe they have a report of one of those being stolen."

"No, sir. Not yet."

Waze's eyes glazed over, his lower jaw jutting forward. "Wolf, you got their phone number?"

"You want me to call them?"

"No. I want you to give me the number. I'll call."

Wolf pulled out his phone and relayed the number while Waze tapped his own screen.

Waze put the cell up to his ear. "I'm not gonna sit around here with my thumb up my ass, ducking calls from senators and governors all afternoon. I need some answers, damn it. Hey, hello?" He walked away to the nearest window. "This Sheriff Brandenburg? Yeah. This is Sheriff Gregory Waze, down in Sluice-Byron County...good. Listen, have you had a report of any stolen vehicles over the last few days? Specifically, a beat-up dark-blue Ford F-150."

"With a scratch and dent on the rear," Rachette said.

"Yes." Waze relayed the info into the phone. "No?"

Waze walked back, shaking his head, running a hand through his hair. He paced back and forth, listening.

"Nothing? Okay. Got it. Listen, I'm going to send up my detectives on this."

Wolf exchanged a glance with Rachette and Patterson.

"Yeah, I understand that, but I have two dead bodies in my county, and we're just as deep into this investigation as you are. We may as well pool our resources and see what we can come up with. Yeah, well, the only lead we have brings us up to you, so..."

Waze walked away quickly toward his office. "I understand," he said, but his tone said otherwise. He disappeared inside the room, still talking.

Wolf followed, stopping outside the office to listen.

"...very capable. Okay? Okay, it's settled. They'll be up tomorrow morning, and you can take it up with him. My lead detective is David Wolf...that's right."

Wolf rounded the corner and looked in through the open door. Waze sat behind his desk with his chair pushed back, a fake grin plastered on his face.

"...great. Ha, don't worry. Look, I have a lot of pressure down here to make moves on this, and I really appreciate it. I'm sure you get where I'm coming from. I'll talk to you soon. You have my number. Goodbye." The smile disappeared as Waze pulled the phone from his ear, pecked at the screen, and threw it onto his desk with a clatter. "Prick."

Waze put both hands to his eyes, rubbed hard, then lowered them. "Wolf! Oh...Wolf, get in here."

Patterson and Rachette were already standing next to him, so the three detectives walked inside.

"What was that?" Wolf asked.

"You guys are going up to Doyle. They're expecting you tomorrow morning."

Wolf blinked. "Okay."

"We need answers, and we've run into a brick wall here. I'm not sitting on my ass for who knows how long while we wait for these guys up in Doyle to relay what they have or haven't figured out. They couldn't even call Patterson back earlier, and we were going to let them run this investigation? We need to know what they know."

Patterson and Rachette eyed one another.

"How long are you planning on us being up there?" Wolf asked.

"How long?" Waze scoffed. "As long as needed. How about that? You get me answers fast, and everyone will be happy."

"I'll go up myself," Wolf said.

"We'll go, too," Rachette said.

Patterson remained silent.

"Don't you guys have a baseball game to attend tomorrow?" Wolf asked.

"The job comes first," Patterson said. "Our families know how it goes."

Wolf shook his head. "I'm going alone."

Waze stared hard at Wolf, nodding. The color in his face had cooled to his normal tan. His breathing was long and relaxed now. "Good. Yes. You two stay. You can deal with our end of things and see your kids play baseball. You don't want to miss that type of stuff. Pretty soon, they'll be out of the house and calling you once a year."

Patterson nodded. "Yes, sir."

Rachette nodded reluctantly.

"Why don't you two leave me and Wolf to talk privately, please."

Patterson and Rachette left, shutting the door behind them on the way out.

Waze stood, folded his arms behind him, and faced the window, presenting his back to Wolf.

"Everything okay, sir?" Wolf asked.

"Yeah," Waze said, turning around and putting on the same fake smile he had used with the Brandenburg phone call.

"What kind of pressure are you dealing with here? The council? The governor?" Wolf shook his head. "They can't exactly demand you solve cases with the snap of a finger. These things take time. Sometimes, they're not solved at all."

"Yeah, about that." Waze sat down. He pulled himself up to his desk and folded his arms. "Sit, please."

Wolf sat.

"My first few months here have been quite a transition for me...in and out of the office. I'm sure you have deduced by now that I've quit drinking."

"Yes, sir. Good job."

Waze flicked a hand. "It sucks. But I needed to do it."

Wolf said nothing, watching as Waze shuffled his thoughts.

"I hear you did the same thing," Waze said.

"That's right."

"How was it?"

"It sucked. But I needed to."

The sheriff raised one side of his mouth. "The pressure they're laying on...it's complicated."

"Try me," Wolf said.

"Thatcher," Waze said.

Wolf prickled with annoyance. "What about Thatcher?"

"He's not happy about Jorel."

"Yeah. You already told me. Tell him to join the club. The two suspects who killed Jorel and disposed of his body in some unknown way are dead. Their mother, the only person who could possibly know anything, is not talking." Wolf turned up his hands. "I'm not sure what Thatcher would have us do."

Waze smiled, but his eyes remained troubled. "Jorel's father has been a lifelong congressman from New Hampshire. Did you know that?"

"We met him last year after Jorel's disappearance," Wolf said, sensing a troubling turn to the conversation. "What about him?"

"Senator Jorel and Thatcher, combined, are quite the influential duo. And...I'll just be frank here...they've chosen you as their scapegoat for Jorel's disappearance."

Wolf shook his head.

"I know. I know." Waze stood up again and walked to the window. "I'm just telling you what I know. Jorel's father and Thatcher are certain types of men who need balance in a situation. A debit and a credit."

"And I'm the...debit?"

Waze turned around and looked hard at him. "When the governor mentioned to me this morning that we'd better be looking very good on this case, or, and I quote, 'We'll be looking for you to make some big changes with your new department,' you can see why I'm feeling a bit on edge here."

Wolf shook his head. "Bastards."

"Yes. They are all bastards." Waze sniffed. "But they are bastards that control everything that really counts when it comes down to it."

"So...what?" Wolf asked.

"So...do your job," Waze said. "And do your job well. Just like you've always done. Personally, I want to look good while I'm in office, and losing my best detective is not the way to do that. Right now, they don't have a stone to stand on. Don't give them one."

Wolf stared back at Waze. "Stones can be made out of thin air pretty easily. Especially by a billionaire and a congressman."

Waze shrugged. "And what are you going to do about that?"

Wolf stood up. "I guess all I can do is my job."

"Keep me posted."

"I will."

CHAPTER NINE

Rachette sat in the front seat of his SUV, staring at the small house silhouetted in the orange glow of the setting sun behind the western wall of the Chautauqua Valley.

At one time, he'd been jealous of the place. A small two-bedroom set among the trees, a baseball throw from the river. Now, as he stared out of the bug-stained windshield of his truck, the place looked run down. The flower boxes sprouted weeds, and the lawn surrounding the place was sporadic and unkempt. The garden gnomes that at one point spiced the place up now looked like partygoers standing among discarded beer cans.

He tapped and pinched his cell phone screen, zooming the camera into the license plate of the Ford Fiesta parked behind Yates's truck in the driveway, and took a photo. He would run the information tomorrow at the station to get a hit. Rachette had never seen the vehicle before but certainly didn't like the guys driving it. They had the look of dangerous drug dealers. At least, the passenger of the car had looked mean. He was muscular, covered in tattoos, and had a look that said he'd hurt a lot of people. The driver—a tall, skinny guy with long hair and a dumb smile—not so much.

A TV flickered in the window, showing an episode of Friends. *Friends.*

Rachette scoffed aloud.

Inside the window, the tall guy stood up from the couch, no longer carrying the paper bag he had taken in. He counted a stack of bills and put them in his pocket, solidifying Rachette's earlier guess of drug dealers.

Dealers. For what? How far had Yates slipped? How far had Rachette let him slip? That second question was like a punch in the gut.

He rechecked the quality of the picture and pocketed his phone. Then he shoved another handful of fries in his mouth.

Damn, he loved these fries. It had been at least two years since he'd allowed himself the indulgence. Ironically, it had been Yates who had turned him around back then, getting him to realize the weight he had put on was doing nobody any good. It had been Yates alone who had pushed him to get back in shape. Now Rachette couldn't believe how much Yates had let himself go.

Rachette ignored the churning bomb about to explode in his gut and unwrapped another burger, finishing it in a few bites. He washed it all down with a supersized Coca-Cola, closing his eyes at the sweet, salty taste as it slid down his throat.

What was Rachette doing, relapsing like this? Something about coming here had freed all those inner demons he'd locked away twenty-four months ago.

The phone rang, beeping in the speakers as the dashboard system took the call and displayed Charlotte's number.

"Shit." He slid his tongue around, swallowing the final pieces of his last bite, and pressed the answer button. "Hey, babe."

"Hey, where are you?"

He turned down the volume. "I'm just...finishing up some calls."

"I didn't see you when I left the squad room."

This was the problem with working in the same freaking building with his wife. Any time he took a shit, she knew about it. "I'm just out. Okay?"

"Okay..." she said.

"Listen, sorry. I'm just a little shaken up about today. I'll see you later. You guys can eat without me."

"Shaken up? Where are you? I'll pick you up when you want to come home."

"No," he said, irritation rising in his voice. "Look, I'm not drinking. I'll just be home in a bit."

She hesitated, then said. "Okay. I love you."

"I love you too."

"Bye."

He poked the dash screen and ended the call.

He shut his eyes, relaxing the tension in his jaw. When he opened them, he set aside the food and opened the door.

Wiping his hands on his jeans, he marched to the house with long, purposeful strides.

He stepped up onto the porch and pounded the door three times.

"Who is it?" a voice said, muffled.

"Who is it? Your mom, asshole! Open up!" He tried the door, but it was locked.

A commotion inside, somebody saying to stay back.

The door opened, and the first thing that came out was the barrel of Yates's personal Glock 19.

"Get that shit out of my face," Rachette said, pushing the gun aside.

"What the hell are you doing here?" Yates lowered the gun, eyes bulging, barely visible through the slits of greasy hair that hung low on his forehead. His beard was almost down to his chest, streaked with two silver plumes that would have been cool had it not been for the knots that proved it hadn't been washed since inception.

"Who's this?" Skinny-Guy stood by the television. His tone was incredulous.

Rachette turned his head slowly, raking his eyes from the greaseball's flip-flopped feet to his pimple-scarred face. "I'm your worst nightmare, asshole."

"Okay." The guy laughed, and Rachette let his face go blank.

Thick-and-Dangerous, the source of Skinny-Guy's confidence no doubt, stood up from the couch. "Hey," he said. "Why don't you turn around and leave, huh?"

Rachette smiled brightly. Mocking the guy's tone precisely, he said, "Hey, prick, why don't you go fuck yourself, huh?"

"Okay, Rachette, dude." Yates put the gun in the back of his pants and held up his hands. "Relax."

Thick-and-Dangerous walked up and stood chest-to-chest with Rachette, looking down from at least a head taller height.

Rachette punched him in the jaw at a diagonal angle, knocking him out instantly. Knees buckling, he landed in a heap, but before he was on the ground, Rachette was already stepping over him toward Skinny-Guy.

Yates tried to stop him, but being such a slow-weak version of his former self, Rachette slapped him away easily.

"Hey, man! Chill ou—" Skinny-Guy didn't get the words out because Rachette grabbed him by the shirt, pulled, and launched him out the door. The guy windmill-stepped twice and tumbled off the deck in a cloud of limbs before rolling down the stairs.

"Ah!"

Thick-and-Dangerous stirred awake, so Rachette kicked the side of his head, putting him back to sleep. Then, he grabbed him by the feet and pulled all two-hundred-fifty pounds of him out of the house, down the stairs, and to the back door of the car.

The exertion took every bit of his strength and then some. Dropping the guy's beefy legs, he screamed in triumph into the blood-orange sky and flexed his arms. "Ahhhh!"

Again, he turned to Skinny-Guy and pointed at the rear door. "Open it."

"Okay. Yeah, okay." The guy got up and snapped to attention, opening the rear door.

"Get him in."

Thick-and-Dangerous groaned, trying to get up.

Rachette pulled his own gun from the rear of his pants.

"Whoa, man! Get in, Calvin! Get in. He's getting in."

Rachette put the gun to the head of Thick-and-Dangerous. "Get up and get in."

The guy did.

Rachette shut the door and pointed the gun at Skinny-

Guy. "If either of you come back here ever again, I'll shoot you dead and throw you in an abandoned mine shaft."

"Yes. Yes, sir. We're leaving." He ran around the car, jammed his bony limbs behind the wheel, and fired up the engine.

Rachette watched the vehicle back up and sputter away.

Then he vomited. All the food he'd just packed into his belly came out in a torrent onto the ground.

Eyes watering, he turned to the blurry form standing in the doorway.

"Ho-ly shit," Yates said.

Rachette wiped his mouth. "Hey, man."

"What the hell is wrong with you?"

Rachette laughed, not having to act to make it sound psychotic. "Mind if I come in?" He wiped his eyes, putting the gun in the back of his pants as he stepped up the stairs.

Yates backed up, watching him with a defiant, untrusting glare.

It was the loss of trust that really pissed Rachette off. After everything they'd been through, he was looking at him like he was some stranger off the street, like less of a friend than those two assholes that had just sold him death in a bag. But Rachette remained silent, shutting the door behind him. He took in the interior of the place.

The blank walls were the first thing that struck him. A few months ago, back when Yates had been on the good track, healing his body, mind, and soul and on his way back into the detective squad, he had been in the thick of his relationship with Gemma Thatcher. Back then, the walls had been covered in a style beyond Rachette's comprehension.

In some way Rachette would never understand, Yates had won the woman's heart during a case involving her restaurant. After his gunshot wound to the chest, she had taken it upon herself to nurse him back to health, and they had fallen in love. The kind of love that made Rachette jealous and a little bit sick. Like...how could two people get along so well without even the occasional misunderstanding? Rachette had never witnessed so much as a millisecond of awkwardness between them. Only hand-holding, and kissing, and laughing. *Nauseating.*

When she'd moved in, although ludicrously quick for Rachette's taste, the whole thing had seemed normal. In-line with the rest of their whirlwind relationship. And she hadn't just moved in; she had transformed the place with furniture, paint, and rugs, all paid for with a diamond-encrusted credit card.

But then something had happened, and she was gone. Rachette was pretty sure she'd left all the stuff. So...where was it?

His eyes went to the corner. It lacked something. And then it all came to him.

"Where's your guitar?"

Yates said nothing.

"You sold your guitar? The guitar your dad gave you?"

Not a hint of shame shone in Yates's dead eyes. "Hocked it."

"You sold the guitar your dead father gave you for drugs."

Yates's eyelids lowered to half-mast.

"And that's where all the decorations went, too?"

Yates shrugged.

"Geez, man. That's pathetic." He walked around the

living room, taking in the place like he was on a house tour in an episode of *Lifestyles of the Broken and Disturbed.*

As he approached the pitted Barcalounger, Yates was clearly using with a vengeance, the smell of body odor intensified, along with the scent of stale beer. It was like they were standing in Beer Goggles on a Saturday night.

"Found two dead bodies yesterday."

Yates said nothing.

"Yep. Couple of biker dudes from Sons of the Void. They were shot and killed. We're looking for the killer now. Strangely enough, it looks like it might have been some old guy. Doesn't look like a killer at all. Wolf's going up to northern Colorado. Place called Doyle. You been there?"

When Yates remained silent again, Rachette looked at him.

"Are you listening?"

"I'm listening. I just don't particularly care."

The words spit in the face of Rachette's temper, but he kept himself calm. He took a few breaths, just like Patterson had been yammering on about with her martial arts training. Surprisingly, it somewhat worked. After the anger went away, he felt the sucking emptiness that filled the room.

"It's really sad in here," Rachette said, his voice low. "I don't like seeing you like this."

Yates's eyes flashed. "Oh, you're sad? Well, go fuck your-self with your tiny dick. That will give you a real reason to be sad."

"Okay." Rachette picked a brown paper bag up off the table next to the chair, making sure to knock over a few beer cans as he did so. He pulled out two plastic bags filled with hundreds of pills each. Pounds of them.

He lifted the bag and looked at the markings. "Hydrocodone. Percocet."

Yates's eyes flashed again, this time with possessiveness.

"Are you kidding me?" Rachette opened one of the bags and pulled out a pill. "These are real?"

Yates said nothing.

"I'm assuming so. Otherwise, you'd be dead a hundred times over, taking this much counterfeit stuff. You do remember counterfeit pills laced with deadly amounts of fentanyl from your job as a detective with the local sheriff's department, don't you?"

Yates rolled his eyes. He went to an end table next to the couch and brought over a handful of blue-tipped paper strips. "Fentanyl test strips. I pick a few random pills and have them test them in front of me. Any presence of the stuff and I pull the plug. But I trust them. There's never been any fentanyl. They're real."

"How are you getting these?" Rachette asked, holding both bags up to the light.

Yates pointed out the window. "The two guys you just beat the piss out of."

"How are they getting them?"

Yates shrugged.

Rachette shook his head, lowering the bags. "You remember me coming over a few weeks ago?"

The look in Yates's eye said no.

"You were passed out in the chair here. The door was open, so I came in. I woke you up. We talked, but I wondered if you would remember any of it."

"I wondered why I found my pills in the fireplace."

Rachette smiled. "Good detective work. Although...

that's not what you are anymore. Right? Now you're just a junky."

Yates raised his chin.

Rachette looked him up and down. "Look at yourself."

"Give me those."

"You know they're gunning to bring in another detective."

Yates stared at the bags of pills.

"You haven't spoken to Dr. Hawkwood. You haven't come in to talk to Waze. You're ignoring his calls."

Rachette went to the fireplace, kicking aside another beer can. The carpet was covered in crumbs, thousands of multicolored flecks of snack food crushed into bits.

"You dumped a billionaire's daughter. Do you recall that? Does that even register in your mind? She was in love with you. A *billionaire's* daughter! A lifetime of sipping wine on mega yachts, and you dumped her. You said, 'Hey, I'd rather hang out with a couple of losers,' and you kicked her out of your place."

"Don't put those in there."

Rachette reached the wall and flicked the switch. The fireplace ignited with a woosh. He tossed the bags in.

"No!" Yates rushed over, stumbling to his knees, almost going into the fire headfirst. Without hesitation, he thrust his arm into the flames and pulled out the melted ziplock bags. Pills scattered everywhere, some in the fire, but most onto the carpet.

"Ah, shit." Yates sucked on a finger. "Bastard!"

Rachette watched in silent horror, the room filling with the scent of burnt plastic and arm hair.

Yates scooped the pills into piles and shoved them into the pockets of his sweatpants. Gathering every last salvageable one, he stood up and walked through the empty dining area—the one that used to hold a modern-designed hand-carved wooden table and six chairs—and entered the kitchen.

He put the pills away somewhere and then came back, this time with the gun in his hand.

Rachette remained where he was, his legs warming from the fire next to him. Sweat slid down the side of his face from his hairline and streaked down the tense muscles of his neck.

"What are you doing? Pussy?"

To Yates's credit, a bit of sanity was left in there and he kept the gun dangling at his side. "Just get out. I don't want you here."

"No."

"Get out!" He stepped up to Rachette and pointed the gun at his face.

Rachette slapped his hand away and took the gun with a fluid-twisting movement that was disturbingly easy.

Yates attacked, punching him hard in the side.

Rachette reared up with his elbow, connecting with Yates's forehead.

Yates stumbled backward and crashed into the corner of the room, slid down the wall, and landed on his backside.

"Just stay down."

Yates sat there, breathing heavily. He put a hand to his chest, panic flashing in his eyes.

"Are you alright?" Rachette stepped toward him.

Yates composed himself, and his face transformed into a mask of rage. He bared his teeth and shook his head, a hate-filled grunt rumbling in his body as he stood up.

"Yeah," Rachette said. "There you are. There's Yates!"

"Get the fuck out of here!" Spit flew from his lips. The words choked his throat. "Get out! And don't ever come back!"

Rachette walked to the door and opened it. He under-hand tossed Yates's Glock on the Barcalounger.

"No," he said. "That I'm certainly not going to do." And then he left and shut the door behind him.

CHAPTER TEN

Wolf stood at the side of the desolate highway, relieving himself into the base of a wind-bent sagebrush.

A thread-worn blanket of clouds draped over the sun to the east, still low in the sky and failing to warm the landscape of northern Colorado after a cold night. A pair of hawks circled overhead, squealing at each other.

The land in every direction was covered in green grass, sage, and greasewood that carpeted rolling hills. To the north, the land rose again for the first time since Rabbit Ears Pass down south of Steamboat Springs, but not in the jagged, snow-capped way he was used to in Rocky Points. Further up the highway where he was headed, the tops of the mountains were like long swells covered in pines.

The scene reminded him of a painting Lauren had done and hung in the bathroom when she had lived with him. Funnily enough, he'd spent many moments just like this, staring at that painting.

The floodgate to memories of Lauren and Ella had apparently opened. It didn't take Sigmund Freud to know why. He still hadn't told Piper about the plans she'd shown him.

The prior evening, Wolf had returned from work to find an empty house. Piper had been gone to a working dinner, a task she did frequently now that her boss had learned she was not only a crack investigator for the firm but also an expert schmoozer for prospective clients. When she returned, he'd already been sound asleep.

He knew he needed to break through his mother's mantra. He wasn't *complaining* by telling her what was on his mind. Piper had a right to know she was accidentally jabbing an icepick into his heart. But for some reason, waking her before dawn and telling her that just hadn't felt right, so he'd kissed her on the cheek and left quietly.

And now here he was, stewing in his inaction, regret mixing with the trepidation Waze's words had given him yesterday.

He walked to the SUV and got in, the cab a sound booth compared to the breezy conditions outside.

The GPS told him he had another seventeen miles to his destination, and his dashboard temperature light said it was fifty-eight degrees. The forecast was calling for mid-sixties.

Two miles south of Doyle he stopped at a gas station, filled his tank, and continued up the highway as it entered a wide, low valley flanked on either side by pine-covered hills. Traffic in either direction was sparse. A river came down from the mountains to the west and sidled up next to the highway, hidden beneath a wall of towering oaks, quenching green hay fields, and cattle.

At 8:12 a.m., he passed a sign reading *Doyle: Population 1,183* and entered the town.

Just like down in Rocky Points, the speed limit dropped to thirty miles per hour, and the road became Main Street, according to signs posted at crossroads. Looking down the length of the thoroughfare and then at the GPS map, only a half dozen streets were shown before the town ran out and the road continued into the valley.

Following the directions, he slowed and took the first right. Small, cubed houses squatted underneath old-growth trees. Manicured lawns were lined with bursting flowers.

Two blocks up, he turned into a parking lot and parked in front of a one-story building, squeezing between two trucks emblazoned with the Anniston County Sheriff's Department logo.

He shut off the engine and got out into the still, pleasant air, smelling of cut grass and pine trees. A mirror-finished window reflected his image, and he sensed someone inside watching him arrive. Wasting no time, he stepped onto a crumbling sidewalk and opened the front door.

The interior was quiet, far from the bustling interior of the county building down in Rocky Points, with three vacant desks. The fourth was occupied by a deputy.

The deputy watched Wolf enter, a tired-looking smile creasing his handsome face, and stood. "You must be from Rocky Points."

"Yes, sir."

The man walked over, showing he was equal to Wolf's above-average height but much more muscular.

"Deputy Nichols." He held out a massive hand, standing ramrod straight. Sandy-blond hair stood up in a mess on top, cut short on the sides. The man obviously had a penchant for the gym that would have rivaled Rachette's. "I thought there were two more detectives."

"Just me," Wolf said, shaking his thick hand. "The other two stayed back."

"Oh. Well, nice to meet you. You're even earlier than we thought you'd make it."

"I got an early start."

Nichols looked at the wall clock. "I'll say. Doesn't it take four hours to get here from Rocky Points?"

"Something like that."

Nichols chuckled. "Got ourselves an early riser here."

Wolf's eyes caught movement in another room beyond, where a sign on an open door read *Sheriff Brandenburg*.

A man appeared a second later. "Wolf?"

"Sheriff Brandenburg?"

"That's me. It's good to meet you." Brandenburg stepped on tree-trunk legs attached to a medicine ball gut. He offered a hand attached to a well-insulated arm, suggesting the man took his eating regimen as seriously as Nichols did his weights. His hair was spiked in a silver cube on top, shaved close on the sides. He wore a tan uniform and a toothbrush-bristle-length mustache of the same frosty color as his hair.

"Welcome to Doyle." He splayed his hands like they were in the center of a vast warehouse, then pointed to a coffee machine on a table against the wall. "You need coffee?"

"I'd love some, sure."

Brandenburg gave him a paper cup off a stack, waited for Wolf to pour a cup, and then poured himself one.

Nichols sat down at his desk again.

"Come on in." Brandenburg waved Wolf to his office.

Wolf followed, looking down a hallway toward a pair of doors.

"Holding cell," Brandenburg said, following his gaze. "Just one of them. I've had a few drunks in there, sobering up on the cot, but as far as criminal activity goes...it's normally pretty quiet here. Even with those biker hooligans so close."

Wolf sipped his coffee. "You just have the two of you?"

Brandenburg sat down with a grunt behind his desk. "One more deputy out on patrol. A cohort of volunteers around the county. You must know how it is. Back in the days before Sluice County merged with Byron, you were smaller, right?"

Wolf nodded, although he had never worked for such a tiny department.

"Please, have a seat."

Wolf scoped the wall as he sat in a plastic chair in front of Brandenburg's desk. There were framed photographs of the sheriff as a younger man, a hundred pounds ago, some dressed in green with palm trees in the background, others with the current tan uniform he had on now.

His eyes stopped on a different man, one much older, with a white beard and a beaming smile.

"That's Aldridge," Brandenburg said.

"Aldridge?"

"The former sheriff. I took over after his death back in... when was it?" He looked up at the ceiling, sucking in a breath as he thought. "Must have been five years ago now. He was a good man. His whole life was this job."

Wolf sat back, facing the current sheriff.

"So," Brandenburg said, sipping his coffee.

Wolf cleared his throat, reading into the man's expression. He was less than enthused to have him there. Wolf had two ways to think about the situation: One, he was stepping on their toes and needed to tread lightly. Or two, he had two dead bodies down in his county, one of which came from here, chased by a troublesome gang of bikers squatting nearby. Wolf was out of a job if he didn't come home with some resolution.

Wolf chose the latter and sat back. "How are things going?"

Brandenburg sputtered his lips. "Great."

"You said you rarely see criminal action like this up here."

"That's right."

"Unfortunately, I have some experience with stuff like this."

Brandenburg blew on his coffee, staring at Wolf through the rising steam.

Wolf cleared his throat. "Right. Well, I'd like to hear exactly what happened at the biker gang compound the other night."

Brandenburg moved without hurry as he set down his coffee, opened the top drawer, produced a manila folder, and set it on the desktop.

He sat forward as if digging into a meal, opened the folder, and spread out the pictures.

Wolf sat forward, too, and scanned the photos. One picture showed two white males with heavily tattooed skin lying in twin beds that were set along different walls of the same room. The mattresses underneath them were soaked in blood. They were dressed in underwear, and one of them was half-in, half-out of the bed as if he'd been awakened by the shots that killed the guy next to him.

"Sons of the Void," Brandenburg said. "The four victims we spoke about."

"Sir?" Nichols's voice came from behind them.

Brandenburg looked up, nodded, and lowered his eyes to the photos again.

Nichols walked into the office, sitting next to Wolf. The floor bounced, and the chair creaked as his muscled frame settled in.

Wolf glanced over. Nichols sat ramrod straight in his chair and eyed the photos.

"We got the call Saturday morning, at three a.m.," Brandenburg said.

Wolf looked at another few photos, which were zoomed closer. Just like the two victims down near Ashland, each man was covered in tattoos. The inked artwork showed the stuff of nightmares: skulls, fires, chains, demons, and guns.

"You have names for these men?" Wolf asked.

Brandenburg pulled out a list of names and read them off. One was Donald Cruz.

"Donald Cruz," Wolf said. "Remember, one of the victims we found in Ashland was Benny Cruz. His brother. The bike he was riding on was registered to an address here in Doyle." Wolf pulled out his phone, found the address in a note file, and read it off.

Brandenburg nodded. "Yep. That's the address of the compound."

Wolf pocketed his cell. "You said they called in the shooting?"

"They needed an ambulance," Brandenburg said. "It was not good. Like a war zone."

"And this is, what? Their main clubhouse?"

"They call it a compound," Nichols said. "And they have

a few of them around the west. This is not the main one. This is just the local one."

Wolf eyed Brandenburg. The sheriff seemed unperturbed by his deputy taking point in answering the question.

"How many of them live here?" Wolf asked.

"It's fluid," Brandenburg said. "There can be upward of thirty or forty of them there at a time, depending on...whatever it is it depends on."

"They have barracks," Nichols said. "A couple of buildings with bunk beds. Just like the military."

Wolf pulled a photo near him that showed a different pair of dead men than the two in the beds, both similarly covered in tattoos, also scantily dressed for sleeping. They had been run down and stopped by bullets in a hallway. Blood streaked the walls on either side of them.

A tattoo painted an arc across one of the men's bare back reading *Sons of the Void*.

"Have you guys had any run-ins with them down south?" Nichols asked.

Wolf shook his head. "No."

"They keep more north," Brandenburg said. "This is their southern compound."

"Where is this place from here?" Wolf asked.

"Southwest, about five miles outside of town," Brandenburg said. "Sits on a hundred or so acres. Big house, with two other buildings. Surrounded by woods."

"You said things are normally quiet around here," Wolf said. "They keep their noses clean with you guys?"

Brandenburg shrugged. "They keep on their best behavior. I think they have some strict don't-shit-where-you-eat rules about that."

"Are the feds active on them?"

"Not as far as we know," Brandenburg said.

"How long have they been there?"

"This is the tenth or so year."

"So, what? Do they keep their distance? Or..."

"A lot of them hang out at the saloon on Main," Brandenburg said. "A place called the Dusty Thorn."

Wolf sat back. "What did they tell you happened?"

"They said a gunman came in shooting up the place," Brandenburg said.

"A single man?"

"Yes."

"Thirty or forty men and nobody got a well-placed shot off?"

"They only had a few others there that night," Brandenburg said.

Wolf nodded. "And they didn't tell you who it was."

"Nope."

"Description?"

"They didn't have a good one. They just told us it was fast. Bam-bam-bam, in and out."

"What about the vehicle?"

"They didn't see one," Brandenburg said.

"That's it?" Wolf asked. "No other specifics?"

Brandenburg chuckled under his breath, his neck wobbling. "These guys are cagey. They just wanted the ambulance. That was pretty clear."

Wolf folded his arms. "I told you we found a GPS unit and a duffle bag."

"We figure that's why they didn't tell us anything," Nichols said. "They wanted to keep the chase to themselves. They wouldn't want cops finding them first and taking the money."

Wolf looked at Brandenburg and raised an eyebrow. "You think it was money?"

Brandenburg hesitated, a hint of annoyance at his deputy showing for the first time. "I think it was drugs, guns, or money. Like I told you before, that's what they deal with."

"And people," Nichols said.

"Thank you, Deputy," Brandenburg said.

Nichols appeared unaffected by his boss's admonition.

"Our ME found traces of money fibers inside the bag," Wolf said.

"Oh, okay then," Brandenburg said. "My deputy's assessment makes sense then. They were keeping the man's identity quiet so they could get their money before anyone else did. Is that your assessment?" he asked Wolf.

Wolf nodded. "We also learned from the cabin owner down in Ashland that the man paid cash to rent the place for a week. A lot of cash."

Brandenburg's eyes narrowed. He folded his arms on his belly and rubbed his chin. "And this cabin owner didn't get a name?"

"The man told him to call him Adam."

"So, he was using a pseudonym."

Wolf nodded.

"And what was this cabin owner's description of the man?" Brandenburg asked.

"Vague. Gray, black hair and a beard of the same color. The gas station owner told us pretty much the same. The cabin owner described a dark-blue Ford F-150 truck. One with a large scratch and dent in one of the rear sides."

"So we heard," Brandenburg said, "and read on the APB you guys put out."

They sat in silence as Wolf scanned the photographs again.

"Well," Brandenburg said. "You're here. What would you like to do with your time?"

"I think the only thing we can do that makes any sense is visit the Sons of the Void compound."

Brandenburg's eye twitched. Nichols's chair creaked.

When neither spoke, Wolf realized fear had dropped into the room. "We found two of their members," he said. "Shot dead. We found their duffle bag. They'll want to know about it. I haven't told them. Have you?"

Brandenburg nodded, his jowls wobbling as he sucked in a breath. "You're right. They'll be grateful we're delivering the news at least."

Wolf nodded, then scooted forward to stand, noting it took a full second longer for Brandenburg to snap out of his thoughts and do the same.

"You'll ride with me," Brandenburg said. "Nichols, you can hold the fort down."

"I can go, too, if you want more men," Nichols said. "Larkin's coming in this morning."

"No. Stay here."

Nichols nodded, looking slightly disappointed.

"Refill before we leave?" Brandenburg asked, lifting his coffee mug and walking out of the office with quick steps. Whatever hesitation he had before was long gone.

"Yes, please," Wolf said as he followed him out.

CHAPTER ELEVEN

"Here you go, ma'am."

The barista handed the cup of tea to Piper. She sipped the boiling liquid and burned her lips as she walked to the booth. It still tasted amazing. Not double-shot-latte amazing—she had already drunk her fill of caffeine for the day, any more would kick in her fight or flight reflexes—but a delicious blend of lavender and berries, nonetheless. She often came here on breaks from work in the afternoons to have this brew.

Margaret Hitchens, real estate entrepreneur, mayor of Rocky Points, longtime friend of David's, and Piper's coffee date this morning, had a phone pressed to her ear. She nodded at Piper's arrival.

Piper slid into the booth across from her and waited patiently, listening in as Margaret spoke to someone about an inspection gone wrong with one of the hundred-plus real estate transactions the woman's company facilitated each month.

Hammered metal bracelets jangled on her wrists as she

poked the air, rings glimmering on thin fingers. She wore a blouse covered in an abstract splash of paint that Piper could never pull off but that made the other woman's face come even more alive as she ripped into some poor soul on the other end of the call.

Piper hoped she had this much passion for work at sixty. It was highly unlikely. The investigations at the law firm were interesting and varied in nature on a case-by-case basis, but she couldn't picture going another twenty-five years doing it and looking as energized as Margaret did.

"Okay. Sorry." Margaret put the phone on the table. "It never ends with these assholes." She mumbled something under her breath, then tilted her head, smiling at Piper. "Hi."

"How are you doing?"

"I'm great." Margaret reached out and grabbed Piper's hand. "Geez, woman, you look beautiful. I must not see you enough in person because every time I do, I'm just floored by how incredibly beautiful you are. Those big brown eyes, that skin that looks like a baby's ass. What I wouldn't do to have that skin."

Piper blushed. "Thank you. I was just thinking the same about you."

"Don't patronize me. So, how's living with David going? His house isn't exactly the one we found you up along the creek."

"You're right." She smiled. Piper had loved being up the mountain east of town, otherwise known as Sunnyside. The house had been tucked in an aspen grove, with long views out some of the windows. But she'd been happy to rent it out to a young couple with two kids.

"But I love it out at David's place, too," she said. "We're happy."

"It's tough to beat that plot of land David lucked into," Margaret said. "Listen, tell him to just sell me a few acres, and we'll put up some tasteful condos. Sell them for one point five, two million apiece, multiplied by ten or so. You guys would come out flush with cash on the other end."

Piper smiled. "I, uh..."

"I'm kidding. Kind of. But seriously, talk him into it." Margaret sipped her coffee, sitting back on the booth bench. "So, how's it going investigating for the firm?"

"It's going well. The hours are nice. Interesting work. The pay is good. I can't complain."

"Good. I'm glad." Margaret put her hand on the table. "So, what's up? What did you want to see me for?"

Piper tapped the manila folder she had brought with her. "Well, first of all, thank you for meeting with me. You must be so busy."

"Please. No problem. Hit me."

"Okay. Well, I just wanted to get your thoughts on the wedding plans."

Margaret's eyes widened. "Oh. Yes. Gimme, gimme."

Piper opened the folder, unveiling a packet representing the last couple months of planning: floral arrangements, music, catering, tent-configuration maps, and seating charts. It was all here in a stressed-out stack of paper.

"I see you've been busy." Margaret took the packet and started flipping pages. "What do you want to know in particular?"

"Well..." Piper sipped her drink.

Margaret looked up. "What's wrong?"

"Well," she said again.

"Well, what?"

"It's just that I showed this to David, and it looked like...I don't know how to describe it." She picked out the computer-generated, full-color drawing she'd shown David the night before. "This is what the whole thing is going to look like."

"Wow, I didn't know they did this nowadays. Looks almost real."

"Yeah, they took photos of the field in front of David's house and superimposed everything over it with AI."

"I see that." Margaret made an unsure noise and then a face. She set down the paper and looked at Piper like she was going to tell her about the death of a family pet.

"What? What is it? What's wrong with this? You're acting like David did the other night."

"Honey." Margaret set both hands on hers. "This looks exactly like it did when he was going to marry Lauren."

Piper stared, dumbfounded. "It does?"

"Yes."

"I...I don't understand. The flowers? The color-scheme? What do you mean?"

Margaret studied the picture again. "I mean, pretty much all of it. The whole layout and the location of the tents. I mean, it's been a few years ago now, but this looks like an exact replica to me."

"How? Why? What?" She felt defensive. "Here?"

"Yes."

She raised her eyebrows. "Okay, let me ask this. Where were they going to be married?"

Margaret frowned. "In front of his house. The field in front. Just like this."

Piper's face went slack.

"You didn't know that?"

Her breath caught. The booth tilted. "No."

Margaret squeezed her hand, and she reflexively pulled it away.

"How did I not know that?" she asked, her voice a whisper.

"David didn't tell you?"

She shook her head, the memories coming back like a flood now. It had been her brilliant idea to get married in the field in front of his house. She had been ecstatic to tell him about her thoughts on the matter, the way the valley would open up before them all the way north as they got married out in the majestic surroundings of his home. It would be simple. They were going to move in together anyway, so she would have all of her stuff right there in the house, allowing her to get ready for the ceremony in comfort.

"I'm sorry, honey."

Piper snapped out of her thoughts. "It's okay. It's..." She didn't know what this was. Why wouldn't he tell her?

"You used Debbie Gertman's company for the planning?" Margaret pointed at an invoice.

Piper blinked. "I don't know. It's Chautauqua Valley Weddings. I've been working with a woman named Vanna."

Margaret nodded. "I think that's even the same planner, actually. I think Debbie does more of the corporate event stuff."

Piper yanked the picture closer to her. "It's the same planner that worked with Lauren before me?"

"Yes."

Anger flared inside her. "And she just let me make a spitting image of that wedding that crashed and burned."

Margaret's eyebrows arched in sympathy. Her phone buzzed, and she poked it silent. "I'm afraid so, honey."

Piper's face was red hot. David's reaction, the way he'd frozen looking at the page. He said he was thinking about the case, and she'd believed him. To think the facial expressions of someone looking at photos of their upcoming wedding could have been mistaken for someone thinking of rotting, mangled corpses sucked the life from her.

"It's okay," Margaret offered.

"Yeah," she said. She didn't know what words were coming from her mouth. She was speechless.

"It's not your fault. It's these idiots' fault. They gotta know better than this. I mean, come on."

Piper stared through the coffee shop, in her mind, seeing David's shocked face over and over again.

"Are you okay?"

She nodded.

"I can talk to Debbie for you if you want. There's no way Vanna should have approved these plans without giving you a heads-up."

"What? No. Thanks." She raked the plans back and put them in the folder, not bothering to keep them in order. "I have to get going."

"Okay."

Piper stood, and Margaret rose with her arms outstretched.

"I'm sorry," Margaret said. "I don't know when to shut my mouth."

"No, Margaret. I thank you. You've saved me a hell of a lot of trouble."

Margaret's phone rang again.

"Bye," Piper said, using the diversion to leave, forgetting to bring her tea.

CHAPTER TWELVE

The cab of Brandenburg's truck rumbled as they traveled westward along a county dirt road, the sun glaring off the side-view mirror into Wolf's eyes.

"I read you were sheriff down there, but now you're the chief detective?" Brandenburg looked over at Wolf.

"That's right."

Wolf sipped his coffee from the paper cup, enjoying the cinnamon notes of a foreign blend, looking out the spotless window of Brandenburg's department-issued Ford truck at passing trees. The sheriff kept the interior of his vehicle clean. A car air freshener dangled off the center shifter, filling the cab with a pleasant scent. Wolf had been in much worse vehicle interiors before.

"What happened there?"

Wolf kept his eyes on the passing forest. "I got beat in the election when the counties merged."

"But...I'm talking after that. You had another stint as sheriff, didn't you?"

"They appointed me when MacLean decided to leave. I decided not to run when the elections came up the following year."

"Ah." Brandenburg adjusted his rearview mirror. "You must really not like being sheriff."

Wolf smiled. "Nope. No offense, of course. It's not my calling. It's probably a lot less political up here. Or is it?"

"I don't have much opposition with the county personnel. We all tend to get along."

"Lucky you." Wolf took a sip from his cup.

"You grow up in Rocky Points?" Brandenburg asked.

"Yeah. You from here?"

"Born and raised down in Craig. Had a stint after the academy in Southern California, but that didn't last. Too hectic. I wanted to move back home, so when they were hiring here in '92, I jumped at it. Been here ever since."

Rumbling stuffed Wolf's ears as they traveled over a section of washboard dirt.

When the road smoothed out, Wolf asked, "You were hired by this man, Aldridge?"

"That's right."

"What happened to him?" The night before, he'd done some Googling on Doyle and come across an old article about the former sheriff's memorial service.

"The man liked his whiskey and cigarettes," Brandenburg said. "That's what happened to him. I think he'd tell you he had a long, full life. His wife passed ten or so years prior, and he was always one foot out the door after that."

Gravel pinged off the bottom of the truck. There were puddles and potholes, with the occasional large rock jutting up from the ground.

"Not exactly good roads for motorcycles," Wolf said.

"That's what I always say." Brandenburg shook his head. "And if it's raining, it gets muddy and dangerous. That's how my cousin shattered his hip, falling on his hog on a dirt road in the rain. You ever ride motorcycles?"

"Not really."

"I used to have myself a Wide Glide..."

For the first time, Wolf realized the man was talking with nervous energy like soldiers often do when heading into battle. He looked over and watched him talk. Sweat ran down the side of his face, his eyes glued ahead.

"...but I could never justify having it after that. Just too much hassle."

Brandenburg went silent as they drove through a narrow canyon of trees and emerged into a clearing, this one the biggest so far. Mountains rose three hundred and sixty degrees off the horizon.

A side road ahead cut up the mountain to the right, disappearing into the trees. Way up high, almost at the top, a set of rooftops poked out of the woods.

"Yep, that's it," Brandenburg said.

They slowed and turned, the truck bouncing through a rut as they started up the hill.

The road started out flat, then climbed and turned left, punching back into dense woods. Just before entering the forest, two trucks came into view.

Brandenburg let off the gas. "What's this?"

Each behemoth of a truck was parked on opposite sides of the road, creating a pinch-point they would have to drive through. As they rolled closer, two men armed with rifles across their chests and holsters on their thighs climbed down from open tailgates to the gravel.

"Welcome to the Sons of the Void compound," Brandenburg said quietly. "They're normally not down here like this, though."

Wolf remained silent, feeling the adrenaline pump up his heart rate.

One of the bikers, heavily muscled and tattooed, had a bald head tanned the color of tobacco spit. He wore leather and denim, sunglasses covering his eyes. The other man was considerably thinner, with a head of long hair, also wearing a pair of sunglasses.

The long-haired guy put up a hand, and Brandenburg slowed his truck to a stop.

"Is this private land we're on?" Wolf asked.

"Yes. Starting at the turnoff down the hill. Like I said, they have a hundred or so acres."

Wolf unclipped his seatbelt. "Well. I guess this is our stop, then." He opened the door and stepped down onto the gravel.

Brandenburg shut off the engine, meeting Wolf at the front bumper and facing the bikers, who now stood twenty paces away.

"This is private land," the long-haired biker said.

"Hey there," Wolf said. "How's it going?"

"You're trespassing on private land," the man said. "Please turn around and vacate the premises."

"We'd like to talk to Snake," Brandenburg said. "Is he around?"

Wolf scanned the forest next to him, his eyes stopping on a camera mounted high up a pine tree. It was painted brown to blend seamlessly into the bark of the wood. A tuft of fake pine needles sprouted from its housing. A few minutes earlier or later, he would have missed the light glinting off the lens.

"...so you can turn around." The bigger of the two men were talking now. "We're not buying any Girl Scout cookies today, gentlemen. Goodbye."

Brandenburg turned to Wolf, hands upturned. "I don't know what we can do here."

"Who's Snake?" Wolf asked him.

"He's the leader. When he's around."

"I wasn't listening. Is he here?"

"Yeah. But they said he's not seeing anybody. You're not listening? What are you doing?"

Wolf turned to the two men. "We need to see Snake."

The bald guy took off his sunglasses and propped them on his head. "Maybe you're deaf. We just told him, who just told you, we're not taking visitors today."

"My name is David Wolf. I'm chief detective down in Sluice-Byron County. Two days ago, we found two of your brothers shot and killed down near Ashland. We know they were Sons of the Void members."

The two men said nothing.

"That's two killings down in my county to add to the four you guys had up here," Wolf said. "We're in an emergency situation. Would you not agree to that?"

The men remained silent.

"I'd say so," Wolf said, answering his own question. "We have a killer on the loose. Public safety is at risk. Which means we're going to have to confiscate any and all footage from your cameras." Wolf pointed up the tree.

The two men stared back at him like he was a talking elk.

"Right now," Wolf said.

"You need a warrant for that," Bald-Guy said.

"No, we don't."

Brandenburg cleared his throat but offered no words.

A blast of static came from one of the trucks' open windows, and the bald guy turned away, plucking a radio from his hip. When he turned his back, he displayed a patch sewn onto the leather vest he wore—an insignia of a skull with fire and a bleeding bullet hole in the center of its forehead and the arched words reading *Sons of the Void*. He spoke into the handset and, a moment later, turned back around. He said something to the longhair guy, and they both split, walking back toward their respective trucks.

"What's going on?" Brandenburg asked under his breath.

The two men climbed up onto their tailgates.

"He'll be down in a minute," Bald-Guy said.

Wolf scanned the edge of the trees some more and thought he spotted another camera overlooking the road about fifty yards beyond the trucks. He couldn't be sure without getting closer.

Brandenburg spat on the ground. His chest rose and fell quickly.

"What's this guy's name?" Wolf asked.

"Snake."

"That's his real name?"

Brandenburg opened his mouth to respond but stopped when, high up the mountain, they heard a Harley-Davidson firing up. It revved sporadically at first and then let out an angry blast of noise as it shifted through the first three gears.

"His name?" Wolf said.

"Huh? Oh. I don't know his real name. Listen, Wolf. You

don't want to antagonize this guy. They don't call these guys one-percenters for nothing. They don't respect the law like 99 percent of the rest of us."

"Sounds like they respected you when they called for an ambulance the other night," Wolf said.

Brandenburg remained silent, turning his gaze up the road.

Wolf looked as well, focusing on a right turn that emerged out of the trees two hundred yards beyond the trucks.

The engine noise grew louder until a motorcycle came around the bend, going suicidally fast. Sliding on both tires, the motor revving high, the biker wavered to the edge of the road, his rear wheel almost overhanging a drainage trench. The pitch of the pipes changed, and the biker righted himself, centered the motorcycle on the road, and began accelerating.

"Jesus," Brandenburg said, shuffling in place.

Wolf watched, listening as the bike revved higher still, continuing straight at them. At a hundred yards out, it had to be going sixty or seventy miles per hour. Another fifty yards, a blink of an eye later, and it was going faster. No way it was going to be able to stop in time, gravel or not.

"Shit!" Brandenburg stumbled backward, then fell down on his back side.

Wolf remained where he was, crouching to jump either way. The logical part of his brain told him there was no way this guy was looking to kill two cops.

And then the biker drifted sideways a few degrees, and it was clear there would be no collision, just a psychotic flyby at top speed.

The noise rose to a deafening roar and then punched

Wolf's eardrums as the bike passed. Wind laced with pebbles and dust whipped over him as he shut his eyes, ducking against the onslaught.

He spun on his heel. Brandenburg picked himself up off the ground, spitting dust.

"You alright?" Wolf held out a hand and helped him up.

"Yeah, yeah." Brandenburg patted himself off. "Damn it. God damned psycho."

"Who was that?" Wolf asked.

"That's him. Snake."

Snake was in the process of downshifting through all the gears as he rounded the bend behind them. A few seconds later, slowing to a crawl, he turned around and came back their way.

Safely on the far side of Brandenburg's truck, they stood by the bumper and watched as Snake drove back toward them at a leisurely pace.

The apparent leader of the local Sons of the Void compound was dressed in a T-shirt and jeans, with muscular arms painted dark in tattoos. Every inch of skin from chin down was covered in serpents: scales, fangs, and coiled bodies.

Snake rolled past and parked between the guard trucks. He put down the kickstand, stepped off the bike, turned, and began walking toward them in one impressive motion.

He was pure muscle under the tattoos, his limbs moving easily and powerfully. He raised a pair of sunglasses showing eyes the color of steel, and his gaze locked on Wolf. Without slowing, he walked all the way to Wolf and stopped a few inches short.

Wolf remained still, taking in the scent of cigarettes and hard liquor coming off the man.

"Snake, I take it?" Wolf asked.

"Who are you?"

"I'm Detective David Wolf. Sluice-Byron County. We found two of your men down in Ashland."

Snake's eyes remained still.

"Benny Cruz and Jack Whitcomb. Benny was riding his brother's bike, which was registered here." Wolf shrugged. "So, here we are."

Snake's tongue ran over his teeth beneath his closed lips. His eyes still latched onto Wolf's. The man hadn't blinked yet.

Wolf continued. "We found a duffle bag and a GPS unit that had been smashed. Our forensic team found money fibers inside the bag. It's clear this guy stole some money from you guys, and you went after him, but he got the jump on your two men."

Snake said nothing.

"Who is he?" Wolf asked.

Snake looked to Brandenburg, then back to Wolf, but still remained silent.

"Okay, then we'll need the footage from your security cameras from the night of the shooting here."

"You can't do that," Snake said. His voice was low and menacing. "We have Fourth Amendment rights against unreasonable search and seizure."

"We have four people murdered in cold blood right here on this property, another two down south in my county. The killer in question is at large and a danger to the public. This is an emergency circumstance in which I have the right to seize your surveillance footage so we can do our job in protecting the citizenry."

Snake's lip curled into a snarl, and his eyes telegraphed

violent thoughts. He let his gaze probe Wolf's face, a scientist looking at a skull specimen.

"I tell you what," Wolf said. "You can refuse, and we'll come back with an FBI search team and a warrant. I can see that camera right there, hanging on the tree. I can see another one up the road on that tree." Wolf pointed. "Either get us the footage we need, something that shows exactly who this guy was and what vehicle he was driving, right now, or we'll be back with that warrant. Then we'll do a thorough search of the premises, and we'll take what we need." Wolf shrugged. "And maybe we'll find a few other interesting things in the meantime."

Snake smiled wider now, and then he stepped away. He walked backward, pointing at Wolf. "I like this guy! This guy's got some balls!" He snapped his fingers, pointing at Brandenburg. "You see how a real cop acts, there, pudgy? You see that?"

"We don't want any trouble, Snake," Brandenburg said.

"Trouble?" Snake stopped. "You ever get any trouble from us, Mr. Sheriff?"

Brandenburg shook his head.

"That's right." Snake grinned, showing yellow, tobacco-stained teeth. "We're model citizens up here. We're squeaky clean, isn't that right?"

Brandenburg looked down at the road and folded his arms.

Snake dropped the fake smile and looked at Wolf. "Okay, pigs. You two sit tight. We'll get you your footage."

"Thank you," Wolf said.

"You're welcome. Now, don't you say I never did anything for you!" He walked away in good cheer. "Don't you forget it! I sure won't!"

The bike fired up as he swung a leg over, sounding like an AK-47 on full auto. He revved twice, kicked up the stand, and cranked the throttle. The motorcycle remained in place, spitting gravel back at Wolf and Brandenburg.

They turned around against the onslaught of needle-like projections. A few larger rocks hit Wolf in the back of his legs.

Snake rode away at the same speed he came in.

Wolf and Brandenburg went back to the truck and climbed inside. It was warm and smelled of the coffee they'd left in the cupholders.

"I tell you what, I've had just about enough of you Rocky Points assholes." Brandenburg fumbled with his seat-belt, let it go, slapped his thighs, and then sat back, closing his eyes. A considerable amount of sweat clotted the hair at his temples. "You guys don't take no for an answer, do you?"

Wolf smiled. "I guess not."

"You think that's funny? I don't need this type of shit happening right now."

Wolf could have said a lot at that moment but decided not to. The man was obviously worked up and needed to cool off.

They spent the next thirty minutes in tense silence, sitting in the same spot in the center of the road, listening to country music coming out of the speakers. The windows were down, letting in warm breezes from outside, smelling of pine and dust.

The two sentinels sat outside on lawn chairs in their truck beds, unmoving, sunglasses reflecting the forest. Finally, one of them picked up a radio and said something into it.

"Looks like something's happening," Wolf said.

Brandenburg grunted.

The man talked some more into the handset, and then a few minutes later, a motorcycle fired up somewhere high on the mountain. The sound grew louder until a bike came around the bend ahead. It was going much slower this time, at a sane speed, and as the man drew near, it was clear it was not Snake but somebody else.

"You recognize this guy?" Wolf asked.

"Nope."

"Got my back?" Wolf asked, opening the door.

Brandenburg grunted again, opening his as well.

Wolf walked to the front bumper and waited patiently as the man came up, slowed, and swung in a half-circle in front of him, stopping the motorcycle a few feet away. The man wore mirrored sunglasses the color of fire. He had a beard that hung down to the gas tank. He reached into a vest pocket, produced a USB drive, and handed it over to Wolf.

Wolf nodded his thanks, and he and Brandenburg got back in the truck.

"About time," Brandenburg said, putting on his seatbelt. He turned on the engine, reversed, and turned around. "Let's get the hell out of here."

A few seconds later, they were coasting down the road back toward Doyle.

Wolf looked in the passenger's side-view mirror and caught the three men huddled in the road, watching them leave.

"That better be some damn good footage," Brandenburg said.

Wolf frowned, looking at the sheriff, wondering why the man had such an aversion to doing his job.

Twirling the thumb drive in his fingers, Wolf looked down at the tiny device and saw a skull and crossbones drawn in red ink on one of the sides.

"What?" Brandenburg asked.

"Nothing." Wolf slipped it into his pocket and settled back in the seat.

CHAPTER THIRTEEN

The drive back into Doyle was just as it had been since encountering the man known as Snake: quiet and tense. Brandenburg had started some small talk, asking about Rocky Points and the state of the department, but had little interest in Wolf's responses. The interaction shook the man, and Wolf didn't blame him. They were a small department here in Doyle, a fraction of what Wolf had backing him down south, outnumbered ten or fifteen to one, and they'd definitely kicked the hive.

When they reached the edge of town, Wolf pulled his phone out of his pocket and read a text from Waze.

HOW'S IT GOING? ANYTHING INTERESTING HAPPEN?

Yeah, kind of, Wolf thought, but he typed: FOLLOWING UP A LEAD NOW. I'LL KEEP YOU POSTED.

Waze replied, almost instantly: GOOD. YES, KEEP ME POSTED.

Wolf pocketed his phone as they pulled into the parking lot of the Anniston County Sheriff's Department and parked.

Wolf followed the sheriff inside, which was freezing cold.

"Where's Nichols?" Brandenburg asked, walking straight to his office.

"He's in the bathroom," said the new man sitting at one of the desks. He was large and muscular, with a shock of red hair and pale skin covered in freckles. "Hi, I'm Deputy Larkin." He stood and held out a hand to Wolf.

"Oh, yeah," Brandenburg said, his voice coming from his office now. "That's Larkin. Larkin, that's Wolf."

"Nice to meet you," Wolf said.

"You, too." Larkin sat back down. "So? How was the visit? I heard you guys went to the SOV compound."

"Wolf!" Brandenburg barked. "Back here with that USB."

Nichols emerged from the hallway, rubbing his hands on his pants. "So?"

Wolf fished the USB drive out of his pocket and held it up, walking toward Brandenburg's office. "We got some surveillance footage from the night of the shooting at the SOV compound," he said, using Larkin's shortened term for the gang.

"Oh," Nichols said, watching him enter the sheriff's office.

Sitting behind his desk, Brandenburg held his hand out, fingers flicking impatiently.

Wolf gave him the USB, and Brandenburg bent down to put it in his computer tower. He paused for a moment, looking at the skull and crossbones scrawled on the side of the device.

"Cute, huh?" Wolf asked, sitting down.

Brandenburg grunted and grabbed his computer mouse.

Wolf scooted forward to the edge of his seat and angled himself toward the monitor. The screen crackled to life, and the cursor went to a single folder named *Pig File*. Brandenburg double-clicked on it.

One image inside was named by a string of random digits and letters. The file was two megabytes—nowhere near big enough to be anything but a single image and not security video footage.

Wolf's insides dropped. He didn't like having someone call his bluff, but clearly, Snake had made them all wait for nothing. This was probably a picture of a man's bare ass with *Die Pigs* written in lipstick across the cheeks.

Brandenburg clicked open the file.

It was a real photo, a still shot from the night of the killings.

Wolf blinked. There was a lot to take in from the one picture. The man in the image carried an assault rifle Wolf recognized as a Heckler and Koch.

His face was in full light, staring straight into the lens of the camera. His eyes were green, with dilated pupils. Behind him, two men were lying in the hallway, covered in blood. The picture looked to be taken seconds after the gunman had mowed them down.

Wolf leaned forward. There were words overlaying the image as well. They read:

Lawrence Hunt
14 Antelope Flats
Doyle, CO

Wolf looked at the sheriff. Brandenburg stared, his mouth hanging open. He appeared to collect himself and cleared his throat.

"Lawrence Hunt," Wolf said. "Is that who this is? You know this man?"

"What's happening?" Nichols's voice came from the doorway.

Brandenburg looked at his deputy for a moment, then gestured to the screen. "Our shooter."

Nichols walked in and went to Brandenburg's side, looking at the screen. His face froze in similar astonishment as his boss's, and then he shook his head. "Lawrence Hunt."

"I take it you two know this guy?" Wolf asked.

Brandenburg and Nichols shared a meaningful glance, and then Brandenburg nodded. Nichols's eyes glazed over as if he was now in deep, troubling thought.

"What's going on?" Wolf asked. "Is the man in this photo Lawrence Hunt? From this address here in Doyle?"

"Yes," Brandenburg said.

"Lawrence Hunt was the shooter?" Larkin's voice now came from the doorway. "Is that what I just heard?"

When Brandenburg and Nichols remained silent, Wolf turned around. "Yeah, you know him?"

"Yeah," Larkin said.

"Larkin, please," Brandenburg said. "Nichols, why don't you two head out? Give us some space."

Nichols remained staring at the screen.

"Nichols."

The deputy blinked. "Right." He left, and Larkin followed him into the front room.

Wolf turned to the sheriff and raised his eyebrows inquisitively.

The chair creaking in protest, Brandenburg sat back and folded his arms. He gestured to the monitor. "Lawrence

Hunt came into us last month. His son had gone missing, and he was upset."

"Okay." Wolf narrowed his eyes. "That's interesting. What happened there?"

Brandenburg wiped his forehead. "His name, Lawrence's son's name, is Irving. Twenty-eight years old. Irv, he went by. Grew up here in town."

"And what happened?" Wolf asked.

"He was..." Brandenburg's eyes glazed over. He stood up and shut the door, then came back.

Wolf wondered why the sudden secrecy but remained silent as Brandenburg sat.

"He was running with the bikers," Brandenburg said. "That's what happened. The kid was always a troublemaker, and he was hanging around with the wrong crowd."

"He was with Sons of the Void?" Wolf asked.

"He rode around on a bike, he hung out at the Dusty Thorn with the rest of them, he did drugs." Brandenburg shrugged. "Maybe. We're not sure if he was a true member or not. When Lawrence came in here looking for him, I didn't know what to tell him. His kid could have been up in Wyoming, Montana, Idaho, Oregon, Washington, rolling with any of the chapters these guys have. I told him I couldn't do anything for him."

"Did Lawrence know his son was an SOV?"

"Yeah. Didn't you just hear me?"

Wolf ignored the indignation rising in the man's face again. "So, what made him think his son was in trouble and not just out with them in some other state?"

Brandenburg bridged his fingers. "He made a stink about Irv not checking in like he used to. That, and he said he'd heard something...that Irv was in a fight with one of the other members of the gang." Brandenburg scoffed. "I was like, 'What do you want me to do? Go start interrogating the SOV about getting in scuffles with your kid?'" Brandenburg stood up, turning to the back of the room. "Damn fool. The guy's got hell itself coming after him now."

"So, this is all revenge for his son," Wolf said.

Brandenburg turned around. "It fits."

Wolf stood up as well.

"Well, Detective," Brandenburg said. "You came up and saved the day. We got us an ID. Lawrence Hunt. You can head home and let your boss know he's got some answers. We'll take care of the rest."

Wolf raised an eyebrow. "I'm here to find the man responsible, not learn his name."

"The APB will take care of that."

"We have a blue truck without a license plate. That's not going to help us. Not in this country."

"We'll update the APB with a full description and DMV photo," Brandenburg said.

"What's the resistance here?" Wolf asked.

"No resistance. You're just in a jurisdiction that's not your own. We have capable men who can take over from here. We don't need, nor did we ask for, the help of an outside agent coming in here, telling us how to do things."

Wolf smiled.

Don't give them any rock to stand on. When Waze's last words ran through his mind, the smile faded.

"I'm not telling you how to do things. If anything, just giving good suggestions—ones that produce results." He pointed at the computer screen.

Brandenburg walked to the door and opened it.

"Fine," Wolf said, walking past him. "Fourteen Antelope Flats. I'll stop by Hunt's house myself on the way out."

"You do that, and we're going to have some trouble with each other."

"Not any worse than the trouble I'm going to have going home empty-handed." Wolf nodded at Nichols and Larkin as he walked through the room to the front door. He pushed outside to his SUV and sat behind the wheel, turning on his Mobile Data Terminal to pull DMV information for Lawrence Hunt.

A few seconds later, the front door of the office opened, and Brandenburg came out, Nichols in tow. Nichols went to Brandenburg's truck and sat in the passenger seat, but Brandenburg broke off and walked to Wolf's vehicle.

Wolf rolled down the window.

Brandenburg put both hands on the door, exhaling heavily as he looked somewhere in the far distance.

They sat like that for almost a full minute, Wolf sitting silent and Brandenburg contemplating.

Finally, Brandenburg slapped his roof and turned to leave. "Follow us."

CHAPTER FOURTEEN

Brandenburg took a circuitous route to Lawrence Hunt's place, stopping by a Burger King south of town before heading back in and then out to the east. Wolf had no protest, ordering himself a couple of burgers and fries in the drive-through, watching with interest as Brandenburg waited for him to get his food and then follow him back north on the highway.

He enjoyed the meal, washing it down with a Coke, grateful to be in his own vehicle without the electricity between him and Brandenburg.

The sheriff was clearly territorial before anything else— the kind of alpha male that ran and fell on his backside when it came down to it. Maybe Wolf was judging too harshly, but for now, that was the view he was sticking with.

The drive east of town was over a different terrain than near the SOV compound. The hills were covered in lush grass and sagebrush, and the forest, far more sporadic here than in the southwest, was made of piñons and juniper.

Wolf followed the dust trail of Brandenburg's truck along a county dirt road, winding through rolling hills.

Seeing the reception on his phone was strong, he decided to call Patterson.

"Lawrence Hunt," Wolf said.

"That's our man?" Patterson's voice came out of the speakers.

"That's our man," Wolf told her the address. "Are you near a computer? Let's get his license plate number."

"Yes. I'm searching now." A few seconds later, she read. "Lawrence David Hunt...fifty-five years old. He has a registered Chevy Silverado pickup truck. Color gray. Not our blue Ford F-150 in question."

"Shit," Wolf said. "What else do you have on him?"

"Checking criminal history. Let's see...no prior arrests. His record is clean. Squeaky clean."

"Married?"

The tapping of keys came out of the speakers. "He's a widower. His wife died fifteen years ago in a car accident. Never remarried. Huh, looks like he was a Green Beret."

"Okay," Wolf said, viewing the carnage the man had done at the compound in a new light. It made sense now how the man had been highly trained enough to get in and get the jump on that many dangerous SOV men.

"His son," Wolf said. "His name is Irving Hunt. He's gone missing. Twenty-eight years old, according to the sheriff. Possible member of the Sons of the Void. What do you have on him?"

"Irving...Hunt." More keys tapping. "Irving Hunt. Twenty-eight years old. Has a prior arrest in Steamboat Springs for drug possession. Marijuana. That was ten years ago."

"Anything else on his record? Anything more recent?"

"Nothing," Patterson said. "He went missing? What's the story with that?"

Wolf explained Lawrence Hunt's visit to the department headquarters in Doyle and his report to the sheriff that the SOV had something to do with his son's disappearance.

"Hmm, so we're looking at revenge killings?"

"That's what it looks like. We're headed over to Hunt's house now."

Brandenburg's brake lights bloomed out of the dust ahead.

"I gotta go," Wolf said. "Tell Waze everything for me, okay?"

"Will do," she said. "And I'll look into Lawrence Hunt's cell phone data, see if we can't locate him that way."

"Good. Keep me posted, and I'll do the same."

"Be careful."

"Will do," he said and hung up. He shoved the phone in his pocket and slowed behind Brandenburg's truck.

Lawrence Hunt's house was a single-story building, painted gray, surrounded by a lawn of two or so acres and then the wild elements. A shed crouched in the backyard with an irrigation ditch running behind it.

Brandenburg slowed, stopping at a long driveway leading in. At the top of the drive, a gray Chevy Silverado truck was parked.

The sheriff's brake lights turned off, and the two Doyle men got out.

Wolf parked behind him, keeping an eye on the property as he got out. There was no movement in the windows or surrounding the house.

The air was warm and still, smelling of sage and wild grass. Insects buzzed by on swirling paths.

"That's Hunt's truck," Nichols said. "I looked up his DMV file when you guys were talking."

Wolf nodded, pulling his Glock as he looked at Brandenburg. The sheriff pulled his own gun, then gestured: *after you.*

Wolf led the way down the driveway, Brandenburg and Nichols following silently.

They made it to the Chevy, still without any visible movement from the house.

Brandenburg went to the driver's side door of Hunt's truck. "It's open," he said. He looked in and then gestured inside. "And you can see why."

Wolf pulled his eyes from the house and looked into the truck. Broken glass was strewn over the seat under the passenger side window. The center console was open, along with the glove compartment, and the papers and effects were strewn everywhere.

"SOV," Brandenburg said. "They knew it was him. They would have come here by now."

Wolf nodded and put his attention back on the house.

Nichols took the lead now, walking toward the front door with his gun at the ready. Wolf followed, and Brandenburg came up last.

The house looked more weathered up close than from afar, with warped siding, a front porch built from bleached wood, and windows looking like they hadn't been washed since installation.

The wooden steps to the front porch creaked with an alarming bend as Nichols stepped up to the door. He looked back at Wolf and Brandenburg, then knocked.

"Sheriff's department!" Brandenburg yelled.

A window next to the door was uncovered, but it was impossible to see through the filth into the darkness inside.

Brandenburg stepped in front of them and twisted the knob. The door swung inward, creaking on its hinges, revealing a slice of dark interior.

Wolf and Nichols followed the sheriff inside.

Brandenburg flicked a light switch, and an overhead bulb brightened the foyer.

"Whoa," Nichols said. "The SOV's been here all right."

A room to the left had a dining table covered in papers and clothing, other debris flung to the floor. Chairs were tipped over.

A family room opened to the right, where a green couch and chair had been rifled, the cushions uprooted and swept aside. An old TV lay broken on the carpet, the stand leaning on its edge. A tall hutch along the far wall had been pulled down and smashed face-first into the floor. Shards of ceramic plates and trinkets lay everywhere.

Wolf wanted to tell them they should clear the place but waited for Brandenburg to take the lead.

A few seconds later, the sheriff used hand signals to point Wolf into the living room, Nichols into the dining area, and to show he was going to take the hallway.

Wolf waded through debris into the living room, rounding into another small area and coming into the kitchen from a back entrance.

More ceramic on the ground crunched under Wolf's work boots. Dishes were smashed everywhere, every cabinet emptied and dashed to the floor, and every drawer pulled out and treated the same.

"Clear!" Nichols called from the back hallway.

"Clear!" Brandenburg said, emerging from a room off the kitchen.

"Clear," Wolf said.

They gathered near the kitchen table.

"They were looking for their money," Nichols said.

Wolf walked past them and down the hallway, stopping at the doorway to a master bedroom. Inside, a queen-sized bed sat in disarray, the sheets flung aside, the mattress flipped over. Brandenburg and Nichols stepped up next to him and looked inside.

They continued down the hallway into another room.

Psychedelic posters that had adorned the walls were torn off and tossed on the carpet. An acoustic guitar was smashed into a tangle of strings and splinters. The bed was also dismantled. The closet door was open, and inside lay a few open boxes, the contents strewn about.

"Irving's room, I take it? Back when he lived here?" Wolf said.

"It looks like he had a lot of guns," Brandenburg said from across the hall.

Wolf remained where he was, looking down at a picture frame smashed on the floor. He gently lifted the photo from the wreckage. Two young men in their late teens or early twenties were in the picture. One of them wore a tie-dyed T-shirt with a Grateful Dead logo on it and jeans; the other wore shorts with a tattered purple shirt.

They both had long hair. One, curly brown that settled just above his shoulders, and the other, straight and blond, parted in the middle, hanging down past his chin and covering one side of a carefree smile.

They stood with their arms around each other, flanked by hundreds of people on either side, a concert stage visible far down a hill behind them. Blond-Hair had a tattoo on one bicep dipping into view from under his shirtsleeve.

"Looks like he took them all," Brandenburg said, still in the other room. "Probably used them to shoot up the place. What are you guys doing?"

Wolf turned around. Nichols stood next to him, staring at the photo in Wolf's hands.

"You know these two?" Wolf asked.

Nichols blinked out of a daze and nodded. He pointed at the kid on the left in the tie-dyed shirt. "That's Irving Hunt there."

Wolf nodded. "And the other one?"

He shook his head.

"What's going on over there?" Brandenburg came to the doorway. "What's that?"

Wolf showed him the photo. "Nichols says this is Irving Hunt here. You know this other kid?"

Brandenburg shook his head. "No." He thumbed over his shoulder. "Lawrence Hunt's den."

Wolf took out his cell phone, snapped a photo of the picture of Irv Hunt, set it down, and followed them across the hall to the other room.

Inside, a big wooden desk was overturned, broken glass covering the floor, and pictures of Hunt in uniform spilling from frames on the carpet. A shadow box filled with military memorabilia had been destroyed.

Wolf picked up a beret, the wool soft yet firm under his fingers. The flash on the front—a shield of black with diagonal yellow and red stripes—gleamed faintly in the dim light. Centered on it was the silver crest of Special Forces: a dagger flanked by two crossed arrows. Shaking away the glass, Wolf set it on a shelf. "He's a former Green Beret," he said.

"That fits," Brandenburg said. "With what he did to those boys up at the compound."

Along one wall stood a gun case that could have held dozens of rifles, shotguns, and handguns. Now it stood empty, its case a gaping maw with razor-sharp glass teeth.

"Here was his arsenal," the sheriff said.

Nichols picked through some debris quietly.

Wolf went back out into the hall, back to the master bedroom, and to the ensuite bathroom inside.

The space was smallish and also smashed, with bits of mirror on the ground. There were two sinks sunk into a low counter and a glass-enclosed shower that had been spared.

He stared at a stick of deodorant housed in pink plastic lying on the floor. "There's women's deodorant in here."

"Oh?" Brandenburg asked, appearing in the doorway.

"But his wife died fifteen years ago," Wolf said.

"How do you know that?"

"I talked to my detective on the way here."

"Really?"

"Really."

"Any other interesting information?"

Wolf shrugged. "No. She said his criminal record is squeaky clean. How about you, Nichols? Is that what you found?"

Nichols came up behind the sheriff, nodding. "Yes. No record."

Wolf picked up the roll-on antiperspirant and checked the bottom of the cylinder, finding an expiration date a year in the future. "It's new." He handed it to Brandenburg, who read the date and handed it over to Nichols.

"I didn't know these things had expiration dates," Nichols said.

Inside the shower, there was a clear mix of male-female products—organic and floral women's shampoo and artificially colored and scented men's.

"Do you guys know if Lawrence Hunt has a girlfriend?"

"I don't know," Brandenburg said. "I don't exactly keep up with romance gossip in town."

Wolf looked at Nichols. The deputy shook his head, but his eyes had a faraway look again.

"Everything okay?" Wolf asked.

"What? No."

"No?" Wolf asked.

"I mean, yeah."

Wolf eyed them. He didn't know these two from a hole in the ground, but they still appeared to be acting strange. They knew something he didn't. Were they both lying about the other kid in the picture, and if they knew him? If so, why? Or was it something else? It could have been a hundred different things.

Wolf decided to leave them be and go back into the kitchen.

Nichols and Brandenburg joined him, Nichols kicking aside a plastic bowl.

A rear door led from the kitchen to the field out back. "I'd like to check around outside."

Brandenburg gave him the *after-you* gesture again.

Wolf twisted the lock, pulled it open, and stepped out onto a concrete patio. Old, cracked vinyl chairs were gathered around a plastic table that held an ashtray filled with cigarette butts, half of them with red lipstick smeared on the filter.

Nichols stood next to him. "More signs of a woman."

Brandenburg grunted.

Wolf went to a soccer ball lying on the grass and picked it up.

"It's youth size." Wolf turned to them. "Did Irv Hunt have any kids?"

Nichols shook his head. "No, sir."

"Maybe the girlfriend has a kid," Wolf said, wondering if a woman of the same age as Lawrence Hunt, at fifty-five, would have had a kid needing a youth ball. It looked newish and not a relic from Irv Hunt's past.

"What's up?" Nichols asked.

"Just thinking maybe it's a grandkid."

"Oh."

Brandenburg stepped off the porch and into the grass, looking around the yard.

Wolf's eyes went to the shed that stood on the other side of the lawn, and he walked over to the building. Nichols and Brandenburg's steps brushed behind, joining the burble coming from the irrigation ditch that ran along the back of the property.

The shed stood at a crooked angle and was made of particle board that had warped over time in the harsh high-alpine desert environment. It was painted the same color as the house, with a single rolling door with a handle at the front.

Wolf grabbed the cold bar and pulled. The door slid up on well-oiled track wheels, revealing a dirt-floored space filled with garden tools and a workbench inside.

A riding lawnmower sat along the left wall, but the space

in front of Wolf was conspicuously vacant. Harried boot prints, presumably from the bikers checking the place for any sign of their bag of money, were stamped into the dirt.

Wolf knelt down to inspect and found evidence of knobby tires. "There are tire marks here."

"Yeah?" Brandenburg put his hands on his hips.

"Looks like they're for a four-wheeler."

Nichols knelt down, then looked up at his boss. "He's right."

"So, where's that?" Wolf ducked out of the shed. There was no sign of any vehicle on the property other than Hunt's truck.

He went back inside and noticed a folded sheet of stretchable fabric sitting on a wooden shelf. He picked it up and let it unfurl. The Polaris brand name was stitched onto it, along with the model name of *Ranger*. Wolf was familiar with the model, having recently been looking online to buy one himself.

"Looks like a cover for something bigger than a four-wheeler," Brandenburg said. "Like a side-by-side."

Wolf nodded, wadding it up and putting the cover back on the shelf.

Tracked grooves were worn into the dirt leading out of the shed and then disappeared into the lush lawn. But kneeling down, Wolf found a slight groove worn into the sod that headed toward the edge of the property and a piece of plywood that served as a bridge over the two-foot-wide irrigation ditch.

He walked the trail to the wood, which was streaked black with tire marks. On the other side, the tracks led through some weeds and then to a two-track trail veering around some junipers and into the wilderness behind the property.

"Where does this lead?"

"I don't know," Brandenburg said. "We've got hundreds of miles of trails surrounding Doyle. Could be a connector from his house to one of them."

"Let's check it out."

CHAPTER FIFTEEN

"Which way now?"

Brandenburg's voice came out of Wolf's radio. They were driving the trail behind the house in their trucks. Brandenburg had come to a stop, contemplating a fork in the road.

"Just a second." Wolf shifted into park, got out of his truck, and went to the front bumper of Brandenburg's, looking down at the dirt.

Nichols got out and came up alongside him. "Got anything?"

Little signs of use showed themselves on the rocky, weed-covered trail, but Wolf found some uprooted rocks and a faint wheel impression leading to the right. He pointed them out. "I think it's this way."

Wolf walked back, stopping at Brandenburg's open window, while Nichols climbed back into the passenger seat of his boss's truck.

"I think they went right," Wolf said.

Brandenburg said nothing as he rolled up his window and let off the brake, taking the right turn.

Wolf climbed into his SUV and followed, another round of annoyance at the sheriff's attitude prickling him.

The terrain was relatively flat but thickly wooded with junipers and pines. The way forward revealed itself in hundred-yard chunks, coming around bends and through knots of trees.

Both of Wolf's windows were down, letting in fragrant air scented by the evergreen foliage. Ahead, Brandenburg moved at a good pace, not too slow or too fast, swerving between large rocks and bushes.

After fifteen minutes of travel, they came into a large clearing, and the trail bent toward a house standing in a field dotted with cattle.

Wolf thumbed the radio and put it to his lips. "Whose place is this?"

The answer took a long time, and just before Wolf was going to ask the question again, Nichols's voice came on.

"Looks like a guy named Dean Chancellor's place."

The truck bounced over some ruts, but the two-track was more well-worn here and smoother, and Brandenburg drove faster. Wolf pressed the gas to keep up.

As they neared the house, they passed a graveyard of farm equipment spread around an outbuilding. The place was one-storied, much like Hunt's had been.

A man stood outside, eyeing the two vehicles as they drove up. As they passed by, he rounded the side of the house, keeping them in view.

The trail spilled onto a dirt road ahead, and Brandenburg slowed, rolling over a cattle guard as he turned right and toward the house. Wolf did the same, then followed

Brandenburg a short distance, parked in front of the place, and shut off his engine.

All three got out and stood at Brandenburg's front bumper, a cloud of dust washing over them.

"Mr. Chancellor!" Brandenburg said.

"What d'ya want?" the man responded.

Brandenburg smiled, walking up the driveway toward the house. "We'd like to talk to you."

"Hi there, Dean," Nichols said.

Chancellor was in his fifties, thin and short, dressed in jeans and a flannel shirt, a trucker hat cast shadows over a distrustful glare. He remained ten paces away, standing with folded arms.

"About what?"

"Lawrence Hunt," Brandenburg said.

"What about him?"

"Have you seen him lately?"

"Nope." The man looked to his right, toward the side of the house, and then back at them, his eyes hard, as if he were now engaged in a staring contest.

It was such a peculiar move that they all looked.

Parked near the house sat a Polaris brand side-by-side. The model had two enclosed seats, and the cargo bed was stenciled with white paint reading *Ranger* that matched the exact logo they'd found on the cover back in Lawrence Hunt's shed.

Wolf, Brandenburg, and Nichols exchanged glances.

"Whose is that?" Brandenburg asked, walking further up the driveway toward the vehicle.

"That's mine. And I'd like it if you'd stay away from it."

Brandenburg frowned, looking at him. "Why?" He continued walking.

Nichols followed, but Wolf kept where he was, watching Dean Chancellor closely. The man seemed harmless enough, but he hadn't gotten a look at the full circumference of his beltline.

"You can't just come barging in here looking through my stuff."

"I've been looking at purchasing one of those myself," Wolf said in an amicable tone. "Do you like it?"

Dean said nothing, flicking a glance at Wolf, returning his glare to the two deputies.

Brandenburg reached the vehicle and touched the tires. "The tread matches."

Nichols nodded.

"This is Lawrence Hunt's side-by-side," Brandenburg said, walking toward Dean.

Chancellor's chest was heaving now like he'd just finished walking up a flight of stairs. He swallowed, shaking his head.

"Dean, we know it," Brandenburg said. "We found the cover to it at his place with the same logo. *Ranger.* Come on. It's his."

"So what?" Dean said. "So, what's the problem?"

Brandenburg chuckled. "Well, the first problem is, why did you just lie to us?"

"He gave it to me."

"He gave it to you?"

"That's right."

"Okay." Brandenburg shrugged. "Why did he give it to you?"

"We traded."

"Traded for what?"

Dean blinked. "My truck."

"That wouldn't happen to be a blue Ford F-150, would it?" Wolf asked.

"That's right. Why? What did he do?"

"Why did he have to do anything?" Brandenburg asked, chuckling. "What are you hiding from us? What's with the cagey attitude?"

Dean narrowed his eyes, his hands opening and closing. "If he gave me money from some illegal source for this deal that we had together, do I get to keep it? I mean, I told him, trading straight up like that...that's not enough. I said I needed something more than that beat-up side-by-side. A mini truck for a full-sized truck don't cut it. The F-150 only had ninety thousand miles on it. Brand new drive train. All new tires."

A moment of silence passed.

"Why would you think the money was from an illegal source?" Wolf asked.

Dean shook his head, his stoic face finally cracking, like he'd been holding a secret for ages and finally had somebody to tell. "He was all out of sorts. And he had a bag with him. And he reached in and gave me four stacks of bills this high." He pinched his fingers. "Looked like something out of the movies."

"Do you still happen to have these stacks of cash?" Brandenburg asked.

Dean's eyes went over his shoulder, then down to the ground. A John Deere tractor was parked in the distance. "No," he said.

"You bought yourself a tractor with the money," Brandenburg said.

"I didn't know it was bad money."

"Nobody said it was bad money yet," Brandenburg said.

Dean closed his mouth.

"Why don't you tell us exactly what happened?" Wolf said.

"He came ripping in here on that thing, then knocking on my door...it must have been three a.m."

"When?" Wolf asked.

"Umm..."

"Saturday morning?" Nichols asked.

"Yeah. Saturday. Anyway, I said, 'What the hell are you doing?' And he just said, 'Hey, I need your truck.' And he wanted to trade for it. I told him the truck was for sale for a reason. I gotta get some money for it. And that's when he went back to his side-by-side, dug into a duffle bag, and handed me forty grand. Four bundles of hundreds, ten grand each."

Dean fluttered his lips. "And then he told me I can keep the Polaris, too. I said, sign me up. Here are the keys!"

Brandenburg whistled softly. "That's a pretty good payday."

"Sure is," Dean said. He looked at them, his joy fading. "So...what do you want from me?"

"Do you have any copies of the registration we can take a look at?" Wolf asked. "We need to know the license plate."

"Sure do."

"Excellent."

CHAPTER SIXTEEN

The next few hours were spent up at Lawrence Hunt's place, looking through the house for more evidence that might lead to his girlfriend's identity. When they found nothing, they waited for a tow truck to come get the Chevy.

Meanwhile, Wolf called Patterson and let her know they had a license plate. She updated the APB, rebroadcasting the alert to every department and precinct within five hundred miles.

It was late afternoon as they rolled back into Doyle. Wolf felt another tug of hunger in his stomach, the growing twinge in his back from all the driving, and the desire for a long nap.

The air inside the department building felt like entering a walk-in cooler.

"Good God," Brandenburg said. "It's freezing in here. Can we turn that up?"

Larkin looked up from his computer, then stood and went to a wall thermostat. "Did you guys figure out anything?"

"At least five degrees hotter," Brandenburg said, disappearing inside his office.

The man turned from the thermostat and sat back down.

"Did you finish submitting the paperwork we talked about?" Brandenburg asked, coming back into the room and knocking on Larkin's desk.

"Not yet, sir. I was just working on it."

Nichols entered the building, stripping off his aviator sunglasses.

"Wolf," Brandenburg said. "Back here."

He entered the sheriff's office and sat down.

Brandenburg sat, folding his arms across his mountain of a chest. "So...what now?"

Wolf raised his chin. "I'm interested in seeing this through. I want to help you find Hunt and bring him in. I'd like to follow through on finding Hunt's girlfriend. She could lead us to him. This is where the action is, not down in Rocky Points."

"And how do we find her?"

"Well," Wolf said, "we could start by looking on social media. Why don't you go to Facebook and Instagram and search Lawrence Hunt."

Brandenburg snorted but moved his mouse and clicked the keys.

Wolf leaned forward and watched as the sheriff looked at the two social media platforms and then two more for good measure. There were plenty of Lawrence Hunts, but none were who they were looking for.

Brandenburg sat back heavily against his seat, abandoning the computer. "What else?"

"Boots on the ground."

Brandenburg stared at him. "You have pressure at home to produce some answers?"

"Yeah, I do."

"What's that all about?"

"I have an unsolved that's getting on some influential people's nerves."

"The billionaire's security manager," Brandenburg said.

"Something like that."

A smile played on the sheriff's lips, and then he sighed. "Fine. Where are you gonna stay?"

"You have any good recommendations for hotels?"

"There's The Lamb Motel. And that's it."

"Then The Lamb it is."

"It's on the other end of town."

Wolf nodded. "Thank you."

Brandenburg looked at his watch. "I don't know about you, but I'm about to drop dead if I don't get some rest. Nichols out there has a newborn."

"Really?" Wolf said. "I didn't know."

"How would you?"

Wolf said nothing.

Brandenburg continued. "I'd like my deputy to get home so he can take care of that baby of his and get some rest. It's been a long, long few days up here. We can't just sit here and work twenty-four hours a day. We have to take care of ourselves, or else nothing will get taken care of."

Brandenburg's eyes were rimmed red. Wolf had seen the same in his rearview mirror on the drive back in.

"Fine? Fine," Brandenburg said, remaining in his seat. "We're usually here by seven. We'll see you tomorrow."

Wolf nodded, deciding an invitation to stay in town was a step up in their relationship.

"See you then." He stood, bid the three men goodbye, and went out to his SUV.

The late-day sun had been beating in through his window, and the warm leather seat was like a salve on his lower back.

After punching in The Lamb Motel into MDT, he followed the directions back to Main and headed north.

On the way through town, he passed the Dusty Thorn Saloon and counted five motorcycles parked along the road in front of the place. Neon beer signs hung in dark windows, reflecting his SUV as he coasted past. Getting no view inside, he turned his attention to the motorcycles. They were all Harley-Davidson's with ape hangers and worn leather saddlebags adorned with studded spikes that hung off the seats. The machines were also filthy with mud and dust, suggesting they were well-used, exclusive means of transport for SOV members and not a group of suburban riders up from Denver.

Wolf thought about going in, getting a bite to eat there, and maybe asking some questions about Irv Hunt's disappearance and his father's reaction. Then he thought of his earlier encounter with Snake and decided one encounter with the SOV was good enough for the day.

He was exhausted, and his back was killing him. He needed to check into this Lamb place, take a hot shower, and find a meal elsewhere.

———

The Lamb Motel was L-shaped, marked by a sign on a pole with a bighorn sheep standing next to one of its young. The building was made from logs, stone, and mortar, like something one would see in Yellowstone National Park.

Pulling off the highway into the parking lot, his wheels rolled over warped tarmac threaded with grass-filled cracks. He stopped under a pull-through portico at the reception office and got out.

Stretching his arms overhead, he took in the exterior of the place. Exactly one car was parked along the building, boasting a Montana license plate.

Instead of entering the office, he walked toward the highway and looked back south into the town, taking in the buildings he had missed while distracted by the Dusty Thorn.

There was a mechanic's garage, a feed and tractor supply store, an insurance provider, a gas station, and a few other buildings.

A restaurant called D's Diner sat directly across the street from the motel. Another two motorcycles were parked in front of it. Again, they looked particularly grimy. Through the window, two bearded men were seated at a booth, staring back at him.

Wolf turned back to the motel.

A man watched him from the office window with narrowed eyes as he approached.

Wolf felt like the lone man in an arena.

Ignoring the eyes on his back and front, he walked inside. It was a cool space decorated with old wooden furniture and paintings of bighorn sheep on the walls. It smelled of pipe tobacco.

"Hello." The man said, shuffling away from the window to a reception desk, limping heavily. "You need a room for the night?"

"Yes, sir. Do you have any availability?"

"Let me see here." He looked down at an accounting book and flipped a page. "What is it? June...sixteenth? No, seventeenth. Says here we have a large business conference taking up the whole place." He looked up with sparkling eyes, a smile upturning his craggy cheeks. "You know, Doyle is a big destination for conferences like that."

Wolf looked outside at the vehicle parked in the lot. "Oh."

The man's chest rattled. "I'm just pullin' your chain. Nobody comes to Doyle, but people goin' through Doyle." He put on a pair of glasses and started writing in the book. "I picked the wrong place to put this business. Your name?"

Wolf told him.

"I see that badge on your hip. You're a cop."

"That's right."

"Where from?"

"Rocky Points."

The man kept his eyes on the page. "You'll be in room nine. It's at the end." He pointed out the window to the far end of the building and then shuffled to a series of hooks containing keys. With a shaking hand, he plucked one and dropped it on the counter.

"Good old-fashioned key," the man said. "Bet you don't have those in Rocky Points."

"Thank you." Wolf chuckled. "Probably not."

"We don't have any Wi-Fi, sorry."

"That's okay," Wolf said.

"I haven't gotten around to installing the system. But people tend to enjoy the silence from life without it anyway." The man smiled. "At least that's what a guy told me once. Let me know if you need anything."

Wolf picked up the key. "I do actually have a couple of questions if you don't mind answering?"

The man's joviality vanished. The wrinkles above his eyes deepened.

"I'm investigating a couple of homicides that happened down south."

"Yeah?"

"Did you hear about the killings that happened out at the compound?"

The man said nothing.

"Is that a no? Or..."

"That's a dangerous question to answer, that is."

"Why's that?"

"Because it has to do with them." He pointed an ancient twig finger at the window, then lowered it.

Wolf looked. He had pointed at the two bikes parked across the street.

"Those two bikes are SOV members?"

The man remained silent.

"How about Lawrence Hunt?" Wolf asked. "You know him?"

The man turned his back and closed the accounting book.

"Right," Wolf said. "Dangerous question. Okay, how about this, can you recommend a good place to eat?"

The man turned around and pointed the exact same way he had before.

"D's Diner?"

"That's right. Best food in town. Or you could go down to the Dusty Thorn and get an overpriced plate of trash washed down with a cup of piss. Up to you."

Wolf cleared his throat.

"But let me give you a piece of advice."

"Go for it," Wolf said.

"Cop or no cop. If you go to the Dusty Thorn, don't be asking questions like you been asking me."

Wolf nodded and turned for the door. "Thanks."

"You're welcome. Have a nice stay."

CHAPTER SEVENTEEN

The room was as expected: neat but just south of clean.

He put his duffle bag on the bed, stripped his clothing, and went into the bathroom. The shower head was too strong, the water like needles on his skin, but strong was always better than weak.

With the water burrowing into the top of his head and running over his face, he felt himself relax under the heat.

His thoughts turned to Piper and the doppelgänger mockup of the wedding she'd been so excited to show him. Regret flooded his body. He'd let the whole thing spiral out of control, and he needed to call her immediately. She needed to know the truth, and with each passing minute, it would only get worse when he actually told her.

Drying off with a scratchy towel, he sat on the edge of the bed, listening to the dead silence of the building. He picked up his cell.

He dialed Piper's number, but when he put it to his ear, there was no sound. Looking at the screen, he heard three beeps, and the call was dropped. Where there were usually reception bars, the screen now read *No Service*.

He got dressed, knowing there had been reception back in the sheriff's department parking lot. He could drive there later and call.

No. He decided it would be impossible to even enjoy dinner without getting this conversation out of the way.

He went outside, climbed into the SUV, and drove south into town, keeping one eye on his cell phone. At the Dusty Thorn, the *No Service* indicator disappeared, and two bars came up, so he pulled over.

He looked over at the jet-black windows of the saloon and the bikes parked a few yards from his front bumper, ignored it all, and dialed Piper.

Shifting into park, he listened to the digital trill ring through the speakers five, then six times, then another five times without going to voicemail.

Damn technology.

He hung up and typed out a message.

Hi.

Deciding what to write, he figured a text message was not the place to explain himself, so he kept it vanilla.

I'M UP IN DOYLE. STAYING AT A PLACE CALLED THE LAMB. THINGS ARE GOING WELL. RECEPTION IS BAD. I TRIED TO CALL, BUT IT DIDN'T WORK. I'LL GIVE YOU A RING LATER OR TOMORROW. I LOVE YOU.

He sent the message and put the phone down. Outside, a biker was coming up the sidewalk toward him.

A shot of adrenaline spiked his pulse. It was Snake.

He had a knife hanging off a studded belt, probably another strapped to his leg inside the riding boots he wore. The compound leader's lips moved in an angry conversation with himself. He spit on the sidewalk, then laughed, then cursed and spit again. He slowed at one of the bikes, then stopped dead as if having a premonition. He lifted his head and locked gazes with Wolf through the windshield.

His demeanor relaxed. He swerved through two motorcycles and walked over to Wolf's SUV, stopping at his window and knocking on the glass.

Wolf lowered the window, twisting his hips to readily pull his gun if need be.

Snake grabbed the window of Wolf's door, his fingers curling inside. He smelled of cigarettes and beer.

"Fancy seeing you here, Detective Wolf."

"Snake."

"You guys find Hunt?"

"Not yet. You?"

Snake pointedly didn't answer the question.

"You didn't give us any information on the truck or the license plate," Wolf said.

Snake shrugged, the blue-inked serpents on his veiny, muscular neck writhing as he did.

"It's alright. We know about the truck and got the license plate anyway and updated the APB. We'll find him soon enough."

Snake's eyes remained calm, his lip turned up in the hint of a smile. "What are you doing here?"

"Just making a phone call. Receptions shoddy around here."

"It is." He looked down the road, back the way Wolf had come. "You getting a bite to eat inside? They have a great burger."

"I don't think so."

Snake shrugged again.

"What happened to Irving Hunt?" Wolf asked.

"Who's that?"

"Lawrence's son, the one who's gone missing, and from what I'm gathering, the reason why he came and shot your men, stole your money, and is on the run."

Snake pushed back, shaking his head. "I don't know what you're talking about."

Wolf nodded. "Okay."

"Welp." Snake slapped his roof and turned to walk away. "See you around." He got on his bike, lifted the kickstand, fired up the engine, and accelerated away.

"Apparently so," Wolf said under his breath as he watched Snake's image recede into the distance at high speed. A minute later, the man was gone around a bend, the noise of his engine disappearing behind the sound of Wolf's air conditioner.

He blinked and looked at his phone. The message he'd sent to Piper had been marked *Read*.

Waiting for a response, his stomach groaned again. After sitting for another two minutes, feeling eyes watching beyond the glass of the Dusty Thorn, he finally decided to ditch his efforts. He shifted into drive, turned around, and went back to the motel.

Parking the SUV, he went to his room and looked out the window to the diner across the street. The two motorcycles were gone, which was good because he wasn't in the mood for yet another biker confrontation. He just needed food. And fast.

He put his badge in his pocket, tucked the Glock in the back of his pants, pulled his shirt over it, and went back out.

The owner of the motel sat outside the office on a

plastic chair, puffing a pipe.

Wolf passed him as he walked through the parking lot, nodding a greeting.

"Off to get a meal over at D's?"

"Yes, sir," Wolf said. "Per your recommendation."

"Tell Savannah hi for me."

"Okay," he said. "Will do." But he was thinking about Piper again. She had read his message but hadn't responded. Did that mean she had seen him call and not answered?

Wolf continued walking, crossing the traffic-less street and entering the diner.

A digital bell dinged as he walked into steamy air that smelled of hamburgers.

The place was well-lit, with sixties country music coming from speakers overhead. Rows of booths stretched out to the right and left along the glass, while a long counter in the middle held attached stools. Everything gleamed silver with original-looking chrome. Neon signs hung on the walls, bent in the shapes of french fries and hamburgers.

An elderly couple sat at a booth to the right, eating silently, but it was otherwise empty of patrons.

"Hi, just one?" A woman appeared in front of him. She was in her sixties, gray hair drawn into a bun at the back of her head, held there by a pencil.

"Yes, ma'am," he said.

She rounded the counter, grabbed a menu, and dropped it on the floor. When she bent down to grab it, the pencil fell out of her hair, and she cursed under her breath as she picked it up.

Now red-faced, she led him in the opposite direction of the couple to a booth. He followed in the scent of her flowery perfume.

"Here okay?" she asked.

"Sure."

He squeezed past her, taking the opposite side of the table to watch the entrance. As he lowered himself to the bench, he saw her looking at his lower back.

Her mouth dropped open, eyes bulging briefly at the sight of his weapon.

Cutting off any misinterpretation, he pulled the badge from his pocket. "I'm a cop."

Her eyes widened further, not the reassured expression Wolf was expecting. One eye was bloodshot below the pupil, the lower lid swollen.

He picked up the menu. "What happened to your eye? Everything going okay there?"

She hesitated, then nodded. "Yeah."

She put a hand up to her face, then lowered it. "Oh. Yeah. Just...fell." But her breathing looked quicker now. She turned to leave. "I'll be back with some water."

"I'll take a Sprite, too," he said.

She left with quick steps, going to fill the drinks behind the bar.

"You got it," she said. She dropped one of the plastic cups, which clunked along the floor behind the counter. Again, she cursed and picked it up.

A minute later, she brought the drinks and put them in front of him. "Had a chance to look at the menu?"

He had not, but he handed the laminated sheet back to her and said, "I'll take a cheeseburger, medium, cheddar, please, with fries."

"Coming right up."

She took the menu and disappeared through a swivel door into the kitchen. It had a circular window, and a man's face came into view. He eyed him and then disappeared.

A second later, the same man came out from behind the kitchen. He was younger than Wolf, a head shorter, with blond hair shaved almost to the scalp on the top and sides. He wore frayed shorts and a food-stained gray T-shirt that had Grateful Dead's Steal Your Face skull on it.

Without pause, the man went to the elderly couple's table, took their drinks, refilled them behind the bar, and returned the cups. The old woman smiled and thanked him, the old man concentrated on his food.

"You okay on your drink?" he asked Wolf.

"Yeah, fine. Thanks."

"Food's cooking." He walked back into the kitchen.

Outside the window, a hatchback Subaru pulled out from next to the restaurant. The older woman who had been waiting on him was behind the wheel, alone. She looked both ways and pulled out going south away from the building.

Wolf stared at the woman's receding car, wondering why she had taken his order and left so hastily. She had been disheveled and nervous while waiting on Wolf. Had she just run away? From him? It certainly looked like it.

Outside, the motel manager across the street was getting up from his seat and walking back into his office. Done with his smoke break.

Say hi to... What was the name he'd used? Georgia? No.

Savannah. *Say hi to Savannah for me.* That was what he had said.

The kitchen door pushed open, and the guy with the Grateful Dead shirt came out and slid a plate in front of him. As he extended his arm, a tattoo on his right bicep came into view from under his shirtsleeve: a lightning bolt coming out of a small cloud.

"You need anything else?" the man asked. "Ketchup's right there."

Wolf stared at him.

"Sir?"

"No. Thanks."

The man left, disappearing again through the back door. Wolf watched him walk away. There was a resemblance in the way the man walked when compared to the older woman. Their backsides both curled under and were of similar proportions, and their feet splayed outward with each step.

He pulled out his phone and found the photo he'd taken at Hunt's house. He pinched and zoomed in on the kid next to Irv. The tattoo matched, and the blond hair, an unruly mess in the picture, was much shorter now, but there was no doubt the same person had just delivered his food. But the man was a good twenty years older now, at least.

Wolf put a fry in his mouth, thinking about the old woman's face. It had been similar—they both had the same rounded eyes and small nose. They were related—Wolf would bet money on it. Mother and son? Aunt and nephew?

He didn't know what to make of any of this, nor, he decided, did he care. Right now, he needed to eat, so he did.

The burger was cooked to perfection, juicy, with a thick bun. The fries crispy. Every bite drew him into the next and the next, and only in the middle of the meal did he start thinking about current events again.

That guy in the kitchen was Irving Hunt's friend. He needed to talk to him.

The kitchen door swung open again, and the man came straight to Wolf's table.

"Everything good?"

"Yeah," Wolf said.

"Get you another drink?"

"Please."

Wolf watched as he left with the cup and went behind the counter. When he came back, Wolf laid his badge and the phone showing the picture on the table.

"My name's Dave Wolf," Wolf said. "I'm a detective from Rocky Points. What's your name?"

The man looked at the badge and set the drink down. He didn't answer, though. He was lost in the photograph glowing on Wolf's cell.

Wolf pushed the phone toward him and pointed at the screen. "Irving Hunt. And that's you, right? I recognize the tattoo on your arm."

The man stepped back. "Yeah, that's me. Although a long time ago. What about it? Where'd you get this?"

"I didn't get your name."

"Mitch."

"Mitch, what?"

"What can I do for you?" Mitch said.

Wolf nodded. Okay, no last name. "Nice to meet you, Mitch." He held out a hand, and Mitch shook it, his hand greasy and warm.

Outside, the lighting dimmed, and wind rattled the window. A few drops of rain hit the glass.

"Where'd you get that?" Mitch asked again.

"It was a picture I found at Lawrence Hunt's place, in Irv's room."

"Oh."

"I'd like to ask you a few questions about Irv."

"Okay. Like what?"

Wolf pulled his badge and phone back toward him, pocketing both. "You two have known each other for a while, huh?"

"Yeah."

"You grew up with him here?"

"Yeah."

"I hear he was running with those bikers," he gestured down the street.

Mitch didn't reply, giving Wolf a look as if considering whether to trust him or not.

"Do you know what happened to him?" Wolf asked. "To Irv?"

Mitch shook his head, looking over at the elderly couple. The two ate obliviously.

"Was that your mother that just left?" Wolf asked.

"Huh? Oh, yeah."

"Savannah, is it?"

Mitch's eyes narrowed. "Savannah? Why do you say that?"

"The guy across the street running the motel told me her name. Said to say hi for him."

Mitch looked outside, then back at Wolf. "Okay. Look, I don't know where Irv is."

"What happened to your mother's eye?"

"Her eye? I don't know what you're talking about."

Wolf changed tack. "You've heard about Irv's dad, right? About what he did the other night up at the biker compound?"

Mitch looked over at the couple again. His voice lowered. "I've heard. What of it?"

"We found two bikers killed down south, and we believe Lawrence Hunt did it. We know he killed four of these guys the other night. We think he did it for revenge for what they did to his son."

Mitch didn't seem particularly mollified by Wolf's news.

"We'd like to know where he is. Have you seen him?"

"No."

"And you don't know anything about Irv's disappearance?"

Mitch's eyes went to the window.

There was a rumbling noise outside that Wolf thought was thunder but now saw was a motorcycle. A biker with long hair and a beard pulled up and stopped in front of the diner windows. He jutted the bike out toward the road, then walked it back, his pipes snapping and popping. He wore a leather vest with the SOV insignia on its back. With a booted foot, he flipped down the kickstand, got off the bike, and approached the entrance.

Wind whipped across the table as the door opened with its electric chime. Wolf turned back, but Mitch was no longer standing next to him.

"Get you a table?" Mitch asked the man, picking up a menu from the counter.

The biker was tall, with tanned leathery skin. He pulled off a pair of sunglasses, revealing a set of pale gray eyes surrounded by tan lines. He looked right toward the elderly couple, who stared back at the man. Then he looked left, letting his gaze land and stay on Wolf for a beat.

"I'll sit at the bar," the biker said. He walked to a stool and sat. "Coke."

Mitch nodded and got to work, pouring the drink and setting it in front of him.

"Get you some food?"

The man didn't answer but pulled the menu toward him. He mumbled something and pushed it away. Mitch took it, then walked to Wolf's table, dropped his check even though he wasn't finished with his meal, and disappeared into the kitchen.

There was a wall with a mirror behind the bar counter, and Wolf sat watching the biker in its reflection. The man's eyes never left Wolf's.

Wolf nodded, then picked up his burger and continued to eat. It was cold now, and the fries, too. But he was hungry and finished it nonetheless, all the while feeling eyes on him.

Outside, the storm freshened. Drops on the window multiplied, and quicksilver streaks ran down the glass. Lightning flashed, and thunder shook the building.

The elderly couple remained where they were, sitting with empty plates, staring out the window, the man picking his teeth with a toothpick.

Wolf felt like he'd been onto something here, but if Mitch knew anything, there was no way he'd be talking with the biker here.

He left money on the table and got up.

Wolf approached the biker, entering an invisible cloud scented with cigarettes and body odor. The man was typing a message into his phone, but when he sensed Wolf, he quickly turned it face down on the counter. He turned, leaning on an elbow. His forearm was the color of charred wood, graffitied with faded-to-blue tattoos.

"What?" the biker asked.

"Hey."

The biker upturned his hands. "Who are you? What do you want?"

"I'm a cop from down south. I'm looking for Lawrence Hunt."

"Oh. Okay." His tone was *Who gives a shit?*

"He shot a couple of you guys down in my county. So, I'm up here looking for him."

The man said nothing.

"I heard what he did up at your place last weekend," Wolf said. "What was it? Saturday morning?"

The guy's eyes narrowed.

"I'm sorry for the loss of your friends."

"Yeah. Thanks, pig."

Wolf looked out the window at the rain dousing the man's bike. "You here to watch me? Or what?"

"A bit full of ourselves, are we?"

Wolf smiled. "Catch you around," he said, turning toward the door.

"Sure," the biker said.

Wolf looked toward the kitchen door on his way out, catching a watchful eye disappearing from the window.

He pushed the door open against a spray of rain. Before the door blew shut, he heard a snorting pig sound coming from inside.

Wolf ducked his head against the storm and walked back to the motel.

CHAPTER EIGHTEEN

"Stee-rike!"

"Great pitch!" Rachette yelled.

The kid on the mound's father never showed up to these games, and with his mother sitting there like a sack of sand, staring at her phone, Rachette felt pride in being little Charlie Wall's biggest fan while he was pitching.

"Come on now, Chuck! You got this!"

Rachette looked across the diamond toward Patterson, sitting in the other stands. Her husband, Scott, was standing in the dugout with his son's team. They were on pins and needles, just like he was. Probably even more than their kid.

Their son, Tommy, was at bat for the other team. Bottom of the ninth. Two outs. Runners on first and second. One strike. No balls. It didn't get bigger than this moment.

Come on.

He looked out at center field, where his own son, TJ,

slapped his glove between adjustments of his cup. His eyes wandered to a jet overhead.

"Look alive, TJ!" Rachette screamed.

TJ nodded his head, smacking his glove again.

"Come on! Let's go, Tommy!" Charlotte cheered next to him.

He shook his head slightly, resisting the urge to tell his wife to shut it and stop rooting for the other team. He got it; she was being nice to Patterson's kid, but right now, it was like fingernails on his brain.

"Come on, we need this. We need this," the parent next to him whined.

"We got this," Rachette said, correcting the guy's tone.

Tommy Patterson was a year younger than TJ, with a flop of brown hair that came out of the ear holes of his helmet. He stepped up to the edge of the batter's box with his hand up to the ump, taking his time getting situated, then stepping his toes in.

Just like his mother, the kid was very short but very quick and capable. He was top of the order for a reason: because he usually got a hit. He always got a hit. In fact, he was four for four today. The way he was twirling the bat like a martial arts expert said he was about to get another one.

But he hadn't faced their ringer closer yet. Chuck had the fastest arm in the league.

Let's go. Smoke this past him.

The next pitch came in. Tommy swung this time, missing.

"Stee-rike!"

Rachette smacked his hands together. "Good pitch!"

"Honey. Don't."

"What?" He turned to Charlotte. "One more pitch, and we win. This is it."

"Yeah. I know. Thank you." Her voice was low. Too low for the moment.

"Huh." He waved a hand and looked back at the action.

The third pitch came, and Tommy Patterson swung. The bat slammed into the ball with a loud ping.

Rachette lunged to his feet. "Oh..." the word spilled out of his mouth. The trajectory was straight up the gut, at an angle that would meet directly with TJ's center field position.

TJ backed up a few steps like he had been taught, and then, realizing the ball was hit harder than he originally thought, backed up a few more. Then he turned and ran.

"Shit," Rachette said under his breath. What had TJ been doing playing that shallow? They had to play deeper for top of the order on this team. The first three kids, starting with Patterson's, had power.

Tommy's jet-powered legs already had him rounding first by the time the ball started its downward arc.

But TJ would be there. He had wheels himself, and he had that look that said he had the catch. He always had the catch. Usually.

It was too much. Rachette couldn't look. But he couldn't peel his eyes away, either.

The ball dropped down on its final arc and landed squarely in the center of TJ's mitt. No bobble, no drop, just a sure clench of the glove and the raising of two hands in triumph.

"Yes!"

The stands erupted with cheers, and even Charlotte got

to her feet. Out in the field, the boys ran to each other to celebrate.

The metal stands shook under Rachette's feet. He hugged Charlotte, then exchanged a high-five with the guy next to him. Then, realizing he was probably putting on the cheer a little too thick, he stopped himself and eyed the other stands.

Patterson was on her feet clapping, cheering for her team or both teams, keeping her eyes pointedly away from his. Scott was out on the field, slapping high-fives as they lined up to shake hands. He'd done a good job of coaching tonight, hell, all year, especially with his choice to put that third baseman on the mound in the final couple of innings.

"Where's Harry?" Rachette looked around for his youngest son. He located him over by the trees, still playing with that girl and Patterson's youngest son, Zack. They were gathering flowers, or rocks, or pine needles, or all the above, placing them in stacks, completely oblivious to what had just happened. Oh well. Another couple of years and he would be out on that field, too. If he ever showed any interest in sports.

"I'll go get him," Charlotte said. "Good job, Raptors!"

Yes. It was a good job. With a pride-filled smile, Rachette descended the stands and waited at the dugout for TJ. When he finally came, they embraced, Rachette lifting him up high. A couple of parents slapped him on the back, praising him for snagging the winning catch.

Rachette said nothing to TJ. He didn't have to. He set him down and smacked him on the back, watching him run off to celebrate some more with his teammates.

The sun was setting over the mountains to the west, illuminating the Chautauqua Valley down below the plateau they were on right now. The air was cool and perfectly pleasant. A few clouds spouted rain in the far distance. It was moments like these that he lived for.

The parents mingled with the other team's parents behind the stands on the way to the parking lot. Patterson and Charlotte were engaged in a laughing conversation as they stood with Harry and Zack.

"Better luck next time!" Rachette couldn't resist.

Failing to hide her eye roll, Patterson pasted on a smile. "That was a great game."

"Sure was."

"Great catch by TJ," she said.

"And great hitting by Tommy. What did he go, four for five tonight?"

"Yep."

"Did you guys see any of the game?" Rachette asked the two six-year-olds.

They looked at him like he was speaking Chinese.

"They had fun playing farmer with Camilla again," Charlotte said. "Isn't that right, guys?"

"Yeah!"

The conversation devolved into talk of growing teeth, dentists, and school problems, so Rachette stepped away and met TJ as he finally came off the field.

He put an arm around his son and steered him toward the truck. "You won the game tonight. Do you know that?"

"I don't know about that," TJ said. "I struck out three times."

"That's okay. It's all water under the bridge when you make a game-saver catch like that."

"Yeah. I guess so."

Rachette rubbed his head.

"Hey!" Scott's voice came from behind them. "Great game tonight, TJ!"

They turned around. Scott and Tommy had joined Patterson and Charlotte, and now everyone was walking behind them toward the parking lot.

"Thanks," TJ said.

"Great game out there, Coach," Rachette said, shaking Scott's hand. "That was a good move putting the third baseman in there to pitch. That guy's got a cannon."

"Oh. Yeah. He did well."

"You'll probably be putting him in every game now."

"We kind of do a rotation."

Rachette scoffed, then realized he was serious. "Oh. Well, good timing then."

"Great job again, TJ." Scott patted TJ on the back and walked away with his family.

"See you tomorrow morning," Patterson said, walking away with her son next to her. He stared at the ground, dejected.

"Hey! Good game tonight, Tommy!" Rachette said. But Tommy didn't seem to hear.

They reached Rachette's personal truck, and he opened the back door, keeping wide of a stream of liquid that streaked out from around the tire as he dropped the gear in back.

"What the heck?" he said, looking down. The liquid had a yellow tinge to it. "There's a porta potty right over there!" He would have loved to have caught the son of a bitch pissing next to his truck. He looked around, but there was no sense in it and opened the rear door for Harry.

"Can we get ice cream?" Harry asked.

"Yeah! Ice cream!" TJ said.

"We have to eat dinner first," Charlotte said, climbing inside.

He shut the rear door and climbed in behind the wheel.

"We have ice cream at home," he said. "But we don't have pizza!"

"Yes! Pizza!" the two boys said in unison.

He smiled at Charlotte, who smiled happily back at him.

Firing up the engine, he shifted into reverse to telegraph his intentions to back out into the line of traffic, which inevitably choked up at the exit to the park. The road out swung sideways and descended steeply, where it ended at the highway, and people took their sweet time turning into traffic. At the last game, it had taken them fifteen minutes of rolling at a walking pace to leave.

"Black Diamond?" Charlotte asked.

"Yeah. Of course," he said.

The truck lurched hard and began rolling back. When he pressed the brake there was a strange sensation, like the seat had moved back. Or...no. He stomped his foot, and this time, he got no resistance whatsoever. The brake pedal went all the way down to the floor and stayed dead on the floorboard.

"What the hell?" He jerked his head around. He was careening backward right toward the SUV behind him.

A horn honked, and he jammed the brakes again.

Too late.

After a sickening crunch and everyone lurching in their seat, he shifted back into park.

"What are you doing?" Charlotte yelled.

"I'm not doing anything! Something's wrong with the truck!"

Now, he was jammed into the vehicle behind him. People were all staring.

He put the truck in drive to move forward, and the same thing happened—he couldn't stop, but this time he was rolling straight toward the fields and the people who were still walking past on the grass.

"Shit," he said, jamming the transmission into park again.

The truck skidded to a stop, and he mashed his foot down on the parking brake to engage it.

"Everybody out!" he said, shutting off the engine.

"What is it?"

"Get out! Everybody get out!"

"Okay, kids. Let's get out," Charlotte said.

He opened the door, jumped out himself, and helped Harry down from the back seat, then hurried everybody away from the truck.

"Go with Mommy," he said. "No, get to the front of the truck. The front." If the brakes gave way now, the truck would roll backward.

The vehicle he'd just backed into—an SUV with a family inside he now recognized as the Campos—pulled into the vacant parking spot next to their truck. While the rest of his family sat rigid in shock, the father—Eddie—got out and went to his bumper.

Rachette put up his hands. "Hey, sorry, Eddie! Geez, I don't know what happened. My truck's messed up."

Eddie rubbed the bumper, which had a basketball-sized dent in it.

"Shit," Rachette said. "I've got my insurance information. Just...wait a second."

Rachette walked back toward his vehicle, the initial

shock translating into clear thought for the first time. Something had been wrong with the brakes. The liquid that had been streaming out from under the truck was brake fluid. Not urine.

From this vantage point, the other front wheel had a similar yellow streak coming from it now. He rounded the other side of the truck, ducking down to look under it. There, he found four streams, each beginning where he'd been parked a few seconds ago.

"Looks like you have a brake line problem," Eddie said, following Rachette to his truck. "That's brake fluid."

"Yeah," Rachette said.

"What's going on?" Charlotte stepped up next to him, her voice insistent.

"I don't know. Just...wait." He got to the ground at the front bumper and then, on his back, shuffled underneath.

The braided hoses that went into the brakes had been severed cleanly.

He pulled himself out and looked down the row of cars leaving the lot again. My God, what if he'd pulled out and put it in drive? The collision could have been much worse. What if somebody had been walking in front of the truck?

"What's going on with our brakes?" Charlotte asked.

Rachette stared at the streams of liquid, this time through a crimson haze of rage, knowing at that moment they'd been cut by the assholes he'd beaten up the night before. It was the only explanation.

"Tom!"

"Sorry...yeah, I don't know. They're jacked up." He pointed at Patterson's vehicle, which was about to pass behind them. "Flag them down."

"Heather!" she yelled over the din of vehicles and

stepped out into the lot, flagging them down. After a brief conversation through the window, Scott pulled into the parking spot a few spaces down.

"Go with them!" Rachette said. "I'll deal with this."

Rachette fished his insurance information from the truck, handed it to Eddie, and asked him to take photos of everything. While Eddie got busy, he walked over to Patterson's family SUV.

Charlotte was talking through the still-open window, stopping when Rachette walked up.

"What's going on?" Patterson asked. "Your brakes aren't working?"

"Yeah. Screwed up. I'm not sure what's going on. Can you take these guys home? I'll stick it out and get a tow truck up here."

"You sit here, Charlotte." Patterson opened her door. "I'll wait with him."

"What?" Rachette blocked the door. "Don't worry about it. I got it. You guys head home."

"You sure?"

Rachette pushed the door closed on her. He hadn't thought this through yet, and he didn't want Patterson mucking up his process. She would figure out the lines had been cut and then want to know why. That would lead to his visit with Yates and what he'd done to his friends. She was good like that.

"How do your brakes go out?" Patterson asked. "That truck is less than two years old."

Rachette shook his head. "I took it in the other day. They must have screwed up something. Believe me, I'll be getting compensated for it."

"Who did it?"

He waved a hand. "Come on, boys. Hop in."

"Our stuff's in the truck," TJ said.

"Okay, I'll get it." He jogged away and went to the truck, where Eddie was on his back and looking underneath Rachette's vehicle.

Rachette grabbed the bags out of the bed.

"You know, these lines look cut!" Eddie said, pulling himself up from the ground.

Rachette ignored him, running back with the bags. They were doing a car seat shuffle in the back seat, and then Charlotte got in. He pushed the bags through the window and into the hands of TJ and Harry in the far back, who were engaged in a conversation with Patterson's boys.

Eddie came walking up, his mouth open to say something.

Rachette turned around and snapped at him, then pointed back toward his truck.

Eddie stopped. "I just—"

"I'll be right over. Okay?" Rachette said, tilting his head to get the meaning across that he didn't want to talk about it there. Eddie got the hint two seconds too late and left with a nod.

Patterson stared at Rachette now, her eyes narrowed, that big brain of hers working as she watched Eddie walking away.

Rachette talked fast. "Okay, all set. Thank you very much."

"I need the house key!" Charlotte said.

Damn it. Rachette fished out his key and handed it back to her.

"You sure you don't want me here?" Patterson asked.

"Get out of here. I'll be fine." He pointed past her.

"Scott, thank you!" And then he slapped the roof and walked away.

He went back to his truck.

"Those brake lines of yours have been cut," Eddie said. "I'm sure of it."

"Yeah, you think?"

"Yeah. I do. There's no other explanation. Those are braided steel lines. They don't break like that."

"Thanks for the assessment. We'll let the professionals deal with it, though, huh?" He smiled and slapped him on the shoulder. "Look, you let me take care of everything, okay? Have a good night. I'll call you tomorrow and we'll get all this squared away, no problem. Alright?"

Frowning, Eddie nodded, reluctantly walking away as he said goodbye.

Rachette braved a glance toward Patterson's car and breathed a sigh of relief. They were leaving.

Suddenly he felt a wave of apprehension watching his family go without him. Would they be in trouble without his protection at home?

No, he decided. Charlotte was a desk jockey, sure, but she was one tough cookie who knew exactly how to use the firearm in their bedroom safe. Besides, the men who had done this were obviously cowards—more into the hands-off approach to harming him.

He marveled at their brazenness and stupidity. Well, he would show them what being brazen really was. He felt a level of rock-hard resolve he'd never felt in his life. These two men would be taken down. Hell, maybe he would go the extra step and make them vanish. He could dump them into an abandoned mine shaft up above Cave Creek, and nobody would be the wiser. Either that or out near Dredge, where it was even more remote.

And then?

With a shaky breath, he turned and looked at the sunset again.

And then he would sleep soundly every night for the rest of his life knowing he'd done it. Because that's how much he loved his family.

CHAPTER NINETEEN

Wolf parked in the Anniston County Sheriff's Department lot as the dash clock said 6:55 a.m.

He sat for a few minutes, downing the remainder of his coffee and eating the final bite of a plastic-wrapped pastry he'd bought at the gas station in town. He watched while the phone reacquired a signal for the first time since the previous night.

A message came in from Piper.

DON'T WORRY. I FIGURED OUT EVERYTHING AND CANCELED THE WEDDING PLANS.

He felt like he was in an elevator that just dropped two floors.

What the hell? Had she figured out the plans looked exactly like his previous wedding? Is that what she meant? And had she called off the wedding altogether?

He sighed and pressed the button to call her.

It went straight to voicemail.

Rubbing his forehead, he spoke into the receiver. "Hi. It's me. I...I don't know what to say. I need to talk to you.

Just..." He lined up the excuses in his mind—that he'd wanted to tell her, but the timing never seemed right, that he had let the moment slip away—but they all sounded weak and ineffectual in his mind. "Just call me. Please. As soon as you get this."

He put the phone back in his pocket as the clock ticked over to seven.

Swimming in troubled thoughts, he squinted against the low-angled morning sun and got out into the cool air. He went to the headquarters entrance and found the door unlocked.

The interior of the building was warmer today, smelling of coffee. A box of donuts lay half-devoured on the back table.

Nichols ducked out of Brandenburg's office. "It's Wolf. Good morning. You want a cup of coffee? There's some donuts if you want one, too."

"Coffee, thanks. Donuts, I'd better not. I just had some."

"Your loss."

Larkin pulled up in his truck outside, parked, and walked in carrying a shoulder bag.

"Hi," he said, then walked to his desk. "Good night?"

Wolf nodded.

"Where'd you stay?"

"The Lamb."

"Oh, right. Of course."

Brandenburg walked out of his office and went to the coffee maker. "Wolf. How are you?"

"Not bad," Wolf said, lying, his mind still on Piper. His phone remained silent and still in his pocket.

Shaking the thoughts away, he recalled the night before.

"Listen. Remember that photo I found on the floor of Irving's room?"

Brandenburg frowned.

"This photo," Wolf said, pulling his phone. He pulled up the picture and showed the pic of Irv and the man he now knew as Mitch to Brandenburg.

"Yeah. What about it?" Brandenburg went to the donuts.

Wolf told them about the night prior at D's Diner—of meeting Mitch and the older woman he suspected was his mother and the biker that showed up, clearly watching him.

"Mitch Russell," Larkin said, looking up from his computer.

"You know him?" Wolf asked.

"Yep. Mitch runs the place. With his mom."

"Savannah?" Wolf asked.

"No," Larkin said. "She's Dolores. The 'D' in D's Diner. Savannah's the little girl. Mitch's daughter. Her grand-daughter."

Wolf blinked, looking at Nichols and Brandenburg. They were both staring at Larkin with unreadable expressions.

Larkin upturned his hand. "I eat there all the time. Me and Nichols go in there a lot."

Nichols remained still for a beat, then looked down at Wolf's phone.

"Let me see that again," Nichols said, reaching out a hand.

Wolf handed over his cell.

Nichols squinted, shaking his head. "I'll be damned. That *is* him."

Wolf watched the deputy, wondering if he was acting.

And if so, how good of a job he was doing. The younger Mitch in the photo looked a lot different from the older version in the diner, with a lot less hair on his face and head. But there was the tattoo and there were the facial features. Had Nichols been lying yesterday about not recognizing the man in the picture? Was he lying now?

"Okay, so what?" Brandenburg asked.

"I don't know," Wolf said. "They were acting weird. He wouldn't tell me his last name when I asked him. And she left right after giving me a drink. Like I said, she was skittish. I don't know. And, oh yeah, she had a black eye."

Brandenburg lowered his cup. "A black eye?"

"I think so."

"You *think* so?"

He told them about the bloodshot eye and the swollen area underneath it. "She told me she fell."

"You asked her about it?" Larkin asked.

"Yeah." Wolf stared, a thought coming to him.

"What?" Larkin asked.

"The soccer ball," Wolf said.

"What about it?" Brandenburg asked.

"What soccer ball?" Larkin asked.

"There was a youth soccer ball up at Lawrence Hunt's house. In the backyard. You say there's a little girl?"

"Yeah."

"How little?" *Say hi to Savannah for me.*

"I don't know," Larkin said. "Like, seven? Eight? Something like that? She sits in the diner, sometimes coloring. Reading books or watching her iPad."

Wolf nodded, looking at Brandenburg and Nichols. "It could fit."

"What could fit?" Brandenburg asked.

"That Dolores, *D*, is Hunt's girlfriend. She's the one staying over at his house."

Brandenburg grunted, his eyes flicking back and forth as if the new thought was taking a while to register inside his skull.

"Yeah," the sheriff said. "I guess that could fit."

Wolf turned to Larkin. "What do you think? Have you seen Lawrence Hunt and Dolores together before?"

"I don't know. Maybe? I'm pretty sure I've seen him in there." He shook his head, looking at his boss. "I can't be sure."

Brandenburg sipped his coffee.

"If she is Hunt's girlfriend," Larkin said, "maybe they were roughing her up to get information on where he was."

Wolf nodded. "That's what I'm thinking."

At that moment, Wolf's cell vibrated, still in his hand by his side. He checked the screen and read Waze's name.

"I gotta get this." He put the phone to his ear. "Hey."

Waze's voice emerged from an ocean of static. "We got a hit on Lawrence Hunt's truck."

"Where?"

"Green River, Wyoming. A couple hours northwest of you. I'm texting you the address now."

"Okay. Thanks."

"Keep me posted."

"Will do." He hung up and pocketed the phone.

"What?" Brandenburg asked.

"They found Hunt's truck."

"Where?"

"Green River, Wyoming."

Nichols set his coffee cup down. "I'll drive."

"No," Brandenburg said. "You two stay here and hold it down. Me and Wolf will go." He nodded to Wolf. "I'll drive."

"Okay."

CHAPTER TWENTY

It had been a long time since Patterson had driven the road she was on.

Thinking back, she locked in the timeframe at about a month after Yates had been released from the hospital. She and Scott had come over for a triple-date dinner with Gemma, Yates, Rachette, and Charlotte. They had been a six-wheeled vehicle running on all cylinders that night, the quirky billionaire's daughter laughing hysterically at anything Yates said, Rachette keeping his Rachette-isms to a minimum.

How things had changed for the worse in the few short months since that winter evening. Gemma had moved in with Yates, probably too quickly, but not as fast as she had moved back out. And now Yates was...he was what? Beating himself up about it?

Patterson rubbed a crick in her neck from a bad night's rest. Swirling thoughts had kept her on the edge of sleep all night, not letting her cross into slumber. Ever since Waze had mentioned he was going to be looking for a new detective, she had been thinking about how she had abandoned Yates in his time of need.

Digging for excuses, she could only come up with one: that she had been preoccupied with her transition out of sheriff and into the detective role again. She'd been obsessed with making sure Waze was set up correctly and not dropping balls that needed to be kept in the air. People's livelihoods were at stake, and this drunk newcomer came in, giving her little confidence in his ability to catch anything more than a cold.

So, here she was on the northwest outskirts of town, driving through clusters of houses in the trees on her way to visit Yates, attempting to make good on the one livelihood she *had* dropped the ball on.

Rachette had probably kicked the door down, as was his way. She needed to come in with her own brand of love to offer and let the man know everyone wanted him to get better. She felt better already for finally doing something. Even if it was a hug and a pat on the back, it would help.

She slowed at her destination, taking in the place.

"Shit," she said under her breath, shifting into park.

It looked so different she had to recheck the address beside the door. She was in the right place. But it looked like the house itself had been on a bender the night prior.

The morning sun lit the lawn, and through the overgrown grass, points of light reflected off beer cans. Paper trash and cardboard chunks of pizza boxes were strewn about. A crushed Coors Light can teetered in the wind on the porch wall. It looked like a house on The Hill in Boulder after a Friday night rager.

She shut the engine off and got out.

Yates's car was parked at an aggressive angle on the driveway, the back right tire rolled up onto the lawn, and the bumper close to the garage door.

She walked up the steps, kicking aside a cigarette butt, wondering whose it could possibly be. Yates had always bad-mouthed the habit.

The other side of the porch wall hid much more para-phernalia of a life gone to the dark side: a dozen beer cans, cigarette butts, and cans of Copenhagen snuff flung to the ground.

She rang the doorbell, hearing the chime echo inside.

Her watch read 7:27 a.m.

No movement from inside, and nobody answered. She pressed her face to the window next to the door and scanned the interior with a squinted gaze.

More beer cans. Pizza boxes. Chinese food. Her eyes landed on a plastic bag of pills next to the Barcalounger. She spotted another on the coffee table and one on the end table.

She reached over and knocked, keeping her position to watch the inside. When nobody answered the second time, she twisted the knob and started when the door popped open inwardly. He was completely checked out if his door was unlocked. The man used to access the candy drawer to his desk with a key to keep Rachette out.

She walked inside, her nose turning up at the beer and BO scent emanating from the family room. The television was still on; a European golf tournament flickered on the screen, the announcers murmuring quietly.

With more than a little trepidation at the state she

would find him in, she walked through the kitchen, down the hallway, and to his ajar bedroom door.

Light blazed inside the open shades of his room, illuminating his motionless form lying on the bed, sprawled face-first in a mess of sheets, clothed in sweatpants and a black T-shirt.

For a shocking moment, she wondered if he might be dead, but then his back moved with a slow breath.

"Hey," she said.

Nothing. Not even the slightest of reactions.

"Hey!" This time, she yelled the word.

He jumped, turning with a half-howling noise.

"Get up!"

His eyes narrowed to slits, and his forehead cracked into a thousand folds as he put up a hand to block the light. "What the hell?"

"Yeah. Exactly what I was thinking."

She walked to the window and tugged it open. "It reeks in here. Smells like you shit yourself...last month."

He said nothing, putting his head back down. Two seconds later he inhaled deeply, turning onto his side, sleeping soundly again as if nothing had happened.

She lifted her foot and heel-kicked the bed.

He jolted again. "Ah!"

She got up on the mattress and pushed him hard with both hands until he spilled off. He hit the carpet, knocking his head against the dresser on his way down.

"Holy shit, what is your problem?" He writhed on the floor.

"Get up. I need to talk to you." She helped him back onto the bed. "And stay up this time."

She went to the kitchen and sifted through a heap of dirty dishes for a cup, filled it with water, and brought it back to him.

His eyes were still open; *that was something*, but he was leaning back on his pillows.

"I said up!"

He sat up.

"Here. Drink this."

He took a sip.

"Chug it. All of it."

"Okay, geez."

She watched him suck the water down like he'd been walking through the desert for days. She went and refilled it again and again, watching each time as he sucked it down greedily until the fourth time when he finally settled on sipping.

"You better?"

He looked up at her with the deadest eyes she'd ever seen. "No," he said.

"Really. What is that smell?" A stack of dirty clothes in the corner drew her attention and solved the case.

She was afraid to continue probing the specifics of the place with her eyes, so she locked into his lifeless stare again.

"Listen," she said, "we need to talk."

"About what?"

"About this. About your life. What are you doing here?"

"I don't know." He kept his eyes on hers.

"I'm sorry I haven't been around here more, Yates."

He shrugged.

"What happened with Gemma?"

"Gemma?" He shook his head. "That was months ago."

"What happened with her?"

"She left."

"Why?"

"She's not the kind of girl to hang around losers."

"Are you saying she just left you?"

"You calling me a loser?" He smiled, a disturbing mimic of the facial expression she had known before the gunshot.

"Seriously, Yates. Why did she suddenly move out?"

"I broke up with her."

"What? Why?"

He rubbed his eyes. "It's really none of your business, Patty."

"Yes, it is. You're obviously upset about it. That's why you're sitting here beating yourself up. You were getting better with her in the picture. She's out. And now look at you."

He shrugged. "You got me figured out. What can I say?"

She looked out the window. "What happened when Rachette came over here the other night?"

"Rachette came over?"

She looked at him. "Yeah. Two nights ago. Rachette said he came over. Did he come over or not?"

"Okay, chill. Yeah. He came over and said hi."

"And?"

She waited for more explanation, but none came. "How many pills are you taking a day?"

"I don't know."

"Bullshit. How many?"

"Twenty?"

She didn't know what number she expected, but it hadn't been that high.

"Maybe more," he added.

182   JEFF CARSON

"What kind?"

He shrugged. "Vicodin. Percocet."

She shook her head. "You're not dead yet, so I know you're not taking fentanyl-laced knockoffs. How are you getting all these pills?"

He picked up his glass and sipped again.

"We need you to get better, Jeremy."

He set the cup down, closed his eyes as he sat back, and smiled. And then his face went slack. When he opened his eyes again, they shimmered with tears.

"What do we do?" she asked, her voice low. "They have a couple of places out in eastern Colorado. In-house rehab centers. There are a few up here in the mountains, too."

"I don't need rehab."

"The hell you don't."

Her phone rang in her pocket. She pulled it out. Waze's name was on the screen.

With a sigh, she answered. "Patterson."

"Hey, they found Lawrence Hunt's vehicle."

"Where?"

"Green River, Wyoming."

"Okay. Did you tell Wolf?"

"Yeah. Where are you?"

"I'm on my way in."

She hung up and pocketed the phone.

"We'll talk about this again, okay?"

The tears were gone, and now he stared at her.

"I said we—"

"Yeah, yeah."

She walked to him, sat down on the bed, and wrapped him in a hug. She pulled him in tight, ignoring the slick skin, the moist shirt, the greasy hair pressing into her cheek, and the smell.

"We love you, Jeremy."

He remained frozen and silent, arms hanging limp by his side until she let go.

"We'll talk about this again," she repeated. And then, fighting back tears, she left.

CHAPTER TWENTY-ONE

Brandenburg drove a few miles per hour slower than Wolf would have liked on the way to Green River, even with the flashers on.

It had taken just over two hours to get to the town off I-80 that sat across the border in Wyoming.

Conversations between Wolf and the sheriff had been brief and clipped. Brandenburg seemed preoccupied with something other than their destination.

Wolf had spent the silence listening to the soft country music coming out of the radio and ruminating on Dolores, her son Mitch Russell, the unknown daughter Savannah, and their potential connection to Lawrence Hunt. It all fit. Dolores's black eye and the way that biker came to watch Wolf. Or had he been watching Mitch? Making sure the guy didn't tell Wolf too much?

Then again, maybe none of it mattered. Maybe they were about to find Lawrence right now.

"Coming up on the right," Wolf said, looking at the GPS on his phone.

"Gotcha," Brandenburg said.

They had exited the highway a few minutes prior and coasted into the town, which was a little like a bowl, rimmed by white buttes, plateaus, and cliffs. Boxy one-story houses with siding and chain-link fenced yards lined the residential roads, the inhabitants a blue-collar population drawn to work the shale oil deposits, natural gas, and mining operations in the area.

Four-wheel drives and sedans lined the streets, old clunkers mixed with new models. Up ahead, a cluster of police officers congregated around the elusive blue Ford F-150, parked facing away from them.

"You can see the dent in the side," Brandenburg said, parking his truck.

"The license plate is different," Wolf said, noting a Minnesota plate attached to the rear.

"Must have switched it." Brandenburg shut off his truck.

They got out into the hot air, made hotter by the rising air off the neighborhood tarmac.

A woman in uniform broke off from a group of five men and walked their way.

"Lieutenant Gifford," she said in greeting, holding out a hand to them.

Wolf took the woman's firm grip and shook. "Wolf."

"Sheriff Brandenburg."

"What's happening?" Wolf asked.

"A patrol officer found it this morning," she said. "The plates don't match, but it's definitely the vehicle in question. I checked the registration in the glove box and found Dean Chancellor's name on the paperwork."

"Has anybody touched it?" Wolf asked.

"I have," she said. "But I gloved up. Just to get into the glove box."

Brandenburg gestured for Wolf to take the lead and Wolf walked the half-block up to the truck, Lt. Gifford following them.

"Mind if we take a look?" Wolf said, pulling on a pair of nitrile gloves.

"Be my guest."

He went to the passenger door, opened it, and ducked inside. It smelled of old leather and aftershave. The keys hung from the ignition. A bag of McDonald's was wadded up on the floorboard.

He checked the center console, finding it completely empty—ready to sell. The glove compartment contained the registration and an insurance card with Dean Chancellor's name on it; otherwise, nothing else.

"Have you talked to the neighbors?" Wolf asked, looking under the seats. There was nothing there except a few stray coins.

"I spoke to every neighbor you can see from the vehicle," Gifford said. "Which is those three houses, here, here, and here."

"Those people said the truck has been there since yesterday." She pointed at the nearest house, where an elderly couple stood watching from a window. "They couldn't tell me what time."

"And the others?" Brandenburg asked.

"They didn't know anything."

Wolf ducked out of the vehicle and shut the door. "Nobody got a look at him?"

She shook her head. "Nope."

Wolf looked around. "This parking spot's not in front of a house. Not near any one of them specifically."

Brandenburg grunted in agreement. "Looks like it's been ditched, if you ask me."

"If he ditched it," Wolf said, "he would need another vehicle."

"We know he's flush with cash," Brandenburg said. "Maybe he bought another vehicle. He switched the license plates already. He must have guessed we were looking for this truck."

"Maybe he knows somebody here in the neighborhood," Wolf said.

"A former army buddy," Brandenburg said.

Wolf nodded. "A former Special Forces buddy."

"How is this guy flush with cash?" Gifford asked.

Brandenburg explained how Hunt had stolen cash from the motorcycle gang.

"Oh, wow," she said. "How much?"

"He paid the owner forty grand for this one."

She whistled, then pointed. "So, is that why those bikers are watching us?"

They followed her gesture. Two motorcycles gleamed in the sun at the corner a few blocks away. Two men with long hair and beards, wearing denim and leather, stood smoking cigarettes. One of them was on the phone.

"Yeah," Brandenburg said. "That would be the reason."

"We're going to need to talk to more neighbors," Wolf said.

"Okay," Gifford said. "We'll pound the pavement. We've got his picture from the APB update yesterday."

She walked away toward the other men in uniform.

Wolf and Brandenburg turned and eyed the bikers.

"What do you think?" Brandenburg asked.

"I think they're just as in the dark as we are. Otherwise, they wouldn't be staring at us."

"Good point."

"I'm going to make a call." Wolf dialed Patterson's number and put the phone to his ear.

"Hi."

"Hey. We're here in Green River."

"And?"

"We have the truck, but it's not telling us much. We'll go door-to-door and ask if they've seen anything."

"How can I help?" she asked.

"I'm wondering if you can see if there are any vehicles for sale around here."

"Shouldn't be too difficult. Give me your location, and I'll search within a radius."

He gave her the address.

"Also, he could be here to see somebody he knows," Wolf said. "You learned he was former Special Forces. Maybe you can see if there's anybody living around here that he knew."

"You mean former Green Berets?" she said.

"Yeah. Something like that."

She tapped keys in the background. "Okay. It's going to take me some time."

"I know."

"I'll let you know ASAP."

"Wait a minute," he said.

"Yeah?"

He eyed the bikers down the street again, thinking about Dolores and Mitch Russell. "I might have met

Lawrence Hunt's girlfriend—a woman named Dolores Russell. Her son's name is Mitch. Why don't you look them up while you're at it, please."

"What happened there?"

He told her about the night before.

"Okay, I'll add that to the list and keep you posted." She hung up.

Pocketing his phone, he stared at the bikers.

"What are you thinking?" the sheriff asked.

"I think it's interesting he moved south of Doyle to us, and now he's north."

"In what way?"

"He's hovering around home. He's not running."

"Why?" Brandenburg asked.

"Maybe he's not willing to leave her high and dry. Maybe he knows he's put her in danger."

"Dolores?" Brandenburg asked.

"Yeah."

"If you're right about Dolores."

"I think there's no other explanation there."

Brandenburg grunted. "What now?"

"Let's help them canvass this place."

Brandenburg huffed. "Fine. I guess it doesn't hurt that I get some exercise today."

The next two hours were spent traveling door-to-door, covering every house within the immediate neighborhood and then across a busy main road into another development.

No one had seen or knew anything about Lawrence Hunt. Wolf had been keeping a special eye on any men who answered the door in their early sixties with military tattoos, flags, or visible memorabilia. Plenty of military men answered their doors, but none of them admitted to knowing or meeting Lawrence Hunt, and they seemed to be truthful.

"Damn it, I gotta exercise more." Brandenburg's uniform shirt was streaked with sweat in all the wrong places.

They were standing two blocks from their starting point when Wolf's phone rang. They both stopped. Brandenburg perking up at the sound.

It was Patterson.

"Hi."

"I got a couple hits. I'm sorry it took so long, but there was quite a list and no mapping feature when it came to vehicles for sale. And then the whole former Green Beret thing..."

"What did you find?"

"Well. I couldn't find any former Special Forces men who fit the description, what with deployment area and timing, but I did find what car he purchased last night."

Wolf raised his eyebrows and looked at Brandenburg. "Which car did he purchase?"

"A 2011 Honda Civic. Forest green." She read off an address. "It's two miles from where you found the truck. Clear on the other side of town."

"Good work."

"And as for Dolores Russell and her son Mitch, she's a squeaky-clean citizen as far as I can tell. She's been in Doyle for the last thirty years, where she's owned and operated the diner for the last twenty-one, according to the restaurant's website."

"And her son?"

"Mitch Russell," she said. "Twenty-eight years old. He has two traffic citations, one failure to appear in court back when he was twenty. His wife is deceased. He has a private Instagram account, and it looks like he runs the D's Diner account, where he has a bunch of pictures of him and his daughter, Savannah, eight, both of them mostly posing with food."

"Okay," Wolf said.

"But back to Dolores," Patterson said. "She has a Facebook account where she has posted three photographs of her and her significant other. And guess who that is?"

"Lawrence Hunt?"

"Yep. There are two photos of them down in Mexico on vacation. Another of them out in the woods somewhere. They seem happy," she said. "A cute older couple."

"I need you to update the APB for the new vehicle," he said. "And please send me links to her Facebook, and any photos of the vehicle."

"Already done, done, and done."

"Thanks. Keep me posted. I'll do the same."

He hung up.

"What vehicle?" Brandenburg asked. "What Facebook?"

Wolf told the sheriff about the Honda Civic, Dolores's Facebook account, and the pictures of her and Hunt on the account.

Brandenburg looked more annoyed by the news than interested. He held up a hand to shield his eyes from the sun, but he'd already lost the war. His skin was beet red.

"Where?"

"Two miles from here."

"We're not walking." Brandenburg turned and walked toward his truck. "And then food, damn it."

"Yes, sir," Wolf said, thinking of the measly gas station donuts he'd had six hours prior. "I'm not going to argue with you there."

CHAPTER TWENTY-TWO

"Patterson!"

She jerked in her desk chair. After doing the research for Wolf, she had eaten a huge meal, gotten some paperwork done, and just found herself asleep in an upright position. Her mind coming online, she unfolded her arms and turned, recognizing Waze's voice.

"Sir."

Waze stood at the end of the squad room, a shoulder bag slung across his chest. He had been gone all afternoon at press conferences and meetings. He went to his door and unlocked his office. "Come in here, please."

She stood. What time was it? Her watch said 4:25 p.m.

She jumped up and down a few times to get the blood moving. Her muscles relaxed as she walked through the squad room toward his office. Damn it. She hated that she had been caught sleeping. Maybe he hadn't noticed.

"You in trouble?" Nelson asked.

She gave him a *good-one* smile and went to Waze's door. "Sir?"

"Come in, please. Sit."

She entered and sat down. Annoyingly, he had the blinds to the windows behind him shut against the afternoon sun and the blinds closed to the well-lit squad room inside, creating a dungeon effect lit by the artificial bulbs above. When she'd been in this office at this time of day, she had always let in as much natural light at her back as possible. It had been her favorite time of day in the space.

"I saw your update on the APB."

"Yes, sir."

"What's Wolf doing now?"

She checked her watch. 4:26. A minute had passed since the last time. She sucked in a breath, willing herself to fully wake up. "I'm not sure."

"What's new with the case?"

She told him about Dolores Russell and her son Mitch and the discovery of Dolores's involvement with Lawrence Hunt.

"They're for sure dating?"

"I sent you links to the Facebook account," she said.

He tapped his keyboard, and she waited while he pulled up her email. A minute later, he sat back, staring at the screen. "Okay, yeah. Definitely looks like it. So...what now?"

"Wolf and the sheriff went to talk to the seller of the Honda Civic. They got a phone number Hunt was using to communicate with the man. I did a trace on the number, and found it was shut off immediately after being used up in Green River. Hunt either ditched the phone, or he's using multiple SIMs. And the phone he's using doesn't have GPS."

Waze sat back. "The guy's clever. I'll give him that."

"Former Green Beret," Patterson said.

Waze bridged his fingers. "And what about this call I got from Lorber that Rachette's brake lines were cut last night at his kid's baseball game?"

She blinked, shifting upright. "Excuse me?"

"You didn't hear?"

"No. I didn't. I mean, I was there. He said he had brake issues. I didn't know they were cut."

Waze folded his arms. "Severed with 'sharp ass tin snips,' as Lorber put it."

"Any fingerprints?"

"No. Nothing."

She shook her head. "Shit."

"Yeah. Where's he now?"

"He's home," she said. "Taking the day...after last night. He texted me and said it was a late one."

"But he didn't mention that he took the truck to Lorber and got him to look at it?"

She shook her head.

"Why would he keep that from you?" Waze asked.

"Good question."

"And why would he not be answering my calls?" he asked.

She blinked. "I'm not sure, sir."

"This is big," he said. "That's attempted murder. And now poof. Where is he?"

She shook her head again, thinking back on the night prior. He had been acting so strange, and now she knew he had known right then and there what had happened. Why was he hiding it? She pulled out her phone and checked. No missed calls.

"Are you listening to me?" he asked.

She lowered her phone. "Excuse me?"

"I said keep me 100 percent in the loop on this."

"Yes, sir."

"I'm not liking the direction this is going."

"No, sir." She stood up. "I'll get on this."

Waze turned to his computer. "Bye."

Back out in the squad room, she went to Nelson's desk. "Have you seen or heard from Rachette today?"

"He was in first thing this morning," Nelson said.

"He was? I didn't see him."

"I think you weren't in yet." She must have been at Yates's.

"What did he say?"

Nelson thought about it. "Not much. Actually, he seemed preoccupied...went to his desk, did something on the computer, then left. Haven't seen him since."

She sat back in her chair. "Damn it, Rachette," she breathed, dialing his number. "What are you doing?"

The phone went straight to voicemail without ringing as if it had been turned off. "Rachette," she said. "It's me. Give me a call when you get this. Immediately."

She hung up and tried to get into the mind of Rachette.

His family had been threatened. What would she have done in this same situation? With a lack of evidence, there would be little to do except stay vigilant with her husband and children in plain sight.

She looked over at Charlotte's desk, which sat vacant. She had every second Friday off, and she hadn't been in today.

Patterson dialed her number.

"Hello?"

"Hey, it's me. Is Tom there?"

"No. He's supposed to be with you."

"Oh. Okay, never mind."

"Wait a minute. What's going on? He came home really late last night. He said everything was figured out, but he was acting weird."

"Nothing," Patterson said. "He just left and I thought he went home. I think he was going to get food. I'll call him back."

"I can't get hold of him. It keeps going straight to voicemail."

"He's probably just eating, screening everyone. He does that, you know."

"Not to me."

"It's okay. Listen, I'll keep you posted." Patterson hung up.

"What did he do now?" Nelson asked.

She dialed Lorber's number. The ME answered on the first ring.

"Hey, what's up?"

"Hey," Patterson said, "What happened with Rachette last night?"

"With his brake lines? Did you not hear?"

"Yeah, I know about it. I just want to know what happened last night exactly."

"Okay. He called me at eight or so, all in a fit. Had me come down and examine his truck at the lab. He got a tow truck to bring it in for him."

"And?"

"And it was clear the lines had been cut. Severed with tin snips."

"No fingerprints?"

"None," Lorber said. "I dusted every piece of metal on the underside and outside of that truck, and there wasn't anything but his and his family's prints. Took me three hours."

"Okay. And did he mention who might have done it?"

"No. He said he had no clue."

"Okay. Fine. Thank you."

She hung up and stared out the windows. Without evidence, there was nothing Rachette could do, right?

Unless he had evidence and he wasn't telling anyone.

"You idiot," she said under her breath, standing up. "What are you doing?"

"You need help?" Nelson asked.

She shook her head. "No thanks."

Snatching up her keys, she turned and left, headed to the only person she could picture offering any help when it came to the mind of Rachette: Yates.

CHAPTER TWENTY-THREE

Wolf looked at his phone again. No messages from Piper. Cell reception had been solid the entire way from Green River to Doyle, and Wolf had taken the opportunity to text an apology, with reasons—however weak they sounded to himself—laid out in full.

Now, with the whole day passed, she still hadn't responded.

"Everything okay over there?" Brandenburg asked, sipping a cola cup the size of his head. The man had started the drive in silence and became more talkative after they stopped at the McDonald's drive-through.

"Yeah," Wolf said, pocketing his phone, but not before glancing at Piper's last message one more time.

DON'T WORRY. I FIGURED OUT EVERYTHING AND CANCELED THE WEDDING PLANS.

Both parts of the message brought up questions in his mind. How did she figure out everything? She was an investigator for a law firm and a former cop. She had her ways. The second part of the text was the most concerning. She had canceled the plans. What exactly did that mean? That the wedding was off? What about the rest of their relationship?

"Doesn't look like you're fine," Brandenburg said with a chuckle.

Wolf took a sip of the watered-down remnants of his Coke. "I'm just thinking about Hunt and his new vehicle, that's all."

"Yeah," Brandenburg said, the interior lightbar flash reflecting off his eyes as he turned his gaze back out the windshield.

They were a few miles from Doyle, which rose on the horizon, a cluster of gray buildings and green foliage doused in afternoon clouds that shaded the center of the valley ahead.

"I keep checking every vehicle, thinking it's going to be him," Brandenburg said.

Wolf was doing the same thing, eyeing every car for the green Honda Civic as they overtook them or passed in the other lane.

The seller of the vehicle in Green River had positively identified Lawrence Hunt, reporting he had paid cash for the car the previous evening with stacks of crisp bills, which he showed to Wolf and Brandenburg. The seller had shared the phone number he used for communications with Hunt, which Wolf forwarded to Patterson for tracing. That lead died.

Other than finding out Hunt had shown up on foot, looking tired, wearing a blue sweatsuit, and smelling strongly of body odor, they hadn't learned anything new. The APB had been updated, and now they were returning to Doyle.

Wolf leaned forward in his seat, stretching his lower back. The drive up had aggravated a knot, and the drive back had tripled the tie on itself.

"All right," Brandenburg said. "Here we are."

They passed a sign letting them know they were entering Doyle. Brandenburg slowed down, The Lamb Motel approaching on the right and their current destination—D's Diner—on the left.

Two motorcycles were parked in front, and as they coasted past, the SOV insignia sewn onto the saddle bags came into view.

"SOV," Brandenburg said.

The sheriff hung a left beyond the building, and they entered a rear parking lot. The Subaru was there, along with a few other vehicles. Brandenburg parked, and they got out.

Wolf tumbled more than climbed down out of the truck, pain lancing through the length of his right side. Arms overhead, he stretched, relieving some of the tightness, but until he stopped riding in cars for hours and received a full-body massage from a highly trained individual, he knew the pain was going nowhere.

"You gonna make it?" Brandenburg asked.

"Yeah."

"I thought I was in bad shape." The sheriff led the way around the building.

Wolf limped after him. The scent of cooking food permeated the air, but he was immune to the lure of a meal after the earlier fast food.

They went to the front. Brandenburg pulled open the door, and the familiar electronic bell dinged overhead, barely audible over the din of talking voices and music. The place was packed compared to the previous evening.

Two bikers sat where the elderly couple had been before. They had clearly noted the arrival of the two lawmen but were concentrating on their food.

Dolores came out of the kitchen carrying three plates. She stopped dead as if bears had entered the building. But she recovered quickly, lowering her gaze and delivering the food to a booth nearby.

Wolf nodded to the sheriff to take the lead.

"Hello," Brandenburg said. "Dolores, is it?"

"Yeah, Sheriff." Dolores walked to a stack of menus on the counter. "Two of you?"

"We're not eating," he said. "We'd just like to have a few words if you don't mind."

She looked around. "Not a very good time, Sheriff. It's just me here."

"We won't be but a minute."

She looked at them defiantly, her eyes flicking to the two bikers. "I have to drop some drinks at a table first."

"Go right ahead," Brandenburg said.

They watched as Dolores filled fountain drinks and delivered them to a family. Wolf eyed the bikers. Their table had half-empty drinks on it and no food like they were camped there for surveillance.

Dolores took some requests as she passed other tables, wrote on her pad, went behind the counter, and wiped her hands, looking at them expectantly.

"Well?" she asked.

Wolf and Brandenburg sidled up next to two empty chrome stools.

"We'd like to talk to you about Lawrence Hunt," Brandenburg said.

"Lawrence Hunt?"

"You're dating Lawrence Hunt, aren't you?" Wolf asked.

She picked up a plastic cup, scooped some ice, and filled it with soda.

"Dolores," Brandenburg said.

"Yeah. So what?"

"You are dating Lawrence Hunt?" Wolf said, clarifying.

"Yes."

"I spoke to your son yesterday," Wolf said. "I know you two have heard about what he did out there at the biker compound."

"And?"

"And so, we'd like to know if you've spoken to him in the last week since that happened."

"No." The answer was too quick. "Is that it?"

"Who gave you that black eye, Dolores?" Wolf asked.

"I told you, I fell." She began filling another glass.

Wolf and Brandenburg exchanged glances.

"Did they do that to you, trying to get them to tell you where Lawrence was?"

Once again, her eyes hopped on and off the bikers.

"Is Mitch here?" Wolf asked, looking at the kitchen door.

"No."

"So, who's cooking?"

"A cook we hired," she said. "Imagine that."

Wolf put both elbows on the counter, leaning closer. "Do you know why or how Hunt's son disappeared? Any information that can lead us to Lawrence can help us stop any further bloodshed, Dolores. We're just trying to stop the bloodshed. We don't want innocent people getting dragged into this."

Dolores shook her head, mumbling something under her breath as she filled another glass.

"Where did Mitch go?" Wolf asked.

"He's out of town. With Savannah, his daughter. They left together."

"Where did they go?"

"Well, not that it's any of your business, but they went down to Craig. To see his sister. Now, if you don't mind, I need to keep waiting on tables, or I'm going to have some pissed-off customers."

Wolf put a business card with his name and phone number on the table, carefully keeping it out of view of the bikers behind him. "If you ever want to talk, you can call me any time. Got that?"

She looked at the card, scooped up the drinks, and walked away without taking it.

He put the card on the spill mat next to the drink dispenser and stood with Brandenburg. The two bikers had been watching but turned back to one another and started conversing.

"Well?" Brandenburg asked. "What now?"

"Do you know either of these two?" Wolf asked, gesturing to the bikers.

"I've seen them around. But no."

Wolf nodded, watching as Dolores pushed through to the kitchen. He moved to the door, drawn to the circular window giving a view into the back. Putting his face close, he put a hand up to block the glare, and the kitchen came into view.

A dark-haired man was manning the grill, cutting tomatoes, flipping meat, and preparing plates as if he had four arms. It was not Mitch.

Dolores's head appeared underneath him on the other side, and the door swung out, colliding with Wolf's elbow before he could back away. The door rebounded back, thumping against the body on the other side. The sound of plates crashing to the floor muted all conversation in the dining room.

Wolf fished his fingers into the door opening and pulled, revealing Dolores staring down at a heap of food splattered on the tile at her feet.

"I'm sorry," he said.

She looked at him. Eyes bulging wide, she said, "Get out."

"Hey, uh, Wolf," Brandenburg said, grabbing his elbow and pulling. "I think it's time we leave."

"I'll help clean that up."

"Leave!" she screamed, her voice shaking. Tears welled in her eyes. "I said get out!"

Wolf stepped back.

"Come on," Brandenburg said.

Wolf allowed the sheriff to lead him out the front door.

"Nice one, pig," one of the bikers said as they left.

Brandenburg walked quickly down the sidewalk, around the building, and to the rear parking lot. When he reached his truck, he turned around. "Christ, Wolf. That was bad."

Wolf stared into the distance, scratching the stubble on his chin.

"We have to chill out on this angle," Brandenburg said.

"What angle?"

"Whatever angle you're looking from. Whether it's Dolores and this Mitch guy or a connection to Lawrence's kid. We're going after Lawrence Hunt. He's pissed about what the gang did to his son, and that's that. There's no sense harassing this family."

Wolf put his hands on his hips. "She's holding back. I think she knows more than she's saying."

Brandenburg frowned, jutting his head toward Wolf. "She's picking chicken fried steak off the floor because of us. Because of you. Shit, afraid to talk to us? Two bikers were in there watching. She wants to be left alone. This has nothing to do with her and her kid. This is Lawrence and his kid."

"Why are those two bikers sitting there?" Wolf asked.

"Because they're doing the same bullshit we're doing in there. They're looking for her boyfriend. If he shows up to see his sweetheart, they'll nab him."

Pain zinged through Wolf's back, and he bared his teeth. Closing his eyes, he tried to stretch, but nothing helped.

"Shit, boy. You need some pain pills. Get in. We have some ibuprofen back at the station."

Wolf got into the truck, resisting the urge to call out in agony as he sat in the seat. He felt a vibration in his pocket and pulled out his phone. Piper had finally responded to his message.

It's okay.

He swiped up to see if there had been another response before this one that he'd missed. But there wasn't.

Brandenburg backed out, left the lot, and drove down Main Street back toward the sheriff's department head-quarters.

Wolf pocketed his phone. He had given her a novella typed out with his thumbs, and she'd given him three sylla-bles, vague syllables at that. He repeated the words in his head, this time picturing her saying them with sincerity. Then again, sarcastically.

When they got back to the station, Brandenburg parked next to Wolf's SUV. Shifting into park, the sheriff shut off the engine and looked over at Wolf. "Well?"

The dashboard clock read 5:05 p.m. It had been a long, full day again. And still, they were no closer to finding Lawrence Hunt.

"I think I'll head back to The Lamb. I'd appreciate some of that ibuprofen first, though."

"I'll go get it."

They got out of Brandenburg's truck, Wolf spilling out next to his driver's side door. The sheriff went into the building, and Wolf climbed inside his vehicle, once again savoring the warmth that had accumulated on his leather seat as it radiated into his back.

Brandenburg came out with a handful of medicine packets.

Wolf rolled down his window and took them. "Thanks."

"No problem."

He tore one open and popped two pills in his mouth, swallowing them with a half-filled bottle of scorching hot water left in the center console.

"Listen," Brandenburg said. "I think we've got it from here. We've got the whole of Colorado and every adjacent state looking for this Honda Civic now." The sheriff leaned his hands on the door. "If anybody from Rocky Points asks me, as far as I'm concerned, you've produced results for us."

Wolf nodded, the words ringing hollow to him. But in his current state, he really didn't mind what Roland Thatcher, Gregory Waze, or anybody else who had a problem with him, thought. He had business to take care of at home with Piper, and he was going to deal with it. They had hit dead ends here anyway. Dolores, Mitch, their connection to Lawrence Hunt, Lawrence's involvement with the gang, and his son's disappearance were all problems for these men to deal with in their own territory.

Hunt had killed two people in Wolf's county, and he had done all he could for now to find him.

"I think I'll be heading back to Rocky Points," Wolf said.

"Tonight?"

Wolf considered the question. "I think I'll get a good night's rest and head home in the morning. I'm not sure if my back can take another four hours in the car."

Brandenburg reached in his hand, and Wolf shook it. "Either way, it was nice meeting you. Keep us posted. We'll do the same."

Wolf started the engine. "Will do."

———

Three hours—and another packet of ibuprofen—later, Wolf lay on his motel room bed watching a forecast for the western US on the weather channel. Rain was moving in the next day, starting as thundershowers in the afternoon and continuing with a steady drenching that would last a few days.

Wolf shut off the TV and stared up at the ceiling. He checked his phone and, for the thousandth time, read there was no service, no Wi-Fi, and therefore no new messages. He could have gone up the road to tether himself back home, but his mood and his back kept him on the bed.

There would be time to talk tomorrow when he

returned. It had taken him, Piper, and three movers with a truck two whole days to move all her stuff into the house; he was reasonably sure she would still be there when he got back.

He decided the best thing for now was to rest. So, as the light faded outside and the darkness grew in his room, he shut his eyes and fell asleep.

CHAPTER TWENTY-FOUR

Rachette sat quietly in the front seat of his truck, facing the windshield, binoculars raised to his eyes. The house was mostly dark except for the uncovered window in the living room, which bobbed in the eyepieces.

He lowered the binoculars and rubbed his hands together, still chilly from the earlier reconnaissance of the place he'd done on foot. He had gotten the address easy enough earlier that morning at work by looking up the plates of the Ford Fiesta in the DMV database. A search on Google Maps had shown the place was south of the pass, surrounded by trees, sitting on a good portion of land.

The neighboring house to the north had been furnished inside but was vacant and listed on the property rental sites. Earlier in the day he had gone on his phone and pretended to book it, and the sites told him it was free for the night.

That left the house to the south, which he had just returned from checking out. There had been an older couple inside, looking like they were planted on the couch for the long haul, a TV visible through shutters on the window.

There were no dogs. Not there or here at the house.

He picked up the computer printout of the two men again, looking down at their rap sheets. The skinny guy with the Fiesta was Steven Carlton. He had a prior arrest for possession of Schedule II drugs with the intent to sell. He'd gotten off his first offense with community service and probation. Must have had a good lawyer.

The bigger guy, named Calvin Engelhardt, also lived in the house. He had a more active sheet, with time served in jail down in Denver for reckless endangerment.

Rachette put the paper back on the passenger seat and raised the binoculars again. Everything was a green light except for this chick sitting on the couch. A skinny blonde dressed in a tattered patchwork dress had arrived an hour ago, pulling up in a new Toyota 4Runner. She had gone inside wearing a backpack and had been hanging out on the couch ever since.

She was clearly into Engelhardt, laughing and looking over at the big man every chance she got, and he was giving it back to her, cracking jokes, pleased with himself as he watched her laugh. Even from this distance, Rachette could tell Carlton was into her, too. But she was obviously having none of his skinny ass. He was a third wheel that wouldn't fall off.

It was like a terrible deadbeat reality show, and Rachette was hooked. He lowered the binoculars again and shook his head. Damn it. He'd give it another ten minutes, and then he was going to have to leave. No way he could bring an innocent bystander into this.

Just then, there was movement inside. Glassing the

house again, he saw her stand up, the two men rising with her. She reached up and gave Engelhardt a long hug on her toes, then Carlton a quick obligatory wrap of her arms, and went to the door.

Carlton sat back in the chair, looking at the two of them as they went outside, shutting the door on him.

Rachette followed the girl and Engelhardt as they walked to her 4Runner. Giggling floated through the still air and into Rachette's window.

The two of them kissed, and Engelhardt's hands groped her chest. When he grabbed her backside, she tried to stop him, but he was having none of it and continued to pull her close.

Squealing came through the air now, and Rachette reached for the door handle.

Then Engelhardt stopped, releasing her and backing away, a confident smile on his lips. The woman shook her head with an admonishing grin, then tucked a lock of hair behind her ear and waved with her fingers as she climbed in behind the wheel.

The 4Runner howled to life, and she backed out, turned around, and came straight toward him.

Rachette already had his tinted passenger window rolled up, but he ducked down out of sight just in case as the vehicle passed, rising again when she was long gone.

Now, he was in business.

He got out and shut the door quietly, tucking the unregistered, silenced Heckler and Koch USP Tactical he'd been gifted from a friend in Nebraska sixteen years ago into the back of his pants.

He removed nitrile gloves from his pocket and put them on. He went over the plan again. Like a shipbuilder, he scoured every move he was going to make, looking for leaks in his logic—what was going to be their reaction as he came in, how he was going to make them admit what they had done.

Rubbing his hands together, feeling the synthetic rubber on his fingers, he knew he couldn't actually kill these guys, but the effect of him walking in on them was going to make them shit.

And if he had to? Well...that's why he had the HK.

Damn it, he felt nauseous. He sucked in a deep breath, upping his pace toward the house to a jog. He wanted to catch them while they were still hanging out in the front room. As he approached, he could see Engelhardt was still standing. Rachette wanted to catch him before he receded to a back room or something.

Running full out now, he climbed the steps up onto the darkened porch and rang the doorbell. He pulled the gun and waited, sidling up to one side of the door, aiming.

He heard the TV mute inside and then a long, silent pause. Then the door swung open.

Engelhardt looked outside. His right hand was behind the door, probably holding a gun.

Wearing long black sleeves and pants, Rachette appeared from nothing when he put the silenced barrel to Engelhardt's face.

"Show me your hands," Rachette said. "Slowly."

Engelhardt blinked, eyes crossing as he looked up at the gun, then showed both of his hands, which were both empty.

Rachette kicked the door, and the big man stumbled back. He moved in quickly while Carlton was still sitting on the couch.

"Show me your hands," Rachette said, pointing the gun at him now.

Carlton raised his hands to his side.

Rachette closed the door behind him, locking the deadbolt.

"Move back," he said to Engelhardt, waving the barrel. "On the couch."

Engelhardt remained where he was, looking like he was ready to pounce.

"On the couch!" Rachette said, putting both hands on the grip of the gun.

The big man swallowed whatever thought he had and sat next to his roommate.

Rachette moved quickly to the window and grabbed the string for the blinds with his left hand, keeping his aim and attention on the two men.

The string didn't work as he pulled down. He tried again, angling it the other way, and finally, they lowered with a clang. He fumbled grabbing the bar to twist them shut, but his hands were jittery and ineffectual with the adrenaline coursing through his veins. On the second attempt, he got hold of it and turned the plastic stick. The outside darkness disappeared as the slats closed, along with any view of him inside should somebody walk past.

But they wouldn't. He took a deep breath, trying to calm his racing heart.

"What are you doing?" Carlton asked, his voice tight with fear, looking at Rachette's gloved hands.

Rachette lowered the weapon, eyeing them both with what he hoped looked like a menacing glare.

"Which one of you cut my brake lines?" He watched

their faces. Engelhardt frowned, playing dumb, while Carlton shook his head and closed his eyes.

Rachette aimed at Engelhardt. "It was you."

"No, it wasn't. I have no idea what you're talking about."

Rachette bared his teeth, extending the gun another inch toward the big man.

"You see this silencer on the barrel?" he asked. "These gloves? I have a roll of plastic in the car and some tie-downs, so I can easily move your dead bodies. I have a route planned to a mineshaft over near Dredge, where I'm going to drop the two of you inside. I don't have a phone on me. Nobody knows I'm here. Nobody knows I'm looking for you. I'm not fucking around. I want to know who cut my brakes and tried to kill me and my family."

Engelhardt scoffed. "I don't think you're telling the truth."

"What?" Carlton eyed his roommate. "Dude, shut up. Look, sir. We didn't...we..."

"Yeah, we did," Engelhardt raised his eyebrows, staring at Rachette. "We did cut the brakes on your truck. So, what are you going to do about it?"

Rachette shook his head.

"But you don't have any proof," Engelhardt said. "We ditched the cable cutters. You'll find nothing here. We also didn't bring our phones, so there's going to be no evidence we were ever at that baseball game."

Rachette stared mutely at the man. Never did he expect them to admit what they had done and his bluff to be called so quickly. Never did he think his resolve would be tested so immediately.

"Look at him," Engelhardt said to Carlton. "He's not going to hurt us, are you? You're a cop. You can't do something like that. You can't just kill us in cold blood. Think of what life would be like for you after that."

Rachette shot at the couch next to Engelhardt. The gun snapped, and a blast of fire came out of the suppressor. The cushion next to the big man shifted positions, spitting out a piece of foam from the tiny hole.

"Oh shit, oh shit," Carlton said. "Come on, man. It was him. He did it. It was him. I'll admit it. You don't have to kill—"

Engelhardt reached over and punched his friend in the side of the head, silencing him.

"Ah!"

"Freeze!" Rachette said. "Stop it right now!"

Engelhardt leaned forward and stood up.

Rachette backed away a step, keeping the gun pointed center mass.

And then, a sound came from outside and penetrated through the blood rushing in his ears. It was the low rumble of approaching tires. Light streamed in through the cracks of the blinds, straight on at first and then at a severe angle as the vehicle parked in the driveway.

Engelhardt remained where he was, listening and watching, too. He smiled. "What are you going to do, cop?"

It was the girl, damn it. She had returned.

Rachette shook his head. "I'll arrest you."

"You don't even have any handcuffs, do you?"

Shit. He didn't.

Engelhardt smiled wider. And he took a step forward.

Rachette tightened his grip. His voice shook, and every muscle flexed as tight as ski lift cables. "You step back, asshole. I swear to God I'll kill you right now. I swear to

God. You want to test me? Keep stepping forward. Take another step."

Outside, a car door thumped as it closed.

Engelhardt lifted his other foot. He put it forward, balancing on one leg. He put his arms out to his sides like he was on a tightrope. "You've got two kids. You're not going to throw all that away."

Knocking at the door, an insistent pounding against the wood behind Rachette that made him jump. "What the hell?"

"Rachette!" the voice came from the other side.

CHAPTER TWENTY-FIVE

The doorknob rattled. "Rachette!"

After a second of shock, Rachette recognized the voice.

"Rachette! Open up! It's Yates!" More pounding.

A wave of relief washed over him. "Yates?" He reached over and twisted the lock. As he did, Engelhardt took another step toward him.

Yates busted in with his gun raised, stopping Engelhardt's progress.

"Hands up!" Yates yelled.

Rachette swung the door closed and stood next to Yates. "Sit down!"

"Jeremy." Engelhardt stepped back. "What are you doing?"

"Sit down," Yates said, his voice calm.

Engelhardt turned up his hands. "I thought we were friends."

Yates lowered his gun, ignoring the big man. "What are you doing here?" he asked Rachette.

"These assholes cut the brakes on my truck. I had my

kids in there. My family. We could have been killed. He just admitted it, man. He just told me."

Yates put a hand on Rachette's arm. "Lower the gun, brother."

A tear spilled out of Rachette's eye and ran down his cheek. "We could have died."

"You can't drive a truck after the brakes have been cut," Engelhardt said. "We knew that. We were just doing it to scare you."

"The rest of the car still worked, asshole. I backed into the car behind me. There could have been kids walking behind my truck at the time."

"Well, you're an idiot for not feeling the brake pedal sink to the floor then."

"I told you they could have been hurt," Carlton said.

Engelhardt looked over at his roommate. "Shut up!"

They all stood in silence for a while. The two men on the couch turned against one another, Rachette still aiming his gun, Yates's hand on his shoulder.

"Come on, Rachette," Yates said. "What's the plan here? We can't just shoot 'em."

Rachette blinked, the tears receding as he lowered his gun.

"That's it," Yates said.

"Yeah, that's it," Engelhardt said.

"Shut up!" Yates aimed the gun at his chest.

Engelhardt put up his hands, then made a zipping of his mouth motion, locking it and throwing away the key.

"Asshole," Yates said, lowering his gun.

"I have no proof," Rachette said. "There's no way to prove it. But he's gotta pay. They've both gotta pay. There's no way I'm living out there with my family with these two walking around on this planet as free men. I can't risk it."

"We can bring them in," Yates said.

Rachette looked at him for the first time. Yates was pale, sweating all over like spring slush. His eyes were red-rimmed, and it looked painful for him to be standing and conscious.

"What are you talking about?" Rachette asked. "On what?"

"That girl I just drove past," Yates said. "In the 4Runner. Her name's Chloe Anderson. She works at the Mountain Mart Pharmacy in Ashland. She's in charge of inventory, and she skims from orders coming in and gives it to these guys. These guys sell it, and they split the profit. It's one of the ways they get the legit stuff and not the counterfeit." He turned to Carlton. "Where is it?"

Carlton said nothing, but he looked at a paper grocery bag perched on the end table next to him.

Yates walked over, picked up the bag, which looked as heavy as if it were filled with groceries, and brought it back. He hefted it onto his forearm as a shelf, opened it, and tilted it toward Rachette, showing multiple plastic bags of pills lying inside, identical to the ones that had been over at Yates's house. There were two dozen or more.

"We can bring her in and get her to talk," Yates said. "She has no prior record, and I'm sure she'll be happy to keep it that way by rolling on you two."

"We'll tell them about you," Engelhardt said.

Yates ignored him. "And then there's the fake prescription pads. They have them in the house here somewhere, I'm sure. Carlton here has a friend who's a managing nurse over at the county hospital, a guy named John Jansky. I'm sure he's the one supplying them. They have a network of intermediaries who go to various pharmacies in the state to fill the fake prescriptions. Sit here a week, and you'll see all kinds of people coming in and out. I'm sure they have other means, too, but the girl and the nurse—they'll be enough."

Yates turned back to Engelhardt and Carlton. "Carlton here has a prior with schedule two drugs. A second offense with intent to sell would bring on the hefty sentence of multiple decades in jail as it is. Throw in the elaborate ring you two are running..." Yates clucked his cheek. "I'm not sure if you guys will ever get out. Not in this lifetime."

"You know all of this for sure?" Rachette asked.

"Yeah."

"You just...followed them around in your spare time?"

Yates shrugged. "I'm a detective. What can I say?"

"We'll tell them about you," Engelhardt said again. "You're one of our best customers, Jeremy."

"I don't care. Tell them all you want. My career's over as it is."

"It's aiding and abetting," Engelhardt said. "You followed us around, figured out everything we were doing, and still you bought from us. They'll throw you in jail, too. You were basically an accomplice."

Rachette narrowed his eyes, knowing they could be right, depending on how the DA's office wanted to spin it. He looked at Yates.

"I don't care," Yates said. "The point is, you don't have to throw your life away by killing these guys, Rachette. These guys are already toast."

Rachette shook his head, thinking. How would prosecutors pursue charges against Yates? The district attorney had never liked Rachette, that was for sure. But how about

Yates? Surely, White wouldn't push to bust a former detective who was clearly fighting PTSD after getting shot on duty, driven to desperation for pills he was hooked on due to the trauma of doing his job and saving the life of his fellow detective in the process.

Then again, Rachette couldn't say for sure. The DA had always acted in his own best interest, driven by his track record first and foremost. It could be a scandal. But it could just as easily be a boon for White's next election.

"How about this?" Rachette said. "Either you two spend the rest of your lives in jail."

"Along with your friend," Engelhardt said.

Rachette nodded. "Maybe he faces charges, yes."

"Or?" Carlton asked. "You were going to say something else?"

"Or you two pack up and get the hell out of here," Rachette said.

Yates narrowed his eyes.

"You guys leave town by tomorrow night," Rachette said, "Seven o'clock p.m., or else we get a warrant and come after you. And after that," he looked at Yates, "we let the chips fall where they will. But we bring you two assholes in, and you rot in jail for the rest of your lives."

Engelhardt tilted his head. "And you just forget all about us?"

Rachette shook his head. "No. I don't. You let us know where you went, and I let the local law know all about you —about our suspicions of what you were doing and how. But we don't have any concrete evidence. So, they keep a close eye on you. And you turn your lives around, get legitimate jobs, and quit being the scum of society."

"Done," Carlton said.

Engelhardt looked over at his partner in crime.

"What?" Carlton slid sideways on the couch away from him. "I'm not doing this anymore. I told you it was a bad idea. I told you. I'll leave tomorrow, alone. You can do whatever you want."

Engelhardt looked like he was having murderous ideas about his friend, but Rachette didn't care about them at the moment. He was proud of himself for coming up with such a win-win plan for him and Yates.

"Whatever," Engelhardt said.

"Bullshit," Rachette said. "Not *whatever*. You tell me you agree. That you'll be out of here by seven p.m. tomorrow, and you'll let us know where you end up by the end of the week. Or else we start searching."

"Agreed," Carlton said.

After huffing and then upturning his hands again, Engelhardt nodded. "Okay."

Rachette put his gun in the back of his pants. "Good. That wasn't so hard, was it?"

The two men said nothing.

Yates looked up at Rachette; a hint of joy glimmered out of deadened eyes as he put his own gun in the back of his pants.

They left, Rachette eyeing the two men as he shut the door behind them. Carlton and Engelhardt looked stunned, resigned to their fate.

Outside, the air was cool and thick with the scent of pine. Rachette followed Yates down the steps to his car.

"Are you okay to drive?" Rachette asked.

"Yeah."

"How many pills have you had?"

Yates pulled open his door. "I'm fine."

Rachette grabbed his shoulder, stopping him from getting inside. "Hey."

Yates turned around, and Rachette wrapped him in a hug.

Yates remained motionless for a few moments, arms dangling by his sides, then finally slapped him on the back. "Okay."

"Yeah," Rachette said. "It is okay." He let go of his former partner. With the moonless night, Yates's eyes were puddles of black. "You really saved my ass in there."

Yates said nothing.

"I really was going to kill them. I thought I had no other choice. I was seconds away, I swear. And you frickin' came in there and gave me an out. Shit, man. I don't know what to say. Now, I owe you twice."

"You can thank Patterson. She called me all in a huff, telling me she learned your brakes were cut and she couldn't find you. I knew where you were going."

"And you didn't tell her?"

"No."

"Okay, fine. I owe you three times, then."

"You owe me for three things?"

"Yeah. The way I figure it, if you wouldn't have taken that bullet in the chest last year, that woman would have taken me down. I know that's the truth. So, there's that. And now there's this."

"You owe me for a hell of a lot more than that." Yates turned around and sat down behind the wheel.

Rachette smiled. "Okay, well, consider me following your ass home now, payback for one of them. Give me a ride to my truck."

He walked around the car and got in the passenger side.

It smelled like old food and dust. He shut the door, kicking aside a bag of fast food, and watched Yates for any signs of impairment as he put the keys in the ignition, shifted into reverse, and drove.

"How many pills?" Rachette asked.

"Just a few. Earlier."

Rachette nodded, knowing he was probably lying. He checked the rearview mirror. The house remained dark, save the rectangle of light leaking around the blinds.

"You think they'll leave?" Yates asked.

"I don't know. If they don't, they're idiots."

They rode in silence until they reached Rachette's truck. Yates stopped, and Rachette opened the door. "Wait for me. I'll follow."

Rachette felt fifty pounds lighter as he stepped up and got behind the wheel. He fired up the engine, turned around, and followed Yates down the county road and back out to Highway 734.

Heading north, he steered with his knees as he put the battery and SIM back in his phone and powered it on. The device dinged and vibrated for a good minute, showing he had thirty-two missed calls and ten missed text messages.

"Good lord," he said under his breath and dialed Charlotte.

"Where are you?" she answered.

"I'm fine. I'm with Yates."

"What are you doing? I've been calling you all day. Do you know how worried I was? That I still am? What did you do?"

"Nothing. I know. I'm sorry. I just needed to do something, so I shut off the phone."

"Did our brakes get cut last night?"

"Yes." No sense lying now.

"And you didn't tell me?"

"No."

"Why?"

"Because I was going to do something to the guys that did it."

She breathed into the phone, a ruffling coming out of the speakers. "So? Did you do something?"

"No. And everything's okay now. Alright?"

"Who were the guys that did it? Are we safe?"

"Yes." At least, he hoped so. The HK would stay close to him that night, that was for sure. Carlton sure didn't look like he was entertaining any ideas, but he wasn't so sure about Engelhardt. He decided he would tell Patterson everything, too. Just...not now. In the morning. Right now, he was dead tired.

"I'm coming home," he said. "I'll see you in an hour."

CHAPTER TWENTY-SIX

Wolf turned off the highway and into the gas station, the morning sun glinting off his side-view mirror as he pulled up to the gas pump.

Filling the SUV, he contemplated grabbing another convenience store breakfast or waiting until he reached Steamboat Springs, where he could stop at a diner. The latter sounded better, but he was determined to make good time back to Rocky Points. After Piper's one-line cryptic message, he still hadn't spoken to her, and he didn't plan on doing so either, not over the phone, at least. He needed to see her in person, to see her face as he explained himself.

He decided enjoying a sit-down meal was out of the question.

He stretched his arms overhead, turning side to side, feeling little pain in his back. The Lamb's ancient bed had apparent healing powers. He'd slept like a rock, moved little, and woke up refreshed.

After filling the tank, he hung the hose and walked

inside to use the restroom, then scoped the interior for something he could pass off as a meal.

Settling on a twenty-ounce coffee and some powdered donuts, he walked back to his SUV, vowing to think about health again once he got home.

Sipping his coffee, he took a moment to look at the shiny green landscape, lush with vegetation from the spring rains and creased with early morning shadows.

An older Toyota Tacoma pulled in off the highway from the south, halting at the island on the opposite side. A man climbed out and started filling his tank.

Wolf recognized him immediately as Mitch Russell.

Mitch slid his card into the machine, cursing as he poked his finger once, twice, and then a third time. Shaking his head, he inserted the nozzle into his tank and stared at the side of his truck, hands shoved in his pockets.

"How's it going, Mitch?" Wolf asked.

Mitch looked up with a start. He stared at Wolf for a moment as if trying to place the face and then said, "Oh, hey. It's you."

"Beautiful morning, eh?"

"Oh." Mitch straightened. He looked around. Nodded. "Yeah."

Wolf sipped his coffee. Mitch stared at the gas hose.

The interior of the truck was empty. Still no little girl named Savannah. Dolores had said they were south, down in Craig at Mitch's sister's place, the afternoon before. Wolf wondered if Mitch had heard about his gaffe of blocking the kitchen door and making his mother drop all that food.

Mitch stopped the pump and hung the hose again. It couldn't have filled more than a couple of gallons. He kept his head down and walked back to his truck, ignoring the receipt that spit out of the pump.

The man was an enigma. Even without the two bikers that had been looming in the diner, he was still trying to get away from Wolf without speaking.

Wolf removed the slip of paper from the pump and walked after him. "Hey, here you go. You forgot your receipt."

Mitch turned. "Oh. Thanks."

"I see you were coming in from the south," Wolf said. "Your mother said you were down in Craig yesterday."

"Oh...yeah..." Mitch thumbed over his shoulder as he opened his door. "I work down there sometimes."

"Where at? Another diner?"

"Uh, no. I work for a...natural gas extraction company." He sat down behind the wheel.

There had been a pause in his sentence, and Wolf got the sense he was lying.

"On a Friday night? Like...a night shift or something?"

Mitch nodded. "Yeah. It's a late-day shift into the night. Then I just end up staying down there. Sucks." He reached to pull the door shut. "But whatcha gonna do? It's good money. Anyway. You have a good one."

"Where do you stay?" Wolf asked.

"They have dorms there."

No mention of his sister living in Craig. Either he was lying, or Dolores had been.

"Oh. Okay," Wolf said. "Where's Savannah?"

"Savannah?" Mitch said and pointed. "She's up with her grandma."

"In Doyle?"

"Yeah."

Wolf stared at him.

"See you later," Mitch said, shutting the door. He turned the engine on and drove away, not giving Wolf another glance as he turned onto the highway and headed north toward Doyle.

Wolf stared after the truck as it shrank in the distance. If Savannah Russell was not with her father and not with her grandma, then where the hell was she?

Suddenly, an idea came to mind. And things started making more sense about what might be going on with Dolores and Mitch and why talking with cops was the last thing they wanted to do.

He got back in his truck, swung out onto the highway, and headed north; the accelerator pressed to the floor.

CHAPTER TWENTY-SEVEN

After a few minutes at high speed, Wolf caught up to Mitch Russell on the highway.

He hung back, thinking. He had a hunch that the pieces all fit together, but he didn't have proof. He needed to speak to Dolores and Mitch, confront them with his suspicions, and watch the looks on their faces as he did.

Raising his cell phone, he considered dialing Brandenburg but decided against it, just in case he was completely wrong. Instead, he put the phone down and trailed Mitch at a distance for the next twenty miles until Doyle appeared on the horizon.

Mitch's Toyota slowed and hung a right before the town, and Wolf followed.

The road was dirt, stretching straight for a mile through brush before meandering to the right up into sporadic pines and junipers. The trees grew thicker, and Wolf lost sight of Mitch, but the dust hanging over the road told him he was on the trail.

He rounded a bend, and the dust ended abruptly. He

jammed on the brakes and noticed he'd just passed a driveway leading left into a thick copse of trees.

He reversed and took the drive. There, the road narrowed, choked in by foliage as it led downward and to the right, out of sight. He coasted around the corner, stopping quickly when Mitch's brake lights flared up ahead, no more than fifty yards in front of him.

Mitch's window was rolled down, and he was talking to one of the bikers Wolf remembered from the diner the previous day. He was pointing at Mitch through the window, accusatory, angry. He stopped talking, lowered his hand, and backed away at the sight of Wolf's vehicle.

Wolf rolled forward and saw another man standing in front of Mitch's truck.

Their bikes were parked off the road in the trees.

Wolf kept his foot off the brake and stopped at Mitch's rear bumper. The bikers walked away from the Toyota and toward their bikes, ignoring Wolf.

Mitch let off the brake and moved forward. Ahead, the trees opened, revealing an idyllic setting. A one-story house sat amid a sprawling meadow, with a pond off the back and views of the valley beyond.

Wolf watched the bikers for a beat. They continued to ignore him, speaking to one another as if at a social function. The shorter guy reached into a jacket pocket, produced a pack of cigarettes, and lit one.

Finally, they turned toward Wolf and waved.

Wolf looked forward and let off the brake.

The Tacoma was already down through the clearing, parking in front of the house. Wolf coasted after him and parked next to the truck. Getting out, he turned back. The two bikers were now staring down with great interest.

"What are you doing?" Mitch stood next to his truck.

"Is this your place?" Wolf asked.

"Yeah. Why?"

"I'd like to have a word with you."

Mitch's jaw was set forward. His eyes went to the bikers. "You just followed me from the gas station?"

"Yes."

"Why?"

Wolf eyed the bikers again. One of them had a pair of binoculars raised to his face. The other was speaking on the phone.

"You really want to do this out here?" Wolf asked. "Or do you want to invite me in?"

Mitch shook his head. "It's not a good idea for you to be here."

"Why?"

"It's just not. And it's really not good timing."

"I know about Savannah," Wolf said, watching his face closely.

Mitch's eyelid twitched, closing halfway. His breathing intensified as if someone had sat on his chest. Then he turned around and walked away quickly, stopped, and flung up his hand.

"Fine," he said. "Come in."

Wolf followed him. "Thanks. I appreciate it. I just want to ask you a few questions. That's all."

Mitch opened the door and stepped inside. Wolf followed into a kitchen.

"What is he doing here?" a woman's voice asked. Dolores stood near the sink, looking out a window toward the bikers. She walked to the counter and sat on a stool. She wore no makeup, and a yellowish-purple crescent below her left eye was on full display.

"I didn't invite him," Mitch said. "He followed me."

She looked shaken, her eyes lacking the cool she'd displayed the night before at the diner. "Where were you?" She hissed the words at her son.

Mitch didn't answer.

Wolf stood near the door, watching the interaction. Dolores had been lying the prior afternoon because she didn't know where her son was.

He looked around, taking in the interior. The house was a modest size, with a kitchen and living room that took up equal space in one big room, and a small hallway leading off to the left behind Mitch and his mother.

Dozens of family photographs adorned the walls, and the star of the show was always a little girl with a bright, photogenic smile. Wolf eyed the progression of her as a baby, growing to reach her father's elbow.

His eyes stopped on a young woman who was obviously the mother. She stood holding Savannah as a baby next to Mitch. She was pretty with straight brown hair, standing a head shorter than her husband.

"That's Sally," Mitch said. "She died of cancer after Savannah was born."

Wolf turned to them. "How old is Savannah?"

"Eight," Mitch said.

"And where is she?"

"She's playing soccer," Dolores said, but her voice was weak. "What is he doing here?"

"Last night, you said she was with her father down in Craig," Wolf said. "And this morning, Mitch, you said you were gone all night for work and that Savannah was up here."

They stared at Wolf.

"And now you're telling me you didn't know where your son was, Dolores."

She rubbed the back of her neck, clearly agitated.

Wolf went to the sink window, keeping a few feet back to remain hidden behind the glare. "The bikers have her, don't they?"

He turned and watched their faces. He was right. Tears dripped down Dolores's cheeks, and Mitch glared hard through the room.

"I need you to tell me if I'm right," he said.

Mitch nodded.

"Okay. Why do they have her? Why would they do that?"

"Where were you?" Dolores asked her son again, ignoring him. "They came to the door and asked where you were. I told them I didn't know. I told them you left without telling me, and since they took our phones, I had no clue where you were. They were pissed off, Mitch."

Mitch walked up next to Wolf and looked outside. The two bikers remained where they were, one of them still on the phone, but he was talking animatedly, gesturing at the house.

"The faster you explain it to me," Wolf said, "the better."

"Lawrence raided their place," Mitch said. "He killed a bunch of them and apparently took some of their money. A lot of it, I guess."

"I know that," Wolf said. "But why?"

"He had been asking around about Irv and getting

nowhere. Irv was riding with them, and I really don't know what happened. Nobody does. But...Irv just vanished."

"Okay," Wolf said. "So, he killed them? And took money? I don't get it."

Mitch spoke quickly. "Irv disappeared a month or so ago, and ever since, Lawrence has been digging around for answers. He's gone to the sheriff, the gang, anybody and everybody in town. Nobody was talking. It infuriated him.

"He came over here last week, telling me about how he'd found a back way into the compound, and he'd been watching them. And that he was going to finally do something about their silence. That he had figured out a way to make them talk. And then he just told me to take care of my mom for him, and he left."

Dolores wiped tears from her cheeks.

"So, he went in there and killed some of them," Wolf said. "And he escaped with their money. I see. He held their money for ransom for information about his missing son."

"I guess so," Mitch said.

"Did you talk to him after what he did?" Wolf asked.

"No," Dolores said.

Mitch shook his head.

"But he called me," Dolores said, "from a strange number. I didn't answer it. I never answer those weird numbers. I had been calling his phone, but he wasn't answering. I didn't even notice I had a voicemail from him sitting there on my phone. I'm not good with these stupid phones."

"What did the voicemail say?" Wolf asked.

She shook her head, tears freshening. "I never listened to it. I don't know."

"But Snake did," Mitch said.

"What do you mean?" Wolf asked.

"They came over here Monday morning," Mitch said. "Snake and a bunch more of them. They broke in and woke us all up. They demanded her phone, saw the message, and called the number back."

"Did he answer?"

"Yes. And they spoke to him for just a few seconds. But he hung up on them, and when they called back, he never answered again. That's when they grabbed me, punched my mother, and took my daughter."

"What did they say?" Wolf asked. "What was the conversation like?"

"Snake told him he wanted his money back and that they would get him for what he did. Just...threats. But, then he put down the phone, and he was...he was mad. So pissed. He asked us where Lawrence was."

Mitch rubbed his face with one hand, his eyes welling up. "We didn't know where he was. We told them we didn't know. But we couldn't say anything to make them believe us. I couldn't do anything to stop them.

"They called Lawrence back a few more times on that number. And when he didn't answer, they took our phones. They sent him a text from both. And then showed us the message. It said to bring them the money by midnight Saturday, or the girl dies." Mitch's eyes filled with tears. "And they took her." The last words were choked by rage. "They took my little girl."

Dolores stood up, walked over, and embraced her son.

"Have you spoken to Lawrence since?" Wolf asked.

"No," Dolores said. "Are you listening? They took our phones."

Wolf put up a hand. "I'm just wondering...is there any

indication Lawrence saw the messages they sent? The threat?"

Mitch shook his head. "I don't know. That's the question. I don't know if he even knows they have Savannah, or if he just threw away the phone, or shut it off, or what?"

Wolf sighed deeply, folded his arms, and studied the men outside. The guy on the phone lowered his cell and put it in his pocket. Wolf eyed Mitch. The man's eyes were rimmed red like he hadn't slept in days.

"Where were you last night?" Wolf asked.

"I was looking for the back way into the compound."

"And?"

"And I found it."

"And?"

He shook his head. "I watched. And I think she was in one of the buildings, but I couldn't figure out how to get down there without getting caught. They're on high alert. At least five of them were on an all-night patrol. I couldn't figure out how to get in there without just..." he shook his head and began to sob.

"It would have been a suicide mission," Wolf said. "And you weren't willing to make a poor decision like that unless it was completely necessary. You still had time. You still have until tonight at midnight."

"Yes," Mitch said. "Exactly."

"How many were there in total?"

"I don't know. I counted eleven outside. Five were on patrol, and one of them walked very close to me. But there's a central fire pit area where they congregated. There were lights on inside the buildings."

"What makes you think you found where Savannah was?"

"One of the buildings always had a guard at the door. And one of the men went inside with food once."

"Can you describe the building?"

"It has antlers on it."

"And the others don't?"

"I'm not sure. I don't think so. From my vantage, it was on the left."

Dolores moved toward the kitchen window. "They're coming down here."

The two men were now walking down the drive toward the house.

"How did you find it? Where is the back way in?"

"Off County Road 982. I went onto the satellite maps and looked. There's a two-track road near the point where 982 approaches the rear of the property. There's a cattle guard and a gap in the barbed wire."

"They're coming," she said again.

"And then what?" Wolf asked.

"You take the trail until it stops going up, and then you park and hike up. You can see the compound on the other side from the top of the mountain."

Wolf nodded, making his way toward the door. "What are you two supposed to be doing today? Are you working at the diner?"

"Yes," Mitch said quickly. "It opens at eleven."

"Go to work. Be normal."

"I have a gun. And I know how to use it. If Lawrence doesn't show up, I'm going up there, and I'm getting her. No matter what."

Wolf winced inwardly at the man's confidence. He was willing to die for his daughter; that much was obvious, but life would be much better for everyone involved if they all lived.

He grabbed the doorknob. "County Road 982."

"Yeah," Mitch said.

"Obviously, don't tell them what we've talked about," Wolf said. "Tell them I tried to ask about where you were, Mitch. You tell them you told me that you were gone with Savannah down south."

"My sister lives down in Craig," Mitch said.

"Right."

"I can say I told you I was dropping her off there."

"Good," Wolf said.

"They're getting closer," Dolores said.

He took out a business card.

"I already have your card from earlier," Dolores said.

He put it back in his pocket. "Call me the second you get to work. I want to know that you made it safely."

"Okay."

He went to the door, pausing with his hand on the knob. "When the time comes, we'll come get you, and then we'll go get your daughter."

"When?"

"I'm not sure yet."

Mitch deflated.

"I'll get some reinforcements, and we'll come up with a plan. And we'll get your daughter."

"I don't like the sound of this," Dolores said.

"There's no other way, Mom."

Wolf opened the front door, walked out, and went to his truck, pausing to look at the two bikers as if surprised by their approach. They were halfway to the house, about fifty yards out.

He got in and backed out quickly, then drove, slowing to a stop next to them with his window down.

"What are you guys doing?"

They stared at him.

He shook his head, annoyed, hooking an elbow on the door. "You know, I don't know what all the secrecy is about up here. But I know something strange is going on. You think Lawrence Hunt is coming here? To this house? Why?" He glared at them, waiting for a reply. "That's why you're here, right?"

He couldn't see their eyes beyond the mirrored sunglasses they wore, but he hoped they were twinkling with satisfaction, watching a harried cop clutching for answers.

He continued talking. "I followed Mitch here because I'd like some answers from somebody without you two around, and hey, who do I find? You two again." He leaned out conspiratorially. "What do you two know? Huh? What are you two," he twirled a finger, "and *everyone* else around here not telling me about Lawrence Hunt?"

When they refused to answer again, Wolf turned up one side of his mouth. "Okay. I see how it is." He shook his head and let off the brake.

As he left, he eyed the mirror. The bikers stood there watching him leave but then turned and continued toward the house. He considered going back and stopping them with force, but the rest of the gang undoubtedly knew he was out there at that moment. For the safety of the girl, it was best to play dumb. And that meant playing the part completely.

He continued to drive without pause and watched the mirror as the two men went out of sight.

CHAPTER TWENTY-EIGHT

Brandenburg, Nichols, and Larkin listened with rapt interest after Wolf summoned them all to the main room of the sheriff's headquarters and began relaying the epic story of Mitch, Dolores, and Savannah Russell.

All three men took the news of Savannah's kidnapping in silence. Nichols sat on the edge of his desk, Brandenburg walked to the coffee machine, and Larkin paced behind his desk. They all wore different masks of fear, the news appearing to affect the sheriff most.

Brandenburg filled a cup of coffee, then set it down. Hands on his hips, he turned and faced them. "We can't just go barging in there. That'll end in another shootout. One that's not going to end well for us."

"You're dead sure about this?" Nichols asked.

"Yes," Wolf said.

He told them about the back way into the compound that Mitch Russell had reported finding the night before, the one Hunt had been using to surveil the place.

"Here?" Larkin said, pointing at his computer screen.

They gathered around his desk, looking at the monitor. Larkin had pulled up a satellite map showing County Road 982 cutting through a swath of forest.

"Their place is right here," Larkin said, swirling the computer mouse over a section of woods where three buildings squat in the trees. They were square-shaped, equally spaced in a triangle. A dirt road led into the property from the opposite side off a different county road.

"This is where we came in," Brandenburg said, pointing. "The front entrance comes in from County 17."

The rear entrance was to the north of the property, but County Road 982 cut in from the south and west, making a long bend toward it before heading north and away.

"He must mean right here," Larkin said. "This is the closest the road gets. That's a long way from there to here."

"How far?"

Larkin shook his head, zooming back out. "I'd say an hour. Maybe less. But you have to go all the way down south, here, to catch the road."

He pointed, showing the route taken would be down south on the highway, then west on a different road, before hooking up with 982. It was why Wolf had run into Mitch at the gas station south of town.

Nichols sighed heavily. "We can't go in there, just us."

"I agree," Wolf said. "That's why we'll call in an FBI response team. They have trained individuals to deal with this kind of situation."

Brandenburg remained silent, staring at the screen.

"Sir?" Larkin asked, looking up. "What do you think?"

Brandenburg blinked, then shook his head. "We bring in a bunch of Feds or SWAT...it really is going to turn into a major shootout. They've got firepower up there. Then we're really sealing that little girl's coffin."

"But we have to do something," Wolf said.

"Let me think," Brandenburg said, walking toward his office.

"What's there to think about?" Wolf asked. "Make the calls."

Brandenburg turned around. "Let me think!"

Wolf stood staring at him.

Brandenburg scratched his head. "You think they'll really kill her?"

"You want to wait and find out?" Wolf asked.

"No. Of course not."

Wolf's phone chimed in his pocket, and he pulled it out. Somebody with a local area code was calling. He punched the answer button. "Wolf here."

"They beat him up!" A woman's hysteric voice crackled in his ear. "They came in and beat him up! He's hurt!"

Wolf straightened, recognizing the voice. "Dolores?"

"They broke his legs! We need an ambulance!"

"We'll be right over."

CHAPTER TWENTY-NINE

Patterson looked at the clock again and then over at the empty seat of Rachette's desk.

The bastard. As soon as he came in, she was going to beat his ass. That was if he decided to actually show up.

She pushed her chair back from her computer and rubbed her eyes, stifling a yawn. After another night of fitful sleep, she was here on a Saturday morning. All because of Rachette, who was out there still doing, God knew what.

The night before, she had gotten a late call from Charlotte telling her that she'd heard from him. Rachette told her he was okay and that everything was fine, that he had been with Yates, but Charlotte had no further details. And he still wasn't answering Patterson's calls this morning. Clearly, he was avoiding facing her, knowing she wouldn't put up with half the shit his wife did.

Her email pinged. It was the request from her Special Forces contact down at Fort Carson. She had wanted more information on Lawrence Hunt's time spent in the army, and it looked like they'd delivered on her request.

She read the email. A PDF file was attached with the roster of men from teams Hunt had served with over his twenty-two-year career.

"Hey," a voice came from behind her.

Rachette walked up, dropped a bag next to his desk, sat down, and sipped a cup of coffee. "How's it going?"

She turned slowly, her eyebrows raising. "How's it going?"

Rachette wiggled his mouse and looked at his computer screen.

"I've been looking for you, calling every thirty minutes for two days, and you just waltz in here and ask me how's it going?"

"Hey, Rachette," Nelson walked up. "There you are. We've been looking for—" He eyed Patterson and closed his mouth. Then he backed away, bypassing his desk altogether as he walked out of the squad room.

"Speak," she said.

Rachette swiveled his chair toward her. "Look. I'm sorry. I was in a bad place."

"Why didn't you tell me you knew your brakes were cut?"

"Because I knew who it was, and I was so pissed I thought I might kill them. I didn't want you to stop me because I knew you would." He looked at her with the most sincere expression she'd ever seen on him.

"Okay," she said. "And...what happened?"

He explained how he found the men, had gone to their house, and how Yates had come barging in to stop him.

"If it weren't for you," he said, "Yates would have never been there. So, thanks, Patty."

She nodded. "Yeah. Okay. You're welcome."

"But everything's fine now," Rachette said.

"Fine? What about these two guys who cut your brakes? Did you bring them in?"

He launched into an explanation about Yates and how he had uncovered their method of acquiring illegal prescription drugs and Rachette's decision to make them leave rather than involve Yates in their prosecution, which would have further worsened an already bad situation for the man.

"They have until seven tonight to leave, or else we'll bring them in," Rachette said.

She scoffed. "And you trust these assholes?"

"No. I don't. Which is why I went over to their house again this morning to make sure they were making good on their end of the deal."

"And?"

"And it looks like they are. I went up and parked right there in front of their house and watched while Carlton, one of the guys, packed up his car and left. The other guy was packing, too. But he was taking his time, so I decided I'd give him some space...thought I'd come here so you'd stop calling me."

She shook her head. "I don't know, Rachette."

"Look. I told you the truth, even though I knew you wouldn't like the idea. But I don't care. I'm not putting Yates through more than he needs at this point. It'll work out. Or it won't. Either way, I'll take the hit. This has nothing to do with you."

She leaned back in her chair, watching as Rachette turned back to his computer and clicked his keyboard.

With a sigh, she slid forward, reading the email again.

"How's Wolf doing?"

"I don't know. I haven't heard from him today," she said, clicking the PDF attachment.

"But what's going on up there?"

The file expanded on screen, but she looked over at Rachette with an expression that said *seriously?*

"I heard they still haven't found Hunt," he said.

"Yeah." She turned back toward the screen.

"Okay, fine," he said. "I'll get my info from somebody else." He stood up and stretched his arms overhead.

"Already taking a break, are we?" she said, reading the screen.

There was a list of twelve men in a column, with a short bio detailing their time in service, including specialization on the Green Beret team. A current home address was listed with each man. Her eyes stopped at the third man down.

"Hey," she said. "This guy's in Green River, Wyoming."

Rachette stepped up behind her, looking over her shoulder.

"So?"

She shook her head, then quickly explained how Hunt's vehicle had been found in Green River the day before.

"Oh."

"Yeah." She pointed. "Oh shit, look at that."

Rachette leaned forward, reading. A second later, he whistled softly. "That's not good."

"No, it's not. You call Wolf and tell him about this." She picked up her phone.

"Yeah, okay." He picked up his desk phone. "Who are you calling?"

"Green River PD. I'll see if they can follow up."

CHAPTER THIRTY

Wolf led the way to the Russell house, with Larkin sitting in his passenger seat. Brandenburg followed in his own truck with Nichols behind them.

Turning off the dirt road from memory, Wolf sped down the drive toward the house. The two bikers who had been waiting at the edge of the forest were long gone.

They had left seconds after getting the call from Dolores, but an ambulance had beat them there and was parked in front of the house.

They didn't appear to have been there for long, the two EMTs just entering the house.

Wolf skidded to a stop and ran inside.

Dolores stood over her son, watching the EMTs, a man and a woman, kneeling next to Mitch.

Mitch moaned in pain, his face covered in sweat and blood. His legs were splayed out at unnatural angles; bone poked through one of his shins.

The male EMT had a syringe out and had just finished

shooting something into his arm. "Ketamine for the pain," he said, looking up.

"Dolores," Wolf said, touching Dolores's shoulder. "Let's go outside and let them work."

She allowed him to steer her outside. She walked on shaky legs, her face ashen.

"Relax," Wolf said. "It's okay now. They're here."

"No, it's not okay."

"What happened?" Nichols asked, trailing them outside.

"They wanted to know where he was. They wanted to know what he'd told you," she said and pointed at Wolf.

"And what did he say?" Wolf asked.

"Nothing. We didn't say anything that we'd talked about. He just pretended like he was down at his sister's place in Craig. Like we said."

"Why did they do this?" Larkin asked.

She shook her head, putting a hand over her mouth. "I don't know. They were just so mean. It was the bigger of the two. The other one didn't want to hurt him. But the bigger guy was just..." She stopped talking and closed her eyes. "He wouldn't stop. I told him to stop."

"Coming through."

They stepped aside as the EMTs rolled Mitch out on a gurney.

"You're taking her, too," Wolf said. "She can't drive herself."

"Of course," the woman said. "Hop in, ma'am."

"Where are we going?"

"Craig is the nearest hospital."

"I'm not going...I can't..." Dolores looked like she was hyperventilating now. "What about Savannah? We can't just leave her!"

"You're not leaving her," Wolf said, steering her toward the open ambulance door. "Don't worry. We're going to get your granddaughter back, Dolores."

She looked at Brandenburg, Nichols, and Larkin in turn. "Are you going to? Are you going to get her back?"

The three men said nothing, but Brandenburg nodded with an unsure expression.

"Will you get her back?" she asked, her voice rising to a yell.

"Yes," Brandenburg said. "Yes, ma'am. You go with them. You leave it to us."

"We have to go," the male EMT said, shutting one rear door.

"Dolores," Wolf said. "Go. We'll take care of everything here. Go be with your son."

Face slack, she looked down with a hopeless stare as the female EMT helped her up into the ambulance.

A minute later, the vehicle was gone, the siren's wail dissipating, leaving the four men standing mutely.

"Shit," Larkin said, breaking the silence.

Wolf turned, putting his hands on his hips and tilting his head to the sky. Clouds were building in the northwest, the horizon turning dark. The freshening wind blew across his face. When he turned back, the three men looked at him.

"We need help on this," he said to Brandenburg. "Either you admit it, or I'm going to have to take over here."

"I know," Brandenburg said. "I know." He put up a hand. "I'll make the call."

"To who?" Wolf asked.

"I have a contact in the FBI."

"Me, too. I can call them."

"This is my territory, Wolf," Brandenburg said. "I'm

sheriff of this town, whether you like it or not. And I'll take care of this, God damn it!"

It was the first time Brandenburg had shown so much emotion. He was clearly shaken, but he was moving, his hand already out of his pocket, cell phone in hand.

Wolf nodded.

Brandenburg dialed, put the phone to his ear, and turned around.

Wolf watched and listened as the sheriff launched into a conversation, the gist of which was lost behind the blowing wind.

"Who's his contact at the FBI?" Wolf asked Nichols.

"I don't know," Nichols said.

Larkin's already pale complexion blanched. He was staring at the ground without focus. Nichols stood looking at the sheriff's back. Brandenburg talked, looking over at them, his voice just out of range as he turned away and continued talking.

Impatience boiling over, Wolf walked after Brandenburg and rounded to the front of him, listening in.

"...all right. Yeah." The sheriff looked at Wolf.

"Who are you talking to?"

Brandenburg shook his head, annoyed.

"Who is that?" Wolf asked.

Brandenburg put up a finger. "Listen. I'm going to put you on speaker, so you can let my companion here know exactly what's going on...okay...yeah..."

Brandenburg poked the screen and held the phone between them, with an *are-you-happy-now* expression raising his eyebrows.

"Hello?" A deep male voice came out of the speaker.

"Can you hear us?" Brandenburg asked.

"Yeah. Go ahead."

Nichols and Larkin walked over to join them.

"This is Detective David Wolf, Sluice-Byron County Sheriff's Department. Who's this?"

"Assistant Special Agent in Charge Lance Romero. I hear you guys have a bit of a hostage situation up there, and you need some assistance."

"That's right," Wolf said. "What can you do for us?"

"I was just telling the sheriff we have a team readying up."

"Where are you?" Wolf asked. "Denver?"

"That's right."

"What's your ETA?"

"We're dealing with weather across the state right now. I haven't spoken to my helicopter pilots yet, but there are storms over the metro area. I'd say with prep and flight time, three hours...give or take. Again, depending on this weather."

Wolf shook his head but checked his watch. It was just about noon. They would be coming in well under Snake's midnight deadline, even if it took longer to get there and make a move.

"I was just telling him about the back way into the biker compound you told us about, Wolf," Brandenburg said. "We could go there and do reconnaissance first. You know, get some eyes on the place, and then keep in touch via satphone."

"That's a good idea," ASAC Romero said. "The more info we have going in, the better, obviously."

"Where are your satphones?" Wolf asked Brandenburg.

"Back at the station."

"Along with more weapons, I hope."

Brandenburg nodded. "We have rifles. A couple more handguns."

Wolf nodded, motioning for Brandenburg to continue with the call.

Brandenburg pressed the button and put the phone to his ear. "You there?"

Wolf walked toward the house, again looking at the weather rolling in. The entire horizon was bruised. He pulled out his phone and checked the screen, seeing he'd missed a call from Rachette.

He pressed the number.

"Hey."

"Wolf, what's going on up there?"

He explained to Rachette as best and as fast as he could, watching as Brandenburg wrapped up his own phone call and joined his two deputies near the vehicles.

"Do you need us to come up there?" Rachette asked.

"I don't think so. We have an FBI response team on the way from Denver right now. I'm not exactly sure where or how we're getting into the compound just yet. There's no sense in complicating things. Stay put."

"Okay," Rachette said. "Listen, the reason I called is because me and Patty figured something out about Hunt going to Green River."

"What's that?"

"One of Hunt's former SF teammates lives up in Green River."

"Okay."

"And he was one of the 18Cs on his team. The engineer sergeant. The guys who deal with explosives and demolitions."

Wolf rubbed a hand over his stubble.

Rachette continued. "Patterson has contacted Green River PD. They're headed over to the guy's place right now to talk to him."

"Okay, keep me posted," Wolf said, but he knew he was going into backcountry where his phone would go silent. If there were explosive surprises awaiting them, he would be learning about it firsthand.

CHAPTER THIRTY-ONE

Brandenburg's taillights flickered in the dust cloud kicked up behind his truck, then disappeared when he drove over a hill. The first raindrop hit the windshield, followed by a dozen more.

Wolf steered with both hands, leaning sideways in his seat to relieve the tension on his back.

"You all right?"

Wolf looked over at Larkin sitting in the passenger seat. The big man's eyes were filled with genuine concern.

"I'll be fine," Wolf said. "Just some back pain."

"I slipped a disc once," Larkin said. "Hurt bad. But it went away. Took a shitload of time to heal, though. I had to lie on my back for a month. You ever had to do that?"

"No."

"It's a new kind of hell, let me tell you. Just staring at the ceiling for hours on end. I had my girlfriend screw a TV into the ceiling so I could watch shows on Netflix, though." He chuckled. "She's not handy. I was worried the whole time it was going to rip out of the ceiling and land on my face." He looked out the window and shook his head.

Wolf eyed him and recognized the excited energy coming off the man, much like what he'd witnessed in his army days. Some men would recede inward before missions, others would break into spirited monologues, latching onto any conversation they could get their vocal cords into.

But now Larkin had gone silent.

"You still have this girlfriend?" Wolf asked.

"Yep. But she's back in Fort Morgan. Going to beauty school. She'll be done next semester, then she's moving in with me."

"I bet you're excited for that."

"I am."

Up ahead, Brandenburg's brake lights blossomed, and he took a sharp turn, disappearing into the trees. Wolf slowed and took the turn, the lights ahead coming back into view.

The rain increased, pinging off the roof of his SUV.

Larkin reached down to the floorboard, pulled a pair of rain pants from his bag, and started pulling them on.

"How much farther now?" Wolf asked.

Larkin looked at the MDT screen. "We're close. Three-point-one miles."

The rain fell steadily now, and Wolf turned up the wind-shield wipers. Ahead, Brandenburg's lights smeared and sharpened. Despite the weather, the sheriff kept up his speed, following the same GPS waypoints programmed into his own data terminal.

I canceled the wedding plans.

Wolf pushed the thought away as quickly as it came but felt the aftershock in his quickened pulse. He couldn't stop thinking about Piper, and he just wanted to be home holding her, telling her everything was okay, making up with her. But he would have to face that problem later. Right now, he had to concentrate on getting the girl out of this place, back to her father and grandmother, then he could get his own backside home to Rocky Points.

He picked his phone up from the center console, but there was no reception.

Larkin pulled his own phone from his pocket. "No service. You?"

"Nope," Wolf said.

Larkin shifted in his seat and put on his raincoat: a black slicker that matched the bottoms, with a gold sheriff's department logo emblazoned on one breast.

Wolf's gear was in the back, and it looked like he would get wet putting it on once they stopped. He hadn't thought that far ahead and had the more pressing problem of getting to where they wanted to go. He had no clue how passable or not the road would be once they got there.

They rode the rest of the way in silence, the rain intensifying until the wipers failed to keep up. Finally, Brandenburg slowed, pulling to the left side of the road and coming to a halt.

"This is it," Larkin said. "It's right there." He pointed.

Wolf leaned into the windshield and saw a gap in the barbed wire fence, a cattle guard leading onto a rough-looking two-track road. Rocks jutted up on the other side of steel bars, and huge puddles roiled with the falling drops. Beyond that, the forest was a green smear, obscured by slashing rain.

Wolf pulled up to the passenger side of the sheriff's truck and rolled his window down.

Nichols was in the passenger seat of the sheriff's truck and rolled his down, too.

The rain was deafening, spray coming in at all angles and soaking Wolf's left arm and leg.

"This is it!" Brandenburg yelled. "After you!" He gestured.

Wolf nodded, rolling up his window.

Wolf let off the brake, twisted the wheel, and barreled over the cattle guard. The SUV dipped and lurched upward as they went in and out of many holes. Smooth sections were few and far between, and the vehicle bucked like they were riding out a 9.0 earthquake.

Larkin held the ceiling bar next to him, his other hand on the center console.

"You okay?" he asked Wolf five minutes in.

"Yeah." The movement seemed to be helping rather than hurting his back.

A minute later, the road took a sharp turn to the left and veered up at the same time the rain began to let up. He turned the defroster on high to combat the fog building on the inner windshield.

"A little more," Larkin said, pointing at the screen. "Another 300 yards."

For a while, the road angled sideways, then it cut across the forested slope. Wolf prayed for the tires to keep their grip.

The rain slowed to a trickle, ending quickly, but water continued to hit the glass, cascading down from dense foliage above. A thick fog remained, and the road ahead disappeared into the murk.

"Here," Larkin said. "This is it."

Wolf parked, shut off the engine, and got out, his boots

landing on wet, rocky earth. Icy dollops streamed down and hit his head and neck as he went to the hatchback, opened it, and retrieved his rain jacket.

Larkin met him at the back bumper. Zipping up his own garment against the cold, he pulled the hooded collar tight around his neck and watched Brandenburg's truck come to a stop behind them.

The truck's engine roared like a beast, heat emanating, and then it shut off, whining down to a low hum as the fan kept going underneath the hood.

Wolf closed the rear hatch, putting a hand on his Glock for reassurance, and looked up the slope. Anything beyond fifty yards was hidden in the fog. It was another hundred yards or so to the ridgeline and the vantage of the compound below if the fog lifted.

Brandenburg and Nichols got out, zipping up their own rain jackets.

They had a cache of rifles in their back seat, including a Savage Model 10 for Wolf. He waited for Brandenburg to gather the weapons and hand them out, but the sheriff stood stiffly at his front bumper, eyes darting between the trees.

Wolf felt it, too. They were being watched. As quickly as the thought occurred to him, a green laser point appeared on Brandenburg's chest.

Wolf's insides dropped. Another beam lanced through the fog, landing on Wolf's center mass.

"Drop your weapons," a voice said from their right, impossibly close. Wolf turned and saw a man up in a tree, downslope so as to be at eye level. He was perched in a camouflaged stand, holding a rifle with another laser sight aimed at Larkin.

"Shit," Larkin said.

"Drop. Your. Weapons. You have three seconds, or we start shooting."

"Okay!" Brandenburg said loudly. "We're dropping our weapons!"

Wolf pulled his gun, stretched his arm sideways, and dropped it onto the wet earth. The other weapons clattered to the ground.

Men came out of the fog from up the slope, at least a dozen of them, all carrying assault rifles across their chest, handguns holstered on their hips, dressed in similar camouflaged rain gear.

One drew Wolf's attention, pulling ahead of the pack. It was Snake.

The biker gang leader's eyes were on the terrain in front of him as he walked, then he looked up to meet Wolf's stare.

How in the hell did they know we were coming? Wolf finally had a second to think, and he looked at Brandenburg and Nichols. The two men both had lasers dancing on their chests. Larkin was also under guard. So, who told them?

"Right on time," Snake said, reaching them. The biker hitched his rifle over a shoulder and stopped a few paces away. "Did you guys have a good drive?"

Snake looked between them, not a hint of humor on his face. "Anyway, glad you could make it."

"We have an FBI response team on its way," Wolf said. "They'll be here within the hour."

Snake's eyes squinted almost shut, and he tilted his head. With a familiar deep voice he said, "We have a bit of a delay here down in Denver with the weather. I'm afraid we'll have to ignore your request. Assistant Special Agent in Charge Lance Romero signing off."

He opened his eyes, his lips curling into a brief smile. "I took a lot of acting classes as a kid. Comes in handy in my line of work."

Wolf looked at Brandenburg. The sheriff stared at the ground.

"You piece of shit," Wolf said, looking at Nichols and finding a similar shame-filled expression. "You, too?"

Nichols lifted his chin but kept his eyes averted as if Wolf were a mute apparition.

Wolf turned to Larkin.

"I didn't know," Larkin said. "I had no idea they were working with these guys."

"Okay, shut up," Snake said. He looked at the man next to him. "Keys, phones, pockets."

Rough hands patted Wolf down, leaving no centimeter of his body unsearched. They reached into his pockets and pulled out his wallet, keys, and phone.

Wolf watched with interest as Brandenburg and Nichols were also stripped of their possessions.

"What's this about?" Brandenburg asked.

"Just precaution," Snake said. "You'll get everything back."

One man gathered all the loot in a bag and walked away, putting it on Wolf's hood. With expert hands, he dug inside, dismantling phones and pulling SIMs and batteries.

"Leave the vehicles here," Snake said, turning upslope. "Let's move."

A rifle barrel jabbed into Wolf's back. "Walk."

Larkin was similarly prodded, and again, the sheriff and Nichols were treated equally.

Brandenburg turned around. "Don't touch me with that. This is the thanks I get?"

"Just a precaution," Snake said, his voice distant, already in the fog above.

The man knocked Brandenburg on top of the head with the barrel.

"Ow!"

Then the barrel came down between Brandenburg's eyes, and the sheriff turned around, his arms out to his sides.

The sheriff leaned forward and began slogging uphill, prompted up to speed by the gunman behind him. "Okay, okay. Son of a bitch."

For the first time, Brandenburg looked over at Wolf. His eyes narrowed to slits. "What? You think I had a choice?"

"Yeah," Wolf said. "I do."

CHAPTER THIRTY-TWO

Patterson stood at the window of the squad room looking west. Dark clouds had descended into the valley, and lightning was starting to hammer down.

More thunder rumbled around the building, barely audible behind the thick glass.

Was Wolf in trouble? He could have been. FBI team or not, facing down a biker gang, who were probably armed to the teeth, was bound to be a sticky situation.

And now there was this weather.

"What are you thinking?" Rachette appeared next to her, looking out the window.

"I'm wondering about Wolf."

"Yeah," Rachette said. "Me, too. I just called him, and it went straight to voicemail."

"There's probably no reception where he's at."

Rain streaked down the glass, slapping the road below. A few people outside scrambled from a shop into their car.

Another lightning flash, and this time, the thunder came immediately.

"Call Luke," Rachette said. "Maybe she knows what's going on?"

Patterson nodded. No way she was going to sit here on her hands anymore. They needed information.

She pulled out her phone and dialed Special Agent Kristen Luke's phone number, turning around and walking among the desks of the squad room.

"Sup girl?" Luke answered.

Despite the situation, Patterson smiled at the sound of her old friend's voice. "It's been a while," she said.

"Sure has. What's going on?"

"Listen, I want to talk about the response team they're sending up to Doyle. Wolf's up there. I want to know what's going on."

"I'm in Chicago," Luke said. "So I wouldn't know anything about what's going on in Denver at the moment."

"Who do I call?"

"Well...Archie's back there. You can call him. You have his number?"

"Just a second." She searched through her phone contacts. Special Agent Archie Hannigan's number scrolled up on the screen. "Got it."

"You want me to give him a heads-up you're calling?"

"No," Patterson said. "We know each other well enough, I think."

"Keep me posted," Luke said.

They said their goodbyes and hung up.

Patterson dialed the number and put the phone to her ear, walking back toward Rachette.

"Hannigan," he answered.

"Hi. It's Heather Patterson in Rocky Points."

"Yeah. What's up? Actually, funny enough, I was going to call Wolf here shortly."

"Oh?"

"Yeah. He had me looking into some information about that Sons of the Void biker gang up in northern Colorado."

"Yeah, he's up there now. That's why I'm calling. I want to know what's happening?"

Hannigan hesitated to answer.

"Can you hear me?"

"Yeah. I mean...I don't know what's happening up there. Wolf's the one on location, isn't he? Have you called him?"

She frowned, looking at Rachette.

"Where are you?" Patterson asked.

"I'm at the Denver Field Office."

"Didn't you just send a response team up to Doyle at their sheriff's request?"

"A response team? Not that I've heard of...and I would have heard about it."

She shook her head, lowering the phone. "You told me Wolf said they called up a response team, right?"

"I did," Rachette said. "He did."

"From where?"

"From Denver." Rachette reached for the phone. "Give me that."

She lowered it, poking the speaker phone button. "Are you there?"

Hannigan's voice came out. "Yeah."

"He told me you guys had a team on the way," Rachette said. "I just spoke to him an hour and a half ago."

"He said we did? Are you sure?"

"Yes!" Rachette's hands turned to claws. "He said the Denver Field Office! Yes!"

"Okay, okay, let me make sure, hold on." Hannigan's phone clanked, and he went silent.

Patterson and Rachette stared at the screen mutely.

A minute later, Hannigan came back, his breathing labored. "Nope. No response team."

"You're sure?"

"One hundred percent."

"What does that mean?" Patterson asked. "You're sure?" she asked Rachette.

Rachette's face went mean. "If you ask me that again—"

"Okay," she said. "So, that means he thinks you're sending one up. Which means somebody told him that, and they haven't relayed the request? Or...somebody lied to him?"

Rachette's eyes widened. "He said the sheriff called it in."

Patterson rubbed a hand over her face.

"What's going on?" Hannigan asked. "What does that mean?"

"I think it means you need to send a response team up to Doyle, Colorado. And Archie?"

"Yeah."

"Now."

"I'm on it. Call you back." He hung up.

They went to Waze's office, and Patterson opened the door without bothering to knock.

"Come in," Waze said sarcastically, looking up from his computer.

"Sir, we have a problem."

She and Rachette explained what was going on.

"That's not good," Waze said.

"No, it's not."

"What do you propose we do about it?"

"Get a helicopter prepared," she said, "and let's get up there as soon as possible."

He nodded, then shook his head. "I don't know who to call."

"I do." She picked up the desk phone and dialed.

CHAPTER THIRTY-THREE

Once at the top of the mountain, the fog dissipated into nothing, apparently contained by the valley behind and below.

Wolf breathed heavily through an open mouth as they crested the ridge and started down the other side. Three rooflines poked out of the trees partway down the forested slope, and he recognized the compound from the satellite map.

Brandenburg wheezed loudly behind him, his face bright red, covered in sweat. He looked like he might have a heart attack right then and there. If the sheriff was on the biker gang's side, the gunman behind him didn't show it, poking his back again with the gun.

Wolf listened to the man escorting him cough like he was trying to expel cigarette tar from his lungs. The man carried his rifle lazily and without much regard for what Wolf was doing. Wolf could have taken him within seconds and disarmed him, but there were ten more capable-looking men with guns to their right and left.

Snake had disappeared into the trees ahead of them.

"I see why you guys always had me manning the phones now," Larkin said, talking again to Nichols. "Because you two were out doing shit with these guys."

"Just shut up," Nichols said, his voice low. "You want to survive being with these guys? Just shut up."

Larkin scoffed. "Yeah. Okay. Bastard. Does your wife know about this?"

"Shut up!" One of the bikers said.

Larkin stopped talking and walked down the slope with long, powerful strides.

They continued walking until the terrain flattened out and monolithic granite formations had pushed up from the forest floor. Swerving around and through the rocks sculpted by nature, the buildings came into view ahead.

There was a lot of action going on. Men were tending to the motorcycles, which were twenty or so in number. They strapped bags on and wrapped things to the seats with rope. Some of them stopped to watch the spectacle of prisoners being escorted into the camp, but then they got back to work, hurrying in and out of the buildings.

There were pickup trucks, too, and some of the men loaded cardboard boxes onto them. One was already full, and two men were covering the bed with a tarp.

"Over here!" One of the gunmen behind Nichols said. "Everyone over here!"

Wolf, Nichols, Larkin, and Brandenburg did as they were told, gathering near a firepit surrounded by a semi-circle of camp chairs.

They stood in a rough line facing the chaos with three guards still behind them holding rifles. The other men in the ambush party melted into action. Some stripped off their rain gear, others moved to their motorcycles, and two gathered weapons before darting inside.

Wolf eyed the three buildings. The one behind him and the one to the left had dozens of antlers mounted to exterior logs. Mitch's antler-building description now made sense. He checked the windows, nothing but darkness inside—no signs of Savannah.

The sun was strong overhead now, and steam rose off the ground, whipped into a frenzy by the men rushing back and forth.

Looking into the distance from this high vantage point, he saw jet-black clouds to the east, the storm receding. A dirt road threaded down the mountain through the trees, past the trucks where he'd met Snake the first time, and all the way to the county road below. The two trucks were still parked there as sentinels. No vehicles approached. No sirens or flashing lights. No help was coming.

"Get the four-tens!" Snake said, coming out of a building. "Who's got the four-tens?"

"We've got 'em already," said a man packing a truck.

"Good."

Snake stripped off his rain jacket, unveiling serpent-covered arms. He dropped it on a nearby camp chair and walked over, assessing his new captures.

"What are you guys doing?" Brandenburg asked.

"We're leaving," Snake said.

"Why?"

"In case you haven't noticed, we're fubar here."

Brandenburg put his hands on his hips, shaking his head. "I told you, you shouldn't have killed Irv Hunt. I told you it was going to get out of control. His dad's not a stable man."

"No shit, Sheriff. I remember what you told us."

"So...what does that mean for us?" He gestured between him and Nichols.

"It means you're gonna die."

The sheriff's face dropped. Nichols closed his eyes.

"You can see how that's the only option, right?" Snake splayed his hands. "Unless you can come up with a use for yourselves."

Wolf eyed the three guards behind them. One of them smiled back at him, turning the barrel toward his back.

"Me and Nichols did everything for you," Brandenburg said. "We made you untouchable for the last five years! How about that for a *use?* We buried evidence. We let you do whatever you wanted. We kept quiet."

"And I thank you for that. You did your part well."

"No. We can help you leave. We can make sure...I don't know...that nobody follows after you."

"Thanks to you, we're ghosts as it is, Sheriff."

"You asshole." Brandenburg started crying, shaking his head back and forth. "No. This is not the actions of an honorable man."

"Honorable man? I'm a highly honorable man. Just not by your limited definition."

"I've got a newborn," Nichols said.

"Everybody's got a life," Snake said. "Sorry."

"Where's the girl?" Wolf asked.

Snake looked at him.

"Lawrence Hunt still has until midnight tonight to deliver your money," Wolf said. "And then you can let her go."

"She's gonna leave with us instead," Snake said.

"Why?"

"There are men who will pay us for her." Snake shrugged. "And she will spend her life repaying those men for their investment."

Wolf's insides twisted.

"You sick fuck," Larkin said.

From the corner of his eye, a prick of light caught Wolf's attention. A car had come into view far down in the valley. He squinted as the vehicle appeared to be covering some distance at speed, suggesting this person was in a psychotic hurry.

The car slowed and turned toward the compound. A green Honda Civic.

Lawrence Hunt had arrived.

Snake walked to the edge of the flat compound area and looked down through the trees. He pulled a radio from his belt and spoke into it.

Some of the men stopped what they were doing and rushed to get a view. One of them hollered in triumph, and another few joined the celebration.

Snake held up a hand, the radio at this mouth, and watched.

The car stopped between the trucks below, and the two men, ants from this distance, went to the window of the vehicle.

Snake turned his back on the spectacle and spoke into the radio. "Shoot him and bring the money up here."

A few men laughed. Somebody yelled, "Hell yeah!"

Then, a voice scratched out of the radio.

"Shut up!" Snake said, holding a hand up to his men. He put the radio to his ear. "What?"

The men went silent, and Wolf could hear the response coming out of a few different radios now.

The voice said, "He has a bomb."

CHAPTER THIRTY-FOUR

"He has a bomb?" Snake asked into the radio. "Or he's pretending to have a bomb, so you don't shoot him and take the money?"

"He was in Green River, Wyoming," Wolf said.

Snake's eyes latched onto Wolf. He lowered the radio. "What?"

"He has a friend that lives up in Green River," Wolf said, making his voice loud so more men could hear. "An engineer sergeant from his Green Beret team. You know, the guys in charge of explosives and demolitions. That's why he was up there."

Snake turned and looked down again. He put the radio to his mouth. "Shoot him. We'll come down and disarm the bomb."

The response was immediate. "He has a pressure trigger. If he releases it, the bomb blows."

Snake remained still for a moment, then pressed the button again. "He has the money? You've seen it?"

"Yes, sir."

"All of it?"

A pause. "No, sir. He says he spent some."

Snake nodded, pulling the corners of his mouth down. "Okay. Send him up."

"Yes, sir."

Wolf watched as the vehicle below lurched into motion again, driving through the truck barricade and making its way up the road.

Snake put the radio on his hip and pointed to the antler building. "Bring the girl to me."

The man behind Nichols and Brandenburg broke away and ran over to it.

Wolf and Larkin looked at one another, then the two remaining gunmen behind them.

Wolf's eyes bounced to the handguns holstered on the men's hips. That would be his best chance to gain control of a weapon.

The man behind him read his mind, pulling the pistol and aiming at Wolf's face.

"Don't move, asshole," he said.

Wolf turned back away quickly, raising his hands to his sides, not wanting to antagonize. He heard the pistol go back in its holster.

The activity among the men shifted in tone. A murmur grew, some of them actually getting on their bikes and tilting them upright. One engine roared to life, then another.

Snake shook his head, watching the chaos.

A few seconds later, the girl emerged, escorted by the third gunman.

Wolf recognized her from the pictures in Mitch and Dolores's house, but his heart wrenched at how different, how stricken with fear, she looked. She wore a pink outfit, her blonde hair pulled into a ponytail. Her face and clothing were streaked with dirt. She moved fast, doing as she was told, her face twisted like she was about to cry.

"Come on, honey," Snake said, his voice sickly sweet and repulsive to Wolf's ears. He held out one hand and pulled his gun with the other.

She tried to slow down, but the man with the rifle pushed her forward, making her stumble onto her knees.

"Get up!" Snake said, snapping. "Come on!"

She got up, now crying.

Desperate, Wolf turned around. The man was still watching him close, gun still aimed directly at his back. Any move and he would be dropped with the squeeze of a trigger.

Another motorcycle started.

All eyes went down the road, watching the bend in the distance for the arrival of Hunt's car. They didn't have to wait long. The Honda swung into view, skidding and then straightening out.

More men hopped onto their bikes, kicked up their stands, started their engines, and got out of the way in anticipation of the car's arrival. One of them tipped over. Another man rode straight into the trees, disappearing behind the trunks.

Hunt swerved toward them.

Another man's bike fell as he toppled off it into the drainage ditch next to the road.

And then, just before hitting the men at the rear of the group, Hunt swerved at the last second and turned toward the compound. He sped through the parking area, bounced through a puddle, jammed the brakes, skidded sideways, and came to a stop no more than a dozen paces from Snake and Savannah.

The exodus began, with bike noise rising to an eardrum-shattering din as the motorcycle riders sped down the road.

The door of the Civic opened, and Lawrence Hunt emerged. Hair unruly, face twisted in rage, he walked around the hood of the car with an outstretched fist. Clay-like blocks were strapped to his chest, fastened by circles of duct tape. Wires webbed and weaved, coming off the explosives, leading into a cylinder, and running down his arm to a Jeopardy buzzer he held in his hand—the presumed pressure trigger.

Hunt stopped, looking at Snake and Savannah.

Snake held her by the arm; his other hand held the pistol at his side. "Welcome back, Mr. Hunt!" he said over the fading noise.

"This is five kilos of military-grade C-4," Hunt said. "Five kilos. Anything within seventy-five meters will be vaporized if I release this pressure trigger."

"Which means your little friend here would be vaporized along with us."

"Let her go. Or I'll do it."

Snake looked down. "You think that's a good idea, Savannah?"

"Don't you talk to her!" Hunt stepped forward.

Tears streamed down Savannah's face.

"Where's the money, Larry?" Snake asked.

"It's in the car."

"Go get it. And we'll have a trade."

Wolf heard footsteps behind him and turned. The man who had escorted Savannah was now walking quickly toward the remaining few motorcycles.

"Hey!" Snake said. "Stop!"

The man ignored him, breaking into a jog.

"Shoot him."

A shot rang out, and the man dropped, landing in a motionless heap.

The man behind Larkin had turned and fired. The guy behind Wolf stared in horror at his dead friend; his aim pulled off-kilter and away from Wolf's back.

There was more commotion when Nichols stepped up behind the shooter, pulled the handgun from the man's holster, aimed, and shot him in the head.

The man behind Wolf gained his composure, turned quickly, and shot Nichols. Nichols buckled to the ground.

The action was like a strike of lightning, impossible to predict or react to, and Wolf found himself crouched in the same spot, every muscle in his body tensed for action.

Brandenburg ran, his weight wobbling back and forth as he got up to speed, making his way toward the antler building.

"Get him," Snake said.

This time, when the man behind turned to aim, Wolf lunged, his back spasming with pain as he pushed with all his might from his legs, arms outstretched to grab the gun out of the man's holster.

Larkin moved too, pushing up on the barrel of the man's gun, sending a three-shot burst into one of the buildings.

Wolf pulled the pistol from the man's belt and shot him in the head, then turned and aimed at Snake.

Snake ducked down behind Savannah.

"Let her go," Wolf said.

"Let her go!" Hunt said, stepping close to Snake and brandishing his fist in his face. "I'll do it! I swear, I'll do it!"

Snake swatted Hunt's hand aside like it was an annoying fly.

"You know what?" Snake shoved Savannah away, grabbed Hunt's hand that held the detonator, and then shot Hunt in the head.

Hunt fell. Snake, wrapped up with him, also fell.

"Savannah! Run!" Wolf waved her over.

She ran, screaming bloody murder as she hurried toward him.

"Get her out of here!" Wolf yelled to Larkin.

Larkin sprinted forward, meeting her halfway, grabbed her, then turned and ran past Wolf like an NFL player with a picked-up fumble.

"Haha! I got it!" Snake yelled, still hunched over Hunt. "It's my detonator now! How about that!"

Wolf aimed when he saw Snake had dropped his own pistol but lowered it, seeing there was no sense in shooting him now.

Snake turned to him, a demon's smile stretching his mouth. "Shoot me! Do it! Come on!" He held the detonator now, raising it, his thumb pressed. "Your choice, pig!"

Wolf backed away, looking down at Nichols.

The deputy had fallen back atop the biker he had stolen the pistol from and killed. He was in a reclined position, using the man under him like a pillow. His eyes and mouth were open, his chin painted crimson.

He blinked. And then looked at Wolf.

The pistol was still in Nichols's hand.

Nichols's mouth twitched. "Go." He gargled the word.

Wolf ran.

Spikes of fire hammered into his vertebrae as he

sprinted as fast as he could up the slope, passing between two of the buildings and into the trees.

"Up here!"

He searched, hearing Larkin's voice, and saw an arm waving from behind the nearest granite outcropping, another fifty yards away.

Wolf put his head down and pumped his arms, flinging aside the gun, not needing the dead weight or the worry it might go off.

He swerved behind a tree and, against his own will, looked back down. Between buildings, Nichols was lying motionless. A moment of silence stretched between Wolf's heartbeats as he filled with doubt that the man had been able to live long enough.

Then, fire spat from the deputy's hand.

And an impossibly fast cloud of wood and earth plowed uphill, punching him flat.

CHAPTER THIRTY-FIVE

Patterson sat in the rear seat of the Bell 206 helicopter alongside Rachette. Waze sat in the front seat next to the pilot, a capable man named John Dewer.

A radio communication came through on her headphones. "FBI 1 and 2, twenty minutes to destination."

"Copy that," Dewer said. "Sluice-Byron 1, ten minutes to destination."

"Copy that," the FBI pilot responded.

They were ten minutes ahead of the response team. Considering the storms in the area, they had gotten in the air fast. The flight time north to Doyle was just under an hour on a good day, but they were at the mercy of the weather, which was tacking on minutes.

She looked out the window at curtains of rain falling out of the clouds all around them. They were flying up a hallway of clear sky straight toward the town of Doyle.

Nobody at the Anniston County Sheriff's Department answered any of the phone lines. And her Google search for the Sons of the Void compound near Doyle hadn't produced anything. The FBI field office had no record of an address for that compound, and Wolf had failed to share his location with Rachette, or Rachette hadn't listened if he did.

So, rather than flying blind, they had made Doyle their destination. But then what? Then they would have to start banging on doors for information—a further waste of time she was pretty sure they didn't have.

A jutting patchwork carpet of grasses, pine forests, and farmlands slid by underneath them, and she scanned the woods below for clues.

Rachette sat to her left, bouncing his knee up and down. The movement in her peripheral vision clawed at her brain.

"What's that?" Waze pointed out the windscreen; his voice alarmed through her headset.

A plume of smoke rose from the forest ahead on the port side.

The helicopter banked and leveled out, a new destination on the horizon.

Patterson caught movement on the road below and saw a long stream of motorcycles.

"Got a lot of bikers riding beneath us," Dewer said.

"I see that," Patterson said. "This has gotta be it."

They went radio silent as they approached the scene. Every kilometer closer revealed more details of the destruction below. There had been a powerful explosion. The trees and brush flattened and bowed outward from a crater. Flames licked up from a cluster of trees, sending black smoke into the air.

Dewer hovered over the epicenter of the explosion.

Three buildings were demolished, flung outward, and

shredded into millions of pieces. All sorts of debris blew in the rotor wash. The smoke was pushed away as Dewer lowered the chopper toward a flat, open spot.

"Over there," Waze said.

A tall, muscular man wearing a sheriff's department uniform stood among bent trees, waving his arms overhead. A little girl sat next to him on the ground, wrapped in a rain jacket like a blanket.

"Where's Wolf?" Patterson asked.

Nobody answered.

Dewer set down the helicopter and ramped down the motor. Patterson got out into a cold rush of wind coming off the rotor, ducking as she cleared the blades at a jog. Rachette and Waze hurried and caught up behind her.

With a hand on her gun, she approached the man and the girl cautiously. The deputy was tall, redheaded, muscular, and unharmed by the blast that had leveled everything else around. The holster on his hip was empty, unthreatening.

"Who are you?" Patterson asked.

"Deputy Duane Larkin. Anniston County SD."

"Get away from the girl," Waze said.

The man calling himself Larkin shook his head. "It's okay."

"Step away from her," Waze said, pulling his gun.

"Where's Detective Wolf?" Patterson asked, looking around. Her eyes went to a piece of clothing hanging from a tree, fluttering on the breeze.

"He's fine!" somebody called from behind Larkin.

There were granite rocks up near the trees, and out from behind one of them, an overweight man wearing the same uniform as Larkin walked into view. He was hand-cuffed at the front and escorted by another man.

She sagged with relief. "Wolf."

He walked gingerly, but through a soot and blood-covered face, a white-toothed smile emerged. "Took you guys long enough."

CHAPTER THIRTY-SIX

Wolf drove south along the Chautauqua River, rounding a bend in the road that had become as much a part of him over the years as the hair pattern on his arm.

He turned left and climbed the hill and through the ranch gate of his property.

Venus shone solid above the jagged silhouette of the Chautauqua range behind his house. Lights at the front and side doors were on; the interior darkened. Piper's Toyota Highlander was parked underneath the carport.

He parked next to it and got out into frigid air, grabbing his bag from the back. Dew beaded on Piper's car, streaking down along the windows. He walked to the house, stepped up the stairs to the kitchen door, unlocked it, and walked inside.

The silence pressed on his eardrums. The space was dimly lit by a bulb over the stove.

He walked into the living room, set his bag down, and paused. Piper was curled up on the couch, a feeble blanket draped over her shoulders.

He sat down next to her and kissed her cheek.

She started, then rose quickly, probing his face with her hands. "Are you okay? You have blood on your forehead."

"Stay there," he said, stroking her hair. "It's nothing. Just a scrape."

She laid back, looking up at him. Her eyes shimmered in the soft light coming in through the open blinds. "I'm so glad you're okay."

"Me, too." He smiled wanly.

"How was the drive?"

"Long."

"You could have taken a helicopter ride," she said.

"They had enough to deal with without shuttling me home."

"How do you feel?"

He rolled his shoulders, twisting his trunk, feeling the ever-present tightness at an all-time high. But he was here. The brunt of the blast had been blocked by a thick tree, and he was here. With her.

"I'm amazing," he said, kissing her again, this time on the lips.

"And the girl?"

Wolf nodded. "They brought her to the hospital where they had taken her dad."

"And how's he doing?"

"A hell of a lot better now."

She nodded. "And the situation up there?"

"The feds have taken over."

"And how do you feel about that?"

"I feel like taking a hot shower and crawling in between the sheets and waking up sometime next week."

They sat in silence for a while, watching the light fill the windows one photon at a time.

"We have to talk." She pulled herself up and sat cross-legged.

"That was stupid of me to not be honest with you earlier," he said.

"I know," she said. "And I forgive you. I really do."

He nodded. "Okay. So, what now?"

"Well...I've been thinking. I just don't want to have this wedding."

He blinked and then nodded, his head down.

She grabbed his forearm. "I mean. I want to get married to you. But this wedding? I want to...murder it. With a dull knife."

He raised an eyebrow. "I'm not sure I'm following you."

"I'm saying you don't want to have a wedding that looks exactly like one of the worst memories of your life being reenacted on your front lawn. And I don't want that either. So, we need to start from scratch. With a new venue. Which needs to be big enough to accommodate all the people we've invited. Of which none are available in town. Not at this late notice. Maybe we could do it on somebody else's property." She shrugged.

"Yeah." He felt a familiar weight pressing on his solar plexus, one that had started every time the topic of conversation became wedding logistics. "So, what are you thinking?" He chuckled. "Eloping to Vegas?"

"Why even go that far?" She was dead serious.

"What do you mean?"

"How about the courthouse?"

He took in a breath, trying the idea. "O-kay."

She kept speaking. "And then we keep one of the tents

for next month. Some of the decorations. The catering. The music production company." She outstretched her fingers. "And we put it in Margaret Hitchens's backyard, and we have a wedding celebration. She already agreed to host for us."

She grabbed his arm with both hands, continuing. "We wear normal outfits. We don't take a thousand photographs. There's no..." Her enthusiasm vaporized. "You hate the idea. Oh my gosh, I'm sorry. You want the ceremony."

He kissed her fully on the mouth, then put his hands on her cheeks and looked her in the eyes. "I've never heard a better idea in my life. Ever."

She laughed, throwing her arms around him. He hugged her back, smiling with ecstatic relief and feeling a contentment he hadn't felt in months. He could feel it replicated in her embrace as well.

After another kiss, they stared at each other.

"So, when do we get married then?" he asked.

"I don't know." She shrugged. "We could do it whenever we wanted."

He looked at his watch. "I'm sure if I go to sleep now, I could wake up in twenty-four hours or so. Monday morning? I'm sure there'll be plenty of openings."

"Tomorrow? Are you serious?"

"Why not?"

"Don't you have to make an appointment or something?"

"No. Not when you're me."

"Oh. Aren't we full of ourselves?"

"I am. I'm about to get married to the best woman in the world."

She contemplated, her mouth upturning, eyes lighting with joy.

"What do you think?" he asked.

She kissed him, grabbed his cheeks, and looked him in the eyes. "I think I've never heard a better idea in my life."

CHAPTER THIRTY-SEVEN

Five Days Later: Friday.

The light coming in Wolf's office window played off the platinum hoop on his finger. Years ago, his left pinkie had been shot off while apprehending a criminal, and with the finger missing, it looked strange on his hand. But what his anatomy did to confuse the eye, the simple design of the ring made up for.

Two knocks hit his door, and Patterson poked her head inside.

"Hey, the Russells are here to..." She got distracted, looking down at his finger.

After officially tying the knot Monday, Wolf had taken the next four days off. Judge Zimmerman had performed the ceremony, and Wolf wondered if the woman would spread the rumor. Apparently, being the oldest judge in the district, she had little use for gossip.

"The Russells are what?" he asked.

"Oh," she said. "Yeah. They're downstairs. Did you and Piper get married?"

"Yeah. Send them in." He turned to his computer monitor and clicked shut his email.

"You did? What? Why? How? When?"

"What happened?" Rachette came up, squeezing next to Patterson. "Did you know that family from up in Doyle are here for you?"

"Yeah," Wolf said. "Can you please bring them up?"

Rachette looked at Patterson. When she did nothing, he held up a fist and his other hand underneath it. After a quick rock-paper-scissors, Patterson slapped him on the shoulder. "Better luck next time."

Rachette huffed and stormed away.

"I want answers," Patterson said, stepping into his office.

He shrugged. "We decided to pull the Band-Aid off quickly."

"So, is the ceremony still happening?"

"No. It's not. You'll get an updated invitation in the mail."

"For what?"

"For a party we're having instead."

"Oh. Okay." She folded her arms and started to say something else, but the door opened behind her.

"Right in here," Rachette said.

Wolf stood up. Dolores Russell walked inside, holding the hand of a vibrant, healthy-looking Savannah Russell.

"Here, let me help you," Rachette said, disappearing out the door again.

A second later, he wheeled Mitch in. One of his legs stuck straight out from his wheelchair, the other was bent, both wrapped in casts, but his face was aglow with color and a smile.

Wolf rounded his desk, shook their hands, and then sat on the edge of it, looking at Savannah. "How are you doing?"

She nodded and smiled, joy and pain in her expression. The little girl had witnessed more over the last couple of weeks than most people would see their whole lives.

"We were just on our way to Durango and wanted to drop in and say thanks," Mitch said.

"Oh?" Wolf looked up. "What's down in Durango?"

"My wife's parents," Mitch said. "And hopefully, our new house. We're going to move down there."

"We're going to make a fresh start," Dolores said.

Wolf nodded. "That sounds like a good idea. Are you excited?" he asked Savannah.

"Yeah," she said, with the first word he'd ever heard her speak.

"We're selling the restaurant to our cook," Dolores said. "We'll open something else when we get settled down south."

"Maybe," Mitch said.

"Maybe," Dolores said.

Wolf smiled. "That's great."

Dolores put her hands on Savannah's shoulders and faced Wolf. "We really do want to thank you."

"If it weren't for you," Mitch said, looking at Savannah, "We heard from Deputy Larkin about what they were going to do. Where they were going to..." He shook his head, his eyes welling with tears. "Had it not been for you..."

"I'm glad that you guys are all back together and starting a new adventure."

Mitch wiped his eyes, nodding. "Yeah. Thanks. I'm sure glad, too." He smiled, joy shining through his tears. He leaned forward in his chair and reached out his hand again.

Wolf shook it.

"We're going to leave you guys be now," Mitch said.

"Have a good trip," Wolf said, standing.

"I'll walk you out," Rachette said, grabbing the handles of Mitch's wheelchair and pushing him out the door into the hall.

"Thank you. Oh yeah," Mitch said. "Do you know where we could find some good ice cream around here?"

"Snow White's," a male voice answered from outside. "You're not gonna get any better than that place."

Wolf walked to the door and found Yates standing out in the hall. He was dressed in a pair of slacks and a button-up shirt that lay untucked over a gut Wolf had never seen on the man. His hair was cut short and spiked with gel. His eyes were puffy like he hadn't slept in two or three days.

"Yates." Rachette turned, letting go of the wheelchair.

Patterson walked after Mitch, now coasting unattended. "I'll walk you guys to the elevator. Rachette, you can stay here."

They waved goodbye, and then Wolf ushered Yates and Rachette into his office.

"Yates," Wolf said. "It's good to see you."

"What are you doing here?" Rachette asked.

"I had a meeting with Waze."

"And?" Wolf sat down behind his desk.

"And...hey, did you get married?"

Wolf displayed the ring. "Yeah."

"You got married?" Rachette frowned. "What? But... there's still the ceremony, right?"

"No. We're calling that off."

"When were you gonna tell us that?" Rachette asked.

"I just did."

"So, I'm not gonna be standing up for you anymore?"

Wolf shook his head. "No, sorry. But if it's any consolation, as far as I'm concerned, you stand up for me every day."

"That sucks."

Patterson walked in. "Hey, Yates." She turned to Rachette. "What sucks?"

"Wolf's not having the ceremony anymore," Rachette said.

"So?"

"So...I was gonna look good in my suit up there."

She shook her head. "No, you weren't."

Wolf looked at Yates. "How'd the meeting with Waze go?"

"It went well. I just wanted to, you know, show my face around here. Let you guys know that I'm going to do my best to get back on the squad as quick as I can. That is if you'll have me."

Patterson and Rachette looked at Wolf.

Wolf nodded. "Of course. But, as I'm sure Waze just told you, you have to prove you're better first."

"I know."

"So, what do you need from us?" Wolf asked.

"Well," Yates said, looking at Rachette. "I've booked myself into a remote inpatient rehab center. It's out in rural country, away from distractions. It helps with the recovery, or so I've read. I was hoping you might be able to take me there."

"Me?" Rachette asked.

"Yeah."

Rachette straightened. "Of course. I'd be honored. When?"

"I've got my bag packed at home. I'd just have to drop my car off, and then we'd go."

Rachette looked at Wolf.

"Go ahead," Wolf said, standing. He shook Yates's hand. "Get well. Let us know what we can do. We can't wait to have you back in here."

"Yes, sir."

"Later, Yates." Patterson gave him a hug. "We love you."

"We sure do, brother." Rachette slapped him on the back and started for the door. "Where is this place?"

"La Junta."

Rachette stopped. "Like, a five-hour drive down to eastern Colorado, La Junta?"

"It's like...six and a half. Seven."

They stared at each other.

"Son of a bitch," Rachette said, leaving.

"Thanks, man." Yates followed after him.

Patterson smiled, looking at Wolf. "You need anything?"

"No, thanks."

"I'm going to get back to my paperwork." She stopped in the door. "Oh, and sir?"

"Yeah."

"Congratulations."

He smiled. "Thanks."

CHAPTER THIRTY-EIGHT

One Month Later...

Wolf stood alone at the edge of the woods, watching the tent and the people spilling out.

The sunset on the other side of the valley dazzled like wildfire, with the town lights below like twinkling sparks. A breeze carried the raucous laughter and bluegrass music, the scents of food cooking, the cut grass of Margaret Hitchens's lush lawn underneath his dress shoes, and the pine forest behind him.

From this distance, hidden in the shadows, he watched Jack, Cassidy, and Ryan. His son kissing his daughter-in-law, his grandson chasing a butterfly in tight circles like he was caught in a joy-powered whirlwind.

The phone in his hand vibrated again, and the screen glowed with another message from the same name, putting a cold blanket over the perfection of the moment.

Piper stood out on the deck of the house, talking with

someone he didn't recognize. She spotted him, extracted herself from the conversation, and walked over.

He pocketed the phone and watched her approach. She wore a lavender summer dress that hugged her waist, flaring above the knees, giving her steps a stunning fluidity that drew looks from the men behind her. Her hair cascaded in waves, shining in the magic hour light, a subtle smile playing on her lips, her slender hand carrying a glass of red wine.

"Hi," she said, padding across the grass and standing next to him.

"Hi," he said.

"Pretty great, huh?"

"Yeah."

The obvious question was, *what are you doing out here,* but she remained silent, watching the spectacle in their honor play out. He sipped his soda. She sipped her wine.

She kept her eyes forward. He knew she was giving him space to say what he wanted when he wanted if there was anything to say at all.

"I got a text message," he said.

"Oh?"

"Yeah."

"From whom?"

He pulled out his phone, tapped the screen, and handed it to her.

"Oh," she said, her eyebrows popping high. She nodded a few times and gave the phone back. "What does it say?"

"I don't know."

"You haven't looked yet?"

"No."

"And this is bothering you?"

"Yes."

She nodded again, taking another sip of her wine. "It's understandable. You're at your wedding celebration party... and now she's texting you. I would be a bit apprehensive myself."

He smiled. The phone went dark again.

"Are you going to look at it?" she asked.

"Probably."

"You want me to head back over there? I can give you some space."

"No." He unlocked the phone and tapped the message. "Stay here with me."

She sipped her wine, keeping her gaze pointedly away as he read the two messages that had come in.

Hi David. It's Lauren. I know I'm probably the last person you want to hear from on this day, but I just wanted to say congratulations to you and Piper. I heard about your marriage and tonight's celebration from a friend in town. I've heard Piper is a beautiful, kind, smart, and loving woman. You deserve all the happiness in the world, and I hope you have found it with her.

The second message underneath it read:

Love, Lauren and Ella.

"Well?" Piper asked.

He handed the phone to her.

Theatrically, she took a deep breath, smoothed her hair, steeled her gaze, and read the messages. A few seconds later, she nodded and handed it back. "That's nice of her."

Wolf studied her expression. No hint of jealousy or sarcasm was found.

"I'm sure that was very tough for her to do," she said.

"Yeah."

"So, what are you going to say back?"

"I don't know. Thanks?"

"Yeah. I've got a better idea."

She set down her wine on a nearby rock and held out her hand.

Wolf gave her the phone. She snuggled close and outstretched her arm to take a selfie portrait of them.

"Smile." She snapped a flurry of photos, then let go of him and consulted her work.

"Look at this one. Great picture. You're actually smiling."

"What are you going to do?" he asked, watching her tap and swipe.

"There." She handed back the phone.

"What did you do?"

"I sent her a photo of us."

"Why did you do that?"

She shrugged. "Why not?"

"I don't know. I guess...I wouldn't want to rub it in her face how happy we are. Or something."

"Are you happy?"

"Yes."

"And you don't think she can handle it?"

"I guess that's what I'm saying. Yes."

She snorted. "Then she shouldn't have texted you."

The phone chimed, and another text from Lauren came in.

This time, he angled the screen toward Piper and opened the message. It was a picture of three people: Lauren, a man, and a girl he barely recognized as Ella. She was much taller, with braces and long hair.

"Oh, look," Piper said. "They're so happy."

They did look happy, all three of the people on screen, especially Ella, whose mid-laughter grin was ear to ear.

Another message shot in.

SHE'S BEAUTIFUL. ELLA SAYS SO, TOO. GOOD LUCK TO YOU, DAVID.

He texted back:

GOOD LUCK TO YOU, TOO. AND TO ELLA.

He put the phone in his pocket, realizing he was smiling.

"That wasn't so bad, was it?" Piper asked, her eyes beaming.

He put his arm around her and pulled her close. "No. It wasn't."

They stared out at the tent some more as the light faded.

"I love you," he said.

"I love you, too."

ALSO BY JEFF CARSON

The David Wolf Series

Gut Decision (A David Wolf Short Story) – Sign up for the new release newsletter at http://www.jeffcarson.co/p/newsletter.html and receive a complimentary copy.

Foreign Deceit (David Wolf Book 1)
The Silversmith (David Wolf Book 2)
Alive and Killing (David Wolf Book 3)
Deadly Conditions (David Wolf Book 4)
Cold Lake (David Wolf Book 5)
Smoked Out (David Wolf Book 6)
To the Bone (David Wolf Book 7)
Dire (David Wolf Book 8)
Signature (David Wolf Book 9)
Dark Mountain (David Wolf Book 10)
Rain (David Wolf Book 11)
Drifted (David Wolf Book 12)
Divided Sky (David Wolf Book 13)
In the Ground (David Wolf Book 14)
High Road (David Wolf Book 15)
Dead Canyon (David Wolf Book 16)
Echoes Fade (David Wolf Book 17)
NEW* Silent Country (David Wolf Book 18)

The Ali Falco Series
The Como Falcon (Ali Falco Book 1)
Tuscan Blood (Ali Falco Book 2)

Made in the USA
Middletown, DE
12 December 2024

66787556R00184